Idriel's Children

HAYLEY REESE CHOW

DEDICATION

To my writing tribe,
Whose encouragement made this book possible.

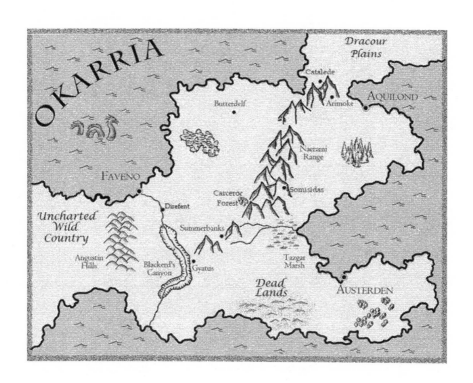

Raging in fire,
The Dragon scattered foul ashes
And roared for more.

Reaping darkness,
The Shadow slicked steel with judgment
And danced with death.

With more life to give,
The Time mended mind and flesh
And bore their pain.

- *The Heir's Way, Chapter 3, Passage 21*

1
SHADOW HEIR

Aza didn't want to kill anybody, but she would if she had to. The forest's branches rustled around the moon-washed clearing, empty save for the small cabin slouching in the night's embrace, as if trying to shrink away from her. With only a thought, Aza drew her *yanaa* from her center and let her shadows flow over her body. In a heartbeat, the color melted away from the world around her, and Aza disappeared from sight.

From deeper in the darkness, a familiar whisper called her from the Shadow Plane. "*Azaaaaaaaaaa.*"

Her lips pressed into a firm line.

"*Azaaaaaaaaaaaaa,*" the voice beckoned again, running like an icy wind through her thoughts.

She shook her head, ignoring the ethereal call as she walked toward the crumbling cabin and drew her black daggers. Each as long as her forearm, their weight sent a surge of adrenaline tingling through her fingers. No fear. No doubt. Only a cold anticipation sharpening her senses.

Ears straining, she could make out the rise and fall of heavy breathing from within. Outside, the horses shuffled nervously, sensing Aza's unseen presence. They had the elegant height of purebred Faveno racers, and the fine leather saddles gleamed in the low light—nothing like the mulish, hungry mounts of the drunken highwaymen she normally dealt with. These belonged to hired blades.

Her gaze ran over the building's rotting wood one more time. Two boarded windows scarred each side, with another higher up, probably indicating some kind of loft. But with no easy exit, the highwaymen wouldn't have bothered going up there. Judging from the mounts, there were four swords inside—three asleep and one on watch, but they wouldn't see her coming.

The prisoner would be bound, gagged, and shoved in a corner, like the other three they'd rescued in the past weeks. Aza rolled her shoulders, still stiff from the nights of little sleep and the hard ride to catch up with these thugs. The pull of yanaa rippled through her muscles as she maintained her invisibility. Her gaze darted back to the tree line that hid the only eyes that could penetrate her Shadow Step. She could almost feel them boring into her shoulder blades—searching for her weaknesses.

She straightened, determined to give nothing away. Even to him.

The splintery door sagged to one side, as if already resigned to what she was about to do. While she detested making the obvious move, the element of surprise was too precious to waste, especially when there was a hostage involved. With one solid kick, the lock on the old door splintered with a *crack* as she burst into the dark room.

A dim lantern flickered in the corner, revealing a spartan room and a cold hearth. But instead of a watchman and three groggy thugs startled from sleep, a dozen pairs of eyes glinted in the weak light. Something soft and loose shifted beneath her boots, revealing her position. *Odriel's teeth.* They'd scattered ashes over the floorboards. A muffled yell drew her eyes upward just in time to see the net drop. Aza dove forward into the feet of one of the men, knocking him over. Heart thrumming, she stabbed a dagger into his leg, his scream cutting through the night.

One down.

Two of the men grabbed at the net while she ducked and buried her other dagger in a nearby belly.

Two.

She threw a knife just as another tackled her from behind. She wrenched him over her back into the other net man. Ripping her daggers free, she punched the steel into each before letting them fall.

Three, four, five.

Aza's hot breath came fast and heavy, leaving only ashen footprints and blood in her wake as she whirled through the room. The highwaymen swung wildly, trying to hit a weaving shadow too fast for their steel.

"Don't move!" a voice called from above. A bearded man shoved a wide-eyed little boy to the edge of the loft. "I'll—"

Aza flung her dagger at the man, finding his eye.

Six.

A man swung his sword where her blade had appeared, and she rolled closer to him, thrusting a knife into his thigh.

Seven.

Another scrambled up the ladder toward the hostage, and Aza sank a blade into his calf before throwing him to the floor.

Eight.

With most of their party dead or bleeding, one called the retreat. "Forget the job—that's a demon."

The men stumbled for the door, but one had the mind to grab a lantern on his way out. "If it's a demon, let it burn like one." He smashed the light against the wooden floor in the doorway, the flame catching easily on the dry, rotted wood and scattered straw.

Curses rattled through Aza's thoughts as her only exit filled with fire. Racing up the ladder, she yanked her dagger from the dead thug's eye and let her veil drop. The young boy jumped at her sudden appearance, his chest heaving with panic.

She cut away the gag and the ropes that bound his hands before sheathing her blades. "I'm here to help."

He flinched as she grabbed him with a gloved hand. Coughing, she pulled him toward the boarded-up window, the black smoke already stinging her eyes and throat. Six warped boards crossed the shattered glass. She pushed the kid aside and drove her heel through the planks, once, twice, three times. Coughing now, she pulled the broken wood away and glanced down. No sign of the highwaymen, but she needed to move quickly before they had a chance to regroup.

She grabbed the boy again, raising her voice over the growling flames and his deafening fear. "Can you climb out?"

The boy didn't move, sweat rolling down his cheeks and his chest pumping with erratic gasps. Not waiting for a response, she lifted his small frame carefully over the shattered glass on the sill, pushing his legs out the window first. Holding his wrists, she let him dangle for a moment, the sharp glass splinters pressing into her leather vest. "I'm letting go now. Roll when you fall, and you'll be fine."

Without giving him time to think, she released him. He landed with a yelp but scuttled away from the building. The structure shuddered, warning of its collapse. Turning around, Aza gripped the edge of the sill, glass shards cutting into her fingerless leather gloves, and back-flipped away from the cabin. She landed on her feet and rolled just as the building toppled in a shower of crackling sparks.

Panting, Aza looked for the child. Her roving eyes stilled on his pale face, whimpering in the paws of one of the thugs, a knife at his throat once more.

"Don't you dare reach for that blade." He dug his glinting steel into the boy's skin, drawing red pearls.

Aza raised her hands—slowly, purposefully reaching for the throwing spike hidden in the spool of her dark hair.

The man licked his lips. "Now, you're going to—" With a sudden grunt, he sagged forward, blood seeping from his temple. The boy shrieked and scurried out from under the unconscious brute.

"I thought you wanted to do this on your own." A shadow in black leather armor materialized from the darkness behind the boy. He sheathed his obsidian blade.

Aza crossed her arms, looking out into the billowing smoke. "I had it, Papa."

He shook his head and reached out for the trembling child. "It's all right now."

"W-w-who are you people?" The boy looked from one to the other.

"I'm Guardian Klaus Thane, and this is my daughter, Aza." Aza nodded, jaw still set, and Klaus flashed a wolfish grin, his hazel eyes glinting in the still-raging fire. The same eyes he had passed on to her. "We're the Shadow Heirs."

The boy swallowed, his voice but a whisper. "Odriel's Assassins."

In the stillness of the deep night, Aza and Klaus sat at their fire while the boy snored gently on Klaus' blanket roll. The forest trees crowded around them, the spring buds on their spindly branches not quite blocking out the winking stars above.

They'd bound the surviving cutthroats, and Klaus had sent a harehawk with a message for the Road Watchers to collect them. The Watchers were responsible for keeping the roads between the State-cities safe, but they were always asking the Heirs for aid. Aza stretched an arm across her wiry body and leaned her neck from side to side. After days of riding and the scuffle in the cabin, she could definitely use a rest, but the call from the Shadow Plane still needled her.

"You lost the advantage when you beat down the front door," Klaus said, interrupting her thoughts.

Aza bristled. "What option did I have? The windows and the back were both boarded."

"You could've made a distraction to draw them out." He crossed his arms and leaned against a fat tree trunk. "If you had a scrap of patience, you could've waited to learn more."

Aza stretched out her legs and leaned forward, touching her nose to her knees. "I thought they'd be asleep." It had been a miscalculation, yes, but one that hadn't mattered in the end. And she wouldn't make the same mistake twice. She never did.

"You assumed that an unknown enemy would be stupid."

"In my defense, they usually are," Aza replied with a shrug.

"Hubris is a weakness. There's no reason to work alone if you don't have to. You put the boy at risk for nothing."

Aza straightened with a laugh. "Pot, kettle. Apple, tree, et cetera, et cetera."

"I'm serious, Aza."

Aza rolled to her feet to stretch her back. "So am I. We got the kid, and it all turned out sunny."

Her gaze flicked to the sleeping child, and she thought back to his parents' plea for his safe return. The villagers had said the boy was well known for his uncanny knack for spotting a lie. The last child they'd rescued could see in the dark, and the one before that could predict the weather. All children born with rare gifts—blessed by Odriel himself, people said. As a girl, Aza's mother, Kaia, had known one of these Odriel's Blessed, a boy who could speak to animals, but Aza had never met one herself. Their yanaa, that Odriel-gifted energy nestled within them, was weaker than the Heirs', but it was unpredictable.

"Speaking of—this is the third kidnapping of an Odriel's Blessed this season." She absently ran a thumb over the long scar that streaked down her cheek like a tear stain. "What do you think is going on?"

"It could be anyone trying to collect power." Klaus leaned back against his tree and closed his eyes with a sigh. "But I fear it has something to do with the Rastgol."

A violent shudder shook Aza's shoulders. The Rastgol clan bred for strength, craved battle as a religious experience, and often decorated themselves with the bones and other body parts of their enemies. The parts they didn't eat, that is. With their unnatural stature and cruelty, sometimes it was hard to believe they were even human. Though they hailed from the lands west of the Faveno river, they constantly harried Okarria's border with their barbaric raids.

"Why?" she asked, her voice a touch hoarse.

"The Rastgol believe they can consume the power of their enemies through their blood." Klaus grimaced. "They hunt out the Odriel's Blessed."

Aza fingered the belt of throwing knives that crossed her chest. "But the Western Guard keeps the Rastgol from crossing the canyon, and we haven't encountered any Rastgol." Now, *that* would have been a real challenge.

"So, someone could be selling the Odriel's Blessed to them."

"Perhaps we should've waited and followed them back to the source."

"And let the child suffer?" Klaus' brow furrowed, his eyes flashing with sharp disapproval. "That's not our way. We're protectors first, Aza, not killers."

Aza turned away so he couldn't see her roll her eyes. He could call them whatever he wanted, but the two walked hand in hand. Wasn't that one of the first lessons he had taught her? The path of the Shadow Heir was dark for more reasons than one. Sometimes, you had to take a life to save one. It set them apart from the Dragon and Time Heirs, and it was one of the reasons the Dragon Heirs never accompanied them on these tasks. Odriel had forged his Shadows with a different metal.

Klaus shifted against the tree. "We'll check our ears in the cities for any rumors. Every predator shows its teeth eventually."

Aza shrugged and sank down onto the grassy forest floor. No use arguing with her father when he had that hardened tone, but she'd be sure to ask her own sources. With that thought, her mind drifted back to the Shadow Plane—to the voice that called her.

"You should get some rest, Aza." Klaus threw a branch on the fire. "I'll take first watch."

Aza nodded and laid her head on her saddle. She'd need some rest to be able to cross into the Shadow Plane later.

Not that she'd tell her father that.

2
A WARNING

Klaus' fingers brushed Aza's shoulder, and her eyes flinched open, instantly awake. The crescent moon still shone high among the silvery wisps of clouds while the boy murmured in his sleep by the fire, and the darkness rested on their camp like a heavy blanket. With the first watch over and his face lined with tired shadows, Klaus half-smiled at her before returning to his side of the fire. Laying his head down on his pack, he shifted his wide shoulders to get comfortable.

Aza rolled to her feet and bent forward to stretch out her legs. By the time she straightened, her father's breathing had already evened into the gentle huffs of slumber. Aza rubbed the back of her leather glove across her face, trying to wipe away her own exhaustion. They'd ridden for nearly three days straight trying to catch up with the thugs. But the weariness was standard on their patrols. At least it made the forest floors comfortable and sleep come quickly.

She flexed her arms above her head. The muscles still ached, but even the brief reprieve had refreshed her. Not full strength, but good enough.

Aza's eyes drifted across the night once more. Her father's chest rose and fell in smooth deep movements, and the boy snored gently by the weak flames. A crescent owl's airy song crooned over the crickets playing their strings in a lulling sonata—all was right here... but elsewhere, something was calling to her.

Aza strode through the trees to where her father's dappled gray Dalteek, Stormshade, grazed in the moonlight. Her own brown mare, Oakhoof, dozed not too far away, but Aza only had eyes for Stormshade. Aza's appreciative gaze swept across the doe's velvety spring antlers already growing tall and her dark lion-like mane. Stormshade's ears flicked forward, and she pushed her velvet nose into Aza's hand in greeting.

The Maldibor clan had gifted her father Stormshade 28 years ago, and yet she showed no sign of aging. Rumored to descend from the uncatchable stags of yore, the Dalteek were one of the few mounts the Maldibor could ride in their cursed, bear-like forms, but they suffered few humans. Stormshade's dark eyes gleamed with the uncanny wisdom that dwarfed even a ragehound's intelligence. But she still loved her sweets.

Aza dug out the yellow slices of dried periapple she kept in her pocket, and Stormshade snapped them from her palm with relish. "There's my girl," she crooned, scratching her between the antlers. "Do you think you can keep watch for me?"

Stormshade nosed at Aza's pocket with a grunt, and she wrinkled her nose before digging out another piece. "Okay, one more. Then when I get back, you can have the rest."

Stormshade whickered softly, and Aza pushed her forehead to the doe's. "Just a few minutes, I promise."

Stormshade lipped at Aza's chin affectionately.

"Thank you," Aza whispered, kissing her nose.

That taken care of, Aza turned and stepped into the shadow of the wood, out of the light of their fire. She unspooled the yanaa from her core, just as her father had taught her, gathering the shadows around her until she disappeared from sight. The Shadow Step plunged her into its perpetual dusk. What little color the moonlight revealed drained from her vision, but she didn't need it. Veiled from the world, only another Shadow Heir would be able to see her, and only if they, too, stepped into the shadows. But there were only two of them left now.

Still, Aza was drawn to the shadows in a way her father never had been. He drilled her in the best ways to use their powers of invisibility to protect and save but didn't Shadow Step more than he had to. Meanwhile, the shadows had always fascinated Aza. She'd walk the shadows until she exhausted herself, and then she'd try again the next day. Then, at fifteen, she discovered the edge of their world and plunged into a new one.

"*Azaaaaaaaaaaaaaa*," the voice whispered.

Aza nodded. *I'm coming.*

She paused for one last moment to survey the peaceful wood. Her father would skin her if he discovered she had abandoned her watch, but Stormshade would alert him of any intruder with one of her warning shrieks. And the old man could certainly take care of himself in any case.

Resolve hardened, Aza tensed her muscles and unraveled spools of yanaa from within, twisting them in and around herself. She churned the yanaa until it spun around her in a vortex. Her breath came fast, and her muscles strained as the world blurred before her eyes. Crossing to the Shadow Plane was like a cork diving to the bottom of the ocean.

The first time she'd crossed over a year ago, the transition felt as though someone had ripped the yanaa from her limbs. She'd been trying to reap more and more shadows, like a performer grabbing a polar lion by the scruff of the neck. Then the world around her vanished, her yanaa carrying her to an entirely new realm. And with it, a wave of empowered euphoria swept through her.

In a swirl of fear and wonder, she'd only lasted five seconds in the Shadow Plane before fainting and returning to the visible world. Her father had panicked at her sudden absence and forbidden such experiments, claiming they were dangerous. But his warning had fallen on deaf ears. Aza stole away to the Shadow Plane as often as she could, building up a resistance to its harsh demands. Her new record was almost four minutes, but only if she stayed perfectly still.

In an intoxicating rush, Aza's surge of yanaa whipped away, and the world twisted and morphed as she left Okarria and entered a world wholly different. A field of empty darkness stretched before her with only blotches of specters dotting the empty landscape. In this silent expanse, her yanaa tingled uncomfortably on her skin with a whitish glow, and even slow movements took concentrated effort. Still, the power of the Plane soaked through her bones, filling her in a way a mere Shadow Step never had.

In the Shadow Plane, she stumbled like a sleepwalker through a dream, her fear driven away by a fierce wonder. Aza had never met another person in the dark realm, but other bizarre creatures with white ethereal bodies wandered the gray fields instead—shadow dwellers.

Aza squeezed her eyes shut to quell the vertigo that threatened to drown her. She took a deep breath and opened her eyes in the mind-bending silence. A field of long silvery grass carpeted the blackness, and the peculiar, disturbing creatures that roamed the Plane were nowhere to be seen, but that was expected. In the last few weeks, she'd been seeing fewer and fewer of the shadow dwellers. They'd fled like birds ahead of a coming storm, disappearing to who knew where, and that wasn't even the worst of it.

"*Azaaaaaaaa*," the wind whispered. The voice had been calling her for weeks now, but it still sent a shiver down her spine. "*Azzzaaaaaaaaa.*"

Aza opened her mouth to answer the call, when she noticed what looked like a headless child cutting across the Plane. With strained steps, as though wading through mud, she made her way to intercept it. Her yanaa uncoiled feverishly, the loose tether binding her to the Plane fraying by the second.

The creature had one eye in the center of its chest and a gaping mouth where its neck should have been, but Aza had no fear. Here, even the most peculiar sights seemed natural—the surreal landscape blunting the sharp edges of alarm. The headless child stopped and stared at her when it noticed her approach.

"Greetings," Aza called.

The shadow dweller said nothing.

"What news?"

"To get you must give," the creature said tersely from its gaping wound of a mouth. The words spewed out quickly like the thing was in a rush, but it kept oddly still.

"*There is much death*," the wind hissed.

The creature gave no sign that it heard the wind. Ignoring the voice for a moment, Aza considered the shadow dweller's request. "Someone's stealing Odriel's Blessed. I want to know more."

The headless thing blinked its single eye at her. "Monsters claim souls. Turn into nightmares."

"*So much suffering*," the wind echoed.

Aza cocked her head, the spent yanaa straining her every muscle. "What monsters?"

The creature shifted, its shoulders swaying back and forth. "Monsters on the hunt."

Blood-curdling screams of anguish swirled through the air between them, and Aza drew back sharply. The creature started walking again.

"Must go. Not safe here," it muttered.

With little yanaa left to anchor her to the Shadow Plane, Aza felt the visible world tugging insistently on her. "Wait!" she yelled at the creature disappearing into the tall grass. This might be her last chance to get answers, and she had only seconds left. "Why isn't it safe?"

The screams were all around them now, growing ever louder—hair-raising cries of the dying, screaming babies, sobbing women. The headless child turned around one last time, staring at her as she struggled to remain for just a few moments longer. Saying nothing, it raised one of its long arms and pointed a claw straight at her.

Aza released her yanaa, and the shadows shoved her back into the visible world. Her reserves completely spent, Aza fell flat onto her back in the wood outside of their camp. Her ears rang and her body ached as though her bones had been rattled around in her skin. She tried to calm her rasping breath and sat up with burning muscles.

Her father's eyes fluttered open by the fire, his voice still thick with sleep. "Aza, are you okay?"

She plucked up a sturdy stick from the ground and rose to her feet. "Just getting more wood for the fire."

Klaus nodded with a grunt, eyes falling closed again.

Aza let out a slow breath, heart still thrumming in her throat. Above her, the inky sky swirled with dawn hues of navy and indigo.

Monsters on the hunt. She could believe that. All kinds of monsters roamed Okarria—both human and otherwise. But *she* was the reason the Shadow Plane wasn't safe? That didn't make any sense. For centuries, generations of

Heirs had sworn to protect Okarria. Wincing, Aza walked back to the fire and tossed the stick into the flames, her eyes resting on her father.

She couldn't keep a message like that to herself. If the Rastgol were the monsters on the hunt, her father needed to know. *I'll have to tell him.* Grimacing, she put her hands on her hips. *But it's not going to be pretty.*

3
CATALEDE

With the boy returned to his parents and their spring patrol at an end, Aza's unspoken confession still weighed on her mind. The Shadow Heirs led their mounts over the steep green mountainside that overlooked the stone fortress of Catalede Academy and the village below. Two dozen slate-tiled houses gathered together in the valley fields as if to keep out the chill. Higher up the slope, standing apart from the village like a shy guest, the stone walls of the Catalede Academy circled another handful of structures—the barracks, the mess hall, the training grounds, the schoolroom, the barn, and of course, the Thane's sprawling farmhouse. Even from afar, she could see a herd of cerulean blusheep going out to pasture and a scattering of long-necked llamow wandering the swaying grass well above the tree line.

Aza smiled. The Shadow Heirs patrolled Okarria each spring and fall, and coming home always felt like a warm blanket around her shoulders.

Well… almost always.

Shifting in her saddle, Aza sighed, eyeing her father riding tall in his sleek black leather atop Stormshade. She'd been waiting for the right time, but after five days, she had to admit there really might not be a right time for this conversation. But then again, she needed to know what she stood to lose before he lost his temper.

Envy twisted Aza's lips as she watched Stormshade pick her way down the slope on her nimble cloven hooves. Her gaze turned to Oakhoof plodding along the track, and Aza patted her neck. Though solid and dependable, gray hair had started to speckle her face. Soon she wouldn't be able to make these journeys.

What Aza wouldn't give for a Dalteek fawn to replace her. With all the hard patrols they'd been doing, it only made sense, and the Dalteek breeders—the Maldibor—were due for a visit in only a few weeks. But if her father was angry with her, the chances of getting one would go from slim to none. Best to feel him out before she broke the news about the Shadow Plane.

"Hey, Papa, is Tekoa coming to the spring festival this year?"

"He usually does." Klaus looked at her. "Why do you ask?"

Aza tucked her dark hair behind an ear and tried to sound casual. "Well, you know Oakhoof is going to be sixteen this year, and I was going to ask Tekoa if they had any new fawns."

Klaus snorted out a sudden laugh.

Aza wrinkled her nose. "What?"

"I've already told you that you only get one when you take my place one day."

Aza groaned. "C'mon, Papa, that'll be ages. I've been patrolling with you for three years now, and I did just rescue an Odriel's Blessed all on my own, so that should count for something."

"You know how the Maldibor tribe are about their mounts. For them, it's like giving family away." He shook his head with a smile. "It's not happening."

Sagging, Aza watched longingly as the graceful Dalteek trotted down the steep path as nimbly as a mountain goat. Well, at least she'd tried. That confirmed, she really had nothing to lose. Time for the more difficult conversation...

Or maybe not. Was there someone else she could talk to about the Shadow Plane? "What about the magi? Do you think they'd come if we asked?"

The smile faded from Klaus' lips. "No, no one has seen or heard from Everard since Fiola passed away." A shadow of grief flitted across his face. "Sorrow hits the magi especially hard."

"What about his brother... Dorinar, right?"

Klaus laughed again. "Dorinar hasn't left his hovel in I don't know how long." The lookout at the Catalede gate saw them and waved with a shout. Klaus raised a hand and then arched his scarred eyebrow at his daughter. "Why are you asking?"

"Last spring you promised to take me to meet Dorinar and learn more about past Shadow Heirs. I still want to talk to him."

Her father ran an exasperated hand through his short dark hair, and his voice held a note of skepticism. "What, specifically, do you want to know?"

"There's more to the Shadow Plane than we know. Maybe Dorinar knows what it is and how we can use it."

Klaus' mouth flattened into a thin line. "I thought I told you not to cross to the Shadow Plane. Even my father warned me against it when I was a boy.

It's too draining, Aza, and we don't understand it."

"Exactly, Papa! That's why I need to talk to Dorinar. If it's part of Odriel's gift, it must serve a purpose." Aza opened her mouth to say more but stopped herself.

Catching her hesitation, Klaus' eyes narrowed. "And?"

No going back now. Aza licked her lips, choosing her words carefully. "For a while now, I've been hearing voices from the Shadow Plane. Cries for help, whispers of death and—"

"You can understand them?" Klaus pulled Stormshade to a halt, the iron Catalede gate looming before them.

"You can't?"

Klaus' brow furrowed. "They've always just been noises to me."

Aza bristled, drawing up alongside him. "You know there's something going on in the world, and someone is trying to warn us about it. What do you want me to do, just stare at a corner until it comes to our doorstep?"

Klaus turned away with a scowl, the leather reins creaking in his tight fists.

"We need to better understand our gift," Aza pressed.

It was something he had drilled into her early after all—to be sharp, to be strong, to be the best. To command the yanaa as another limb. To be able to protect others… and themselves… She traced the scar along her cheek once more.

Farther down the dirt trail, beyond the stubby briar pines and the early teal dewblooms, the Dragon Heirs opened the wrought iron gates with two ragehounds at their heels. For anyone else, the sight of the wolf-like hounds and Odriel's fire-blessed Heirs might've caused a spike of fear. But to Aza, they'd always just be her mother and brother.

Aza lowered her voice. "And you did promise to take me to Tazgar."

Klaus sighed, pasting on a smile as the ragehounds ran toward them with wagging tails, the Dragon Heirs following behind. "Okay, I'll make a deal. You don't cross to the Shadow Plane until we figure out what it actually is." His hard eyes flicked to hers as he dismounted. "*And* you don't mention the voices to anyone else. I don't want to raise alarm when we don't know what this is. Then, in the summer, I will take you to Dorinar."

Aza twisted her lips. She wanted to leave tomorrow, but perhaps she could wear him down later. For now, she'd have to accept this small victory. "The deal is struck."

"Welcome back." Aza's mother approached them with a smile, her side braid shining copper among her long brown locks. Though her chestnut eyes crinkled with joy, Aza didn't miss the sleepless half-circles that clung to her lower lashes.

"Firefly!" Klaus wrapped his arms around her and spun her around. He sealed it with a kiss and a whisper too soft for Aza's ears.

Aza dismounted and ran her hands through the ragehounds' thick fur as they wriggled and snuffled under her fingers. She knelt down to throw an arm around each hound, one red and one black. Her mother always favored the red-furred pups descended from her favorite hound, Gus, but her brother could always pick out the prettiest of the litter.

"Luna! Sasha! I missed you!" She pulled a few dried strips of meat from her pocket, and they snatched them excitedly from her palms.

Zephyr threw out his arms for a hug with a fake pout. "What about me?"

Aza looked up at her brother with a smile. At eighteen, he was two years older than her, but he hardly acted like it. Floppy brown hair hung down onto his forehead, with orange streaking along the side—just like their mother's.

Though historically only the eldest child inherited the gift of the parent Heir, Zephyr and Aza had been the first progeny of *two* Heirs. But Odriel, Okarria's reclusive spirit-guide who granted the Heirs their lasting gifts, had apparently chosen to grant two Heir children to the two Heir parents, rather than one child with two gifts. Lucky for her—she could only imagine how insufferable Zephyr would've been with fire *and* shadow.

She rose with an exaggerated sigh. "I guess." She spread out her arms for a hug, and then at the last minute feigned a punch to his gut.

He flinched as if she'd really punched him. "Always so cold, Shadow."

"Just trying to keep you on your toes, Dragon." She poked him in the stomach with a finger.

Her mother walked over and wrapped Aza in her strong arms. "We missed you, Azy."

Aza inhaled her mother's scent of embers and wool, and a wave of calm washed over her.

"I hope everything went well," Kaia murmured.

Over her mother's shoulder, Aza's gaze found her father's, and an age-old understanding flashed between them. Something they'd never spoken, but both of them knew. All the darkness of their patrols—the close calls, the ambushes, the death—stayed there. They carried the shadows within them, but they wouldn't cast them on their bright home.

"Of course." Aza squeezed her mother with a smile. "No problems at all."

Aza slipped into her old routines like a pair of worn boots. She woke in the near dawn and started her day with a run up Halsana peak. She always savored the brief moment to herself before her instructor duties swallowed the rest of her day. Sweating and muscles burning, she didn't even stop to admire the view in the crisp mountain air before sprinting back down to Catalede. She stepped into the spacious mess hall with her chest still heaving just as the three notes of the sonorous breakfast bell called the students to eat. With a nod to the cooks and a rumble of her empty stomach, she piled eggs and bacon between two thick slices of bread and stepped out again.

She helped Zephyr with the students' morning weapons classes, correcting form with a nudge or a silent demonstration. The students, or Greens as Zephyr called them, were all close to her age and came from all walks of life—farmers' sons, noblemen's daughters, and even a few orphans with nowhere else to go. They stayed at Catalede to complete their training before swearing an oath to serve if the Heirs should call on them. Then they returned to whatever corner of Okarria they hailed from. A waiting army that Aza's parents hoped they wouldn't need one day—but knew they would. With the Rastgol raging in the west, and the corrupt nobles trying to revive the monarchy, war never seemed far off.

This class was reaching the end of their instruction, and Aza could recognize and name every single one of the sixty students who boarded in the barracks. But she much preferred to let Zephyr do the talking. A brilliant smile lit his handsome face as he joked and tussled with the Greens. They spun around him like a wheel about an axle, and he basked in their reverence. They snuck awed glances and shy smiles at Aza too, but she ignored them. Once she made eye contact, they stuck to her like an old burr. Helping their parents run Catalede Academy might've been Zephyr's calling, but it was Aza's chore.

The midday break found Aza in her usual quiet corner of the grassy courtyard with thoughts of the Shadow Plane churning through her mind. The students chattered as they milled about the dirt paths crisscrossing the verdant grounds lined with budding blush maples. But the gray stone walls and sturdy buildings around them seemed small against the sharp mountain peaks behind. The solitude only lasted a few moments before Zephyr and Luna found her.

With his back against the stones of the courtyard wall, he sagged down beside her with a contented sigh and a plate heaped high with hedge hen, wine rice, and greens. Luna rolled her shaggy dark body in the grass, snuffling with her long tongue lolling, and Aza couldn't help but tickle her belly.

Zephyr stuffed a bite in his mouth. "Whatcha doin'?"

"Who says I'm doing anything?" Aza snatched a bit of hedge hen from Zephyr's plate and let Luna lick it from her fingers.

"You're always doing something."

Aza scratched Luna's neck just where she liked it. "Did you hear Mother last night? She's walking the house again."

Zephyr's smile fell. "The nightmares have been getting worse these last couple weeks."

The last couple weeks. Aza straightened. *When the Shadow Plane whispers started.* "Do you think it has to do with Idriel's Children?" She swallowed; the demon spirit guide and those bestowed with his twisted yanaa were not to be taken lightly.

"I don't know." Zephyr licked one of his fingers absently. "Who are they again?"

Aza resisted the urge to slap the back of his head. "Really, Zephyr? Idriel's warning? The undead Heir killer, Mogens, still stalking the dark?"

"Oh yeah. That. I dunno. Maybe?" He scooped another bite into his mouth. "Could be spiders. I have nightmares about spiders."

"You are so…" Aza trailed off as a long-legged boy strode toward them. She rolled her eyes. "Oh, Odriel take it."

"Hey, chums." The skinny, dimple-cheeked boy slid between them, taking a seat against the wall.

Zephyr slapped his friend on the back with an easy smile. "Hey, Witt-wart."

"Aza, you're looking lovely as always." Witt leaned closer to tousle Luna's ears, his mop of mousy curls falling nearly to his shoulders. "What news from the wide world?"

Aza sighed loudly, debating if she should get up and leave. Witt Corser had been a knot in her hair since they were kids, but his innkeeper father did a lot for Cataclede. A usefulness that bought him approximately two minutes of civility. "Too busy for news."

"Too busy, huh?" Luna snuffled Witt's hand for more attention, and he scratched her furry neck. "What's the body count then?"

Aza raised an annoyed eyebrow. Okay. Maybe only two seconds. "Not so many that I can't add one more."

He brought his hands to his chest as though she had struck him. "Right in the heart, and here I was hoping you'd dance with me at the festival this year."

Aza yawned. "Eat rocks, Witt."

"You'd have better luck with a taiga bear, Witty." Zephyr snorted.

"Well, you can't make sense of a heart's desire." Witt shrugged his bony shoulders with a smile. "Speaking of hearts, I hear you're courting the beautiful Miss Staria this week?"

"She's—"

A shout at the gate interrupted him, and Aza leapt to her feet, more than grateful for the excuse to escape the useless small talk.

"Twoscore soldiers approaching from the northern pass in full armor," the sentry shouted.

Before he finished the sentence, Aza had raced across the courtyard and up the short rampart stairs to the top of the stone wall. Sure enough, a company of soldiers rode their horses down the incline; their armor gleaming in the high sun. In their center, a man with golden blond waves and a flowing purple robe sat atop an alabaster stallion. Though she had only seen him once, Aza didn't need to get any closer to know who graced their doorstep.

The iron gate clanked open as her mother stepped out to meet them, fire already curling from her fists up her arms. As always, her red ragehound, Sasha, trotted stoically at her heels.

Though her father couldn't be seen, Aza knew he walked close to her mother. His apparent absence had a way of making their enemies uncomfortable. The two of them were easily a match for the soldiers, but her mother wouldn't use her fire on the living unless she had no other options.

"Mama, it's—" Aza started.

"I know," Kaia cut her off, her voice abnormally sharp. "Stay there."

Zephyr had crested the wall now and crossed his arms beside her. "What's that sack of filth doing here?"

"Which sack of filth?" Witt asked, tailing close behind Zephyr.

"Valente Conrad," Aza nearly spat the words. The son of the human necromancer who had battled her parents decades ago... and died at her mother's hands.

Witt cocked his head, the light breeze tousling his long curls. "Isn't that the old king's cousin that's trying to revive the monarchy?"

"Third cousin," Zephyr said.

"Allegedly," Aza added, watching the soldiers crawl down the mountain.

Witt nodded. "My father says he's the most powerful man in Okarria." Seeing Aza's glare, he quickly added, "Politically, of course."

"Even though his father used dark yanaa to raise an army of the undead 28 years ago," Aza grumbled. "How quickly the people forget." Though the Heirs had gained some bit of begrudging respect after her parents had saved Okarria from Idriel and the elder Conrad's armies of the undead—the *Lost*—somehow Valente Conrad had escaped any blight to his own reputation.

"People forget because he's blamed it all on the Heirs with his filthy lies." Zephyr cracked his knuckles one by one. "That's why we have to take control of Aquilond's shields before Conrad turns them against us."

Aza rolled her eyes. With the monarchy long dissolved, the defensive shield armies of the State-cities were the only professional soldiers Okarria had, and it was no secret her ambitious brother dreamed of commanding them. "You know Mother and Father hate the idea of meddling in politics."

"Short-sighted." Zephyr shook his head with a scowl. "If we meddle now, it'll save us blood later."

At last, the first soldiers stepped within shouting distance of the front gate, and Kaia let a gush of fire billow up toward the sky. The horses stopped, shifting nervously at the flames, their riders' expressions unreadable under their shining helmets.

"What do you want, Conrad?" Kaia shouted, her eyes alight with the glow of the fire encompassing her body.

Conrad's mount cut through his ranks of soldiers, his violet cloak billowing behind him. "Truce, Dragon. I come bearing news, and..." He paused, flashing a cruel smile. "Something that might belong to you."

Kaia let her flames fade ever so slightly. "Get on with it then and be on your way."

With a look from Conrad, the soldier next to him pulled a black bundle from his saddle bag and tossed it onto the road in front of them.

"Consider this an act of good faith," Conrad purred.

For a moment, Aza stared curiously at it, trying to discern what it could be.

Kaia drew in a soft gasp. "Shadmundar?" Beside her, Sasha barked anxiously.

Aza swallowed. Was it really? It had been years since she'd seen the cursed cat, but she had never seen him so... broken.

"Act of good faith?" Kaia's fire burned brighter, stretching into the blue mountain sky. "Is he even alive?"

The soldiers pulled nervously at their reins at her outburst, but Conrad's smug smile only widened. Kaia took a threatening step toward him before jolting to a stop, as though someone had stopped her with a hand. Closing her eyes, Kaia visibly took a breath, her fire receding again. Sasha whined at her feet.

"Would this be the Shadmundar, servant to the magus, Everard?" Kaia called in a barely controlled snarl.

Aza's eyebrows rose ever so slightly. Her mother had chosen her words carefully. Shadmundar was more of an ensorcelled spy rather than a servant, but Everard would be furious if he saw him treated so badly. And a magus' ire was nothing to take lightly. Even if no one had heard from him in a decade.

"He's alive." Conrad shrugged, the picture of nonchalance. "We found him in a ditch by Direfent. The town was burned to the ground. Not sure if he had anything to do with it."

Kaia visibly flinched. "Of course, he didn't have—"

"The Western Guard has been all but decimated," Conrad continued as if she hadn't spoken. "So we ride to the State-cities to gather shields to defend the west from the Rastgol." He gestured toward the walls. "And perhaps any students from your esteemed academy?"

"Another power grab," Aza growled, but the thought of the Rastgol's hulking bodies and faces scarred with kill tallies sent a chill down her spine.

"And a good one," whispered Zephyr. "If he gathers the armies of the State-cities, who could deny him the throne?"

Kaia spoke quietly to an unseen Klaus hovering somewhere nearby. After a moment, her raised voice echoed over the mountain again. "No need. We will take the Dracour west to meet the threat ourselves."

Aza smiled at the barely veiled warning. With the sinuous four-legged body of a dragon and the scaly torso of a man, the Dracour were the fiercest warriors in the land and one of her mother's closest allies.

Conrad chuckled, his placid expression unchanged. He'd obviously expected this, but what was he playing at? "So be it then, but if you tarry, you can be sure we'll be right behind you." He paused, his white teeth flashing. "For support, of course."

The syrupy threat sent a chill up Aza's spine as though she could already feel Conrad's blade twisting in her back.

"Best of luck, Dragon." Conrad's gaze moved to where Aza stood with the others on the ramparts, and he winked. "And Shadow. Till next we meet." With that, he jerked his head for his retinue to return the way they'd come.

Kaia nodded, and Klaus blinked into sight beside her. Together, they conferred in low tones while the soldiers retreated back up the mountain. Then, with Sasha trailing at her heels, her mother moved with measured, purposeful steps toward the bundle lying in the road.

Without waiting for an invitation, Aza leapt from the stone wall onto the long mountain grass below. Rolling to her feet, she jogged to her parents' side with Zephyr close behind her.

While Klaus still eyed the retreating soldiers, Kaia knelt to assess the injured cat. His paws had been bound together and a rag had been tied around his mouth in a crude gag. Tufts of his dark fur had been torn away to reveal the pale skin beneath. Scabbed and oozing gashes crossed his flanks and neck, and his ribs stuck out from underneath his matted fur. He did not stir at their approach, but his chest pulsed with shallow breaths.

Sasha snuffled at his head with a snort while Kaia burned through the bonds with heated fingers. "Shadmundar?" she whispered.

With something between a groan and a mewl, the black cat opened a single bright sapphire eye. For a moment, the pupil narrowed in confusion, before he focused. Then, he released a deep sigh of relief. "Finally. That took long enough."

"Are you all right?" Kaia whispered, her careful hands gingerly probing his wounds.

Amusement and annoyance flickered across his small black face. "Yes. Perfectly dandy. Why do you ask?"

The wind whistled between them for a moment. Then, Klaus cracked the silence, throwing his head back with a dry laugh.

Relief twisted into a wry smile on Kaia's face. "If you're well enough for scorn, then I suppose you'll survive long enough to tell us what happened." She gently scooped him into her arms.

Shad grimaced at the movement, but he didn't resist. "Well, I've been imprisoned in Conrad's saddlebags for two weeks. But at least I didn't have to listen to two Heirs bicker the whole time I suppose." He blinked slowly. "Small favors."

Zephyr whispered close to Aza's ear, "But I thought he was supposed to change back into a man years ago?"

Shadmundar fixed Zephyr with his one open eye. "That would be why I was searching for Everard in the west to undo this wretched curse. It's only been 108 years." His ears flattened. "Not that I'm counting."

Kaia started toward Catalede with a frown. "I'm sorry, Shadmundar, but we haven't seen or heard from Everard either."

"So, what happened in Direfent? Or did Conrad do this to you?" Klaus asked from Kaia's side, his eyes still on the last soldier cresting the mountain pass.

"It was the Rastgol. They attacked Direfent two weeks ago," Shadmundar said softly, the tip of his tail twitching back and forth.

Aza tensed. Two weeks ago? That *wasn't* a coincidence.

Shad's gaze met Kaia's. "Except the Rastgol were already dead. They roam now as the Lost."

Kaia's strides paused, a long sorrowful sigh oozing from her lips. "So Direfent's Guard really is gone then."

The keen of the Lost echoed in Aza's thoughts. The Rastgol were bad enough… but as the undead? A river of ice ran down her spine. How had the Rastgol learned necromancy? Or had Idriel bestowed the unholy power upon them before her father had killed him all those years ago? Aza clenched her jaw. That's all they needed—more of Idriel's Children stalking the land.

"It will take weeks to even get to the canyon," Klaus said, his face dark. "We must send a message to the Dracour and leave at once before the Rastgol reach Faveno. If we're dealing with the Lost, their ranks will only swell as they kill."

Zephyr stepped forward with a smile on his face. "I'm always ready to torch some dead."

"No, Zephyr." Kaia shook her head as she continued toward the gate, shifting Shad in her arms. "You and Aza will stay."

Zephyr's face fell like a disappointed child. "But you and I always go when there's Lost."

Klaus squeezed Zephyr's shoulder. "Yes, but we haven't had to deal with a necromancer for almost thirty years. Much less the Rastgol. This calls for a Shadow and a Dragon."

"Besides." Kaia tried for a weak smile, the worry still gleaming in her eyes. "We need you to run Catalede while we're gone."

Zephyr shrugged—not smiling but perhaps momentarily appeased.

Klaus' gaze flicked to Aza. "And you too, Aza."

Aza met his stare with her own. "But we can't trust Conrad. What if it's a trap?"

"We're not trusting Conrad," Kaia replied. "We're trusting Shad. And if the Lost are involved, then it's our responsibility to destroy them."

"Why would Conrad come here in the first place though?" Aza pressed.

"Because he's a coward," Zephyr said. "He wants us to take care of the Rastgol so he can take credit without getting his hands dirty. Like he always does."

"But Papa…" Aza paused. He had specifically asked her not to tell anyone about the voices on the Shadow Plane, but they were so obviously connected she practically had to bite her tongue. "What about going to visit Dorinar? I don't mind going by myself."

"There are more important things going on in the world right now," Klaus said.

"But maybe Dorinar knows something about it. This could be connected to…" Her father's eyes flashed in warning, and Aza's fists clenched. "Something bigger. We need to ask."

Her mother's face tightened. "Send a harehawk then, Aza. I don't want you going anywhere by yourself with reports of the Lost roaming the land. And even then, you know the magi can be…" Kaia glanced at Shad. "Unpredictable."

Aza swallowed. Between the beastly Maldibor clan and Shadmundar, the magi were well-known for their creative punishments against humans who displeased them. But, Dorinar had dedicated centuries of his life to collecting and preserving Okarria's history. It was more than worth the risk.

"It can wait until the fall, Aza," her father added with finality. "Just have patience."

For a moment, Aza's steely gaze studied her parents as they walked through the gates of Catalede. Her father's eyes were hard and uncompromising while her mother's were filled with love and worry. Aza wouldn't win this argument.

Finally, she forced herself to nod. This was ridiculous. She'd been patrolling the land for three years, had taken more lives than she cared to recount, and had handled a dozen men by herself in the last week. Her fingernails dug into her palms, but her placid features revealed nothing. She would figure it out herself later. Because if she didn't… the image of a rotting Rastgol face with empty eyes flashed through her mind… Well, she knew what monsters were on the hunt now.

4
COINCIDENCE

A week after her parents' hasty departure, Aza drilled out her frustration on the training grounds. A handful of Greens watched her, mouths agape, while another two pairs trained with staffs in another corner. Shad curled against a wall, his fur still patchy over his healing injuries and one eye forever closed, but his poise restored by rest and safety. His remaining blue eye followed Aza carefully, looking for what she didn't know.

Used to having an audience in the training courtyard, Aza blocked them out effortlessly. With a chest plate and a sword made of gravisten, a metal three times heavier than gold, Aza whirled around the empty grass square. She maneuvered the heavy blade with the hard-won precision forged through years of training. Her distinctive style combined the unnatural strength and speed of an Heir with the delicate grace of a shadow. Even her father had trouble keeping up with her now. She sprinted across the grass, rolled, and came to her feet with a twist of her sword before sprinting across the square again.

Her hair whipped behind her and sweat slipped down the bridge of her nose as she thought. Her mother nursed a lingering paranoia after Mogens had…

Aza rubbed her cheek with her shoulder as if she could smudge away the scar. But that had been three years ago. Her parents had trained them relentlessly ever since, both in the training yard and on patrols. She was no longer that thirteen-year-old girl bumbling in the woods. She was a trained killer.

She blew a stray lock of hair from her face and whirled the blade's tip in a tightly controlled pattern in front of her. Her mother's nightmares, the cries of the Shadow Plane, and now new Lost raised again—it was all connected somehow. And yet, they still had no real idea where the Lost had come from. Had the Rastgol learned necromancy? What if the Lost were just bait? Hadn't her father always told her not to make the obvious move? They needed to know more—they needed the magi. She twisted into a backflip, finishing with a thrust of her blade into her imaginary opponent's gut.

The swish of Luna's wagging tail and Zephyr's accompanying footsteps cut through her focus like a knife through meat. With another somersault and a flick of the wrist, she was facing him, blade inches from his smug countenance. The Greens exchanged knowing smiles at the prospect of a match between the Heirs. Between training bouts, exhibitions, and petty quarrels, scuffles between the younger Heirs were more than common at Catalede. Luna retreated to her familiar corner of the training ground and scratched at the dirt before settling down in a heap.

"My, my, aren't you testy this morning?" Zephyr said, his brown eyes twinkling.

Aza rested the blunt blade on her armored shoulder. "What do you want, Zeph?"

Zephyr turned his back to her and walked over to pick out one of the training blades from the rack. "I just wanted to know why you're still in such a tizzy." He swung it experimentally. "We've got the run of the place now."

"Because Conrad is slimy, no one's listening to me…" Aza twirled her blade around her wrist as she spoke. "And something just feels wrong."

She threw the heavy blade in the air and caught it again, spinning it around her other wrist. The Greens murmured appreciatively. Shad leapt onto the top of the weapons rack, his tail flicking from side to side.

"Something feels wrong? What? Did you have a bad dream or something?" Zephyr knocked her spinning blade out of the air.

With two quick steps, Aza caught it and pointed it at him. "All I wanted was to study with Dorinar to find out more about the Shadow Plane. I don't think that's asking a lot."

"That's a terrible idea." Zephyr scoffed. "Not even Mother and Father travel alone, and Tazgar is almost a month-long journey. Besides, Dorinar's not exactly friendly."

Aza beat at his blade, almost jarring it from his relaxed fingers and closed in until her face was inches from his. "I'm a Shadow Heir," she hissed. "I'm more than capable."

Zephyr ducked with a sweeping kick to knock Aza's feet out from under her. She avoided it with a one-handed back handspring. He closed the distance and attacked with three slashes before locking blades with Aza. "Calm your britches! Our parents are *literally* legends. They don't need your help. Why can't you just relax for once? With them gone, I'm going to train an elite class." Ambition lit Zephyr's eyes.

Aza threw him off and hacked at his blade, getting through his defense to slap him on the thigh with the flat of her weapon. "How typical. Our parents are journeying to the war-torn barbarian border to face the Lost and all you can think about is *you*."

"Oh, get off your high horse." Zephyr grabbed her sword arm and flipped her into the dirt. "This is about your obsession with the Shadow Plane, not your *concern* for our parents."

Aza rolled with the throw and sprang to her feet. In another blink, she launched herself at Zephyr once again, battering away at his blade. "I'm *not* obsessed."

Zephyr retreated while he parried and dodged her furious blows. "Oh c'mon, Azy." He grinned. "You're always off in your own little world. It's all you think about."

"At least I'm actually thinking about something, instead of chasing after girls." Aza knocked the light blade out of Zephyr's hand and slashed low at his legs.

Zephyr nimbly avoided the blunt edge of her weapon and dove toward his blade. He picked it up with a roll and came to his feet. "I can't help it if I'm a town favorite." He feinted right and struck quickly at her left. "And they'll love me even more when I convince the Aquilond regent to make me captain of his shields." Aza let him in close enough to clip her on the shoulder. She absorbed the blow, using its momentum to send her into a spinning kick that smashed against Zephyr's chest and knocked him on his back.

"Well as far as I'm concerned, brother, Catalede is all yours. Don't let me stand in the way of your plans."

Zephyr stretched on the ground with a yawn and pillowed his hands behind his head as if there were no place he'd rather be. "I won't."

Aza sank her blade into the dirt, too aggravated for words, and stalked out. There was no talking to her meathead brother. Hot with frustration, she nearly ran over Witt on her way out of the courtyard's stone archway.

"Oh, Aza, are you looking for a sparring partner? Because..." Witt flexed a thin bicep.

She stepped around him without pause. "Try my fool of a brother instead," she called over her shoulder. "He needs the practice."

With a huff of annoyance, she rounded the corner and ran straight into a seven-foot-tall beast. Aza stepped back, the smell of wet dog and animal musk nearly overpowering her. Covered in shaggy wheat-colored fur, the Maldibor wore a huge broadsword strapped to his bear-like torso, a pair of loose breeches, and dusty boots. One of his wolfish ears flicked forward while the other lay half-flopped, and his green eyes crinkled with good humor.

"Hello, Aza."

Makeo.

What were the Maldibor doing here? Of course, the sentry would've let them in—the Maldibor clan were always welcome. But it was a three-week journey from their village in Carceroc Forest, and the spring festival wasn't for another fortnight. Even then it was usually the chief, Tekoa, who visited... not his nephew.

She stepped back and crossed her arms to keep the twisting emotions hidden within. It had been years since she'd even seen Makeo, much less spoken to him. Now, here he was, the cursed beast looming larger than ever. Though Aza would only ever be able to see the light-footed boy with the bright smile he used to be. For the friendly warmth that was Makeo still oozed out of his hulking form, wrapping her in its nostalgic embrace. And all she wanted to do was get away from him.

"Makeo." She nodded. "We... weren't expecting you."

"Our apologies." His tongue lolled out to show his long teeth in the Maldibor smile. "It was an unexpected visit."

A broad-shouldered young woman with short mahogany curls walked up from behind him, a long sword on her belt and a smile on her lips. Though she didn't share her cousin's beastly form, her tense eyes glowed green with the curse she'd pass on to her sons. "Aza," she said, taking Aza by the forearm in the traditional Maldibor greeting. "Good to see you."

"Hoku." Aza squeezed Hoku's forearm in return, her skin prickling. "Is there something wrong?"

Hoku raised her chin. "We seek aid from the Heirs."

Aza's heart turned cold. *Another coincidence.* "I'm afraid you missed them." She fingered the hilt of one of her daggers. "My parents left with the Dracour a week ago to defend the west from the Lost."

Hoku and Makeo exchanged a taut glance.

"That's terrible news," Hoku whispered.

Zephyr emerged from the archway behind Aza with Shad following as a silent shadow.

"Hoku and Makeo! What a pleasant surprise," Zephyr said with a wide smile. He walked up beside Aza and squeezed her shoulder. Her jaw tightening, Aza shrugged his hand away.

"It's good to see you." Zephyr's forehead wrinkled as he took in their grim expressions. "Is there some... trouble?"

"Something disturbs the denizens of Carceroc," Makeo rumbled in his deep bass. "The creatures grow restless and aggressive. We fear we may not be able to stay, so Chief Tekoa requests the strength of the Heirs to ensure the safety of our people."

A shiver ran up Aza's spine. The magi had imprisoned the ancient mankillers in Carceroc to keep humanity safe, and their stories warned of the hypnotizing cylcogres, the childlike cries of the bloodsucking strigans, and of

26

course, the king of darkness—the Dolobra. Though the creatures usually lived peacefully alongside the Maldibor, that didn't stop the elders from scaring their children with hair-raising tales to keep them from straying too far into the labyrinth of Carceroc Forest.

"Well, that can't be a coincidence." Shad curled his tail around his haunches as he sat on the dirt path. "Trouble in the west and disturbances in Carceroc."

Aza raised an eyebrow. At least she wasn't the only one seeing the connection.

Zephyr straightened—all traces of his earlier levity gone. "How long until you have to move?"

"As soon as possible," Hoku said.

For a moment, Zephyr was silent. His gaze swept over Catalede, the mountains beyond, and then back to Hoku. His brows knitted as he weighed the options, and Aza could read the thoughts on his face as if they were scrawled on his forehead. Their parents had left firm instructions to look after Catalede, but... Tekoa was their mother's closest friend. They couldn't abandon the Maldibor in their time of need. Plus, defeating the ancient mankillers of Carceroc? The villagers would love him for it.

The creases in Zephyr's face smoothed into a smile as he made his decision. "Anything for our Maldibor friends." Zephyr looked at Aza, his cheeks practically glowing with excited ambition.

Aza repressed the urge to roll her eyes and nodded. Any action was better than staying here.

"I'll gather the students that are willing and competent and arrange for my uncles to lead in our absence." Zephyr rubbed his jaw as he thought. "We can leave as early as tomorrow."

"Our thanks, Zephyr." The lines eased from Hoku's face. "This means the world to our clan."

"Of course, it's our duty." Zephyr took her hand with his most charming smile and pulled her toward the training ground. "But come, rest and have something to eat while we make the preparations."

Zephyr ushered the Maldibor woman away, and Shad's tail swept across the dirt path. "Just when I thought I was going to get some rest for a change."

Aza arched a brow. "Shouldn't you stay here? You're still weak."

"If the ancient forest of mankillers really is in turmoil, I'd rather not leave it in the hands of overgrown children." Shad's blue eye pierced through her. "No offense."

Makeo laughed in his rough, grating voice, and Aza suppressed the urge to deck both of them. "I thought you, of all people, wouldn't underestimate a young Heir."

"Underestimate? Never." Shad's gaze slid along the scar on her cheek, like everyone's did at one point or another. "But I thought you, of all people, would understand that even Heirs make mistakes."

Aza's muscles tensed, the arrow of guilt finding its mark in her gut.

"Mistakes that are learned from, Shadmundar," Makeo rumbled softly, his soft gaze never leaving Aza.

Shad almost purred. "Well, that remains to be seen."

True to his word, and no doubt motivated by visions of glory, Zephyr assembled the travelers and their supplies before the sun had reached its peak the next day. And not two weeks after Aza had traveled north over the pass, she found herself headed south again with a dozen Greens, one cursed cat, and two Maldibor. Their mounts trailed in a long line through the tall mountain grass, the dirt path curving around the belly of the broad mountain, and the rocky, white-capped peaks staring down on them.

The cold fingers of the spring breeze wormed through Aza's dark cloak, bringing with it the promise of a late frost with the falling sun. Though Zephyr and the Greens chuckled and chattered up ahead, Aza let herself fall behind. Her gaze still followed the others' expressions and gestures, but her mind spun with her own thoughts.

Even though she'd rather be traveling her own way, she'd gone along with her brother's overbearing lead. Every step away from Catalede was a step in the right direction—for now. While she cared deeply for the Maldibor tribe, the world was turning upside down all at once, and if she was going to fix it, she needed to cut out the heart of the problem, not the fingers.

Shad's battered ears poked out of Zephyr's saddlebag, and Aza's eyes strayed to Makeo and Hoku's Dalteek—a flaxen liver chestnut for him and a piebald for her. Makeo's tall ear flicked back toward her almost as if he could feel her eyes. Just looking at him reminded her of all those summers she had spent chasing after the round-cheeked boy with floppy blond hair he had once been—before his family's inevitable curse claimed him in adolescence. Even though they hadn't spoken since he first arrived, it was as if a well of unspoken words filled the space between them. Yet another reason she had to get away.

"I guess I never really had a chance against that Maldibor, huh?"

Aza turned to see Witt Corser smiling at her from the back of a muddy brown gelding. She tried to keep her cheeks from burning. "Witt, you never had a chance against the old scarecrow in our garden." She shook her head. "I thought you would've wanted to stay for the festival."

He shrugged with calculated innocence. "What good is the festival if you're not there to be my dance partner?"

Aza silently cursed her brother for letting this idiot tag along. Although he'd trained alongside them at Catalede for years, it hardly compensated for his annoying personality.

He didn't wait for her answer before going on. "It's actually my first time farther than Aquilond, if you can believe it." He rubbed the leather reins between his fingers. "Since I'm seventeen now, it was the first time my parents couldn't force me to stay."

"Pity."

He continued on, but she didn't hear him, as calculations rattled through her mind. It would take a party this size three weeks to reach Carceroc. From Carceroc, it would probably take her a week to make it over the mountains to Tazgar marsh by herself. She didn't have that kind of time. But... what if she left now and went by sea instead? She could reach Aquilond in three days, and the sea voyage would cut the journey in half.

Her gaze cut to the sinking sun across the lush mountain meadows dotted with the bright orange petals of phoenix clover. They'd be making camp soon, but they'd be cutting west across Glim Pass in the morning. And she couldn't be with them when they did. She wasn't going to make the obvious move again. And if she traveled fast, she might still be able to meet them in Carceroc in a few weeks' time. Armed with Dorinar's knowledge, they could get to the root of the problem instead of hassling with the weeds.

The decision sank and solidified in her chest like cooling metal. With her mind made up, she straightened in her saddle, a smile at last smoothing her scowl. She turned to Witt and was surprised to find that he was, in fact, still talking.

"I've just been dreaming of going with you and Zeph on your adventures since we were kids, you know?"

"Sure, Witt." Her gaze drifted east, away from him. Starting tomorrow Witt, Zephyr, and Makeo could go off on their own adventure. And she could go on hers.

5

PATHS DIVERGE

That night the party gathered around the campfire in a thick copse of trees to break their almost-fresh bread. The Greens' laughter boomed in the shelter of the white trunks of the evergold pines as they bantered with one another, their good cheer brightening the thick dusk. Witt prattled on about the different stews his mother made at the Cataledan Inn as he stirred the pot hanging over their fire. He'd collected some herbs and roots to add to the stout chuckhog that a Green had managed to shoot earlier in the day, and though Aza hated to admit it, the stew smelled delicious.

Aza's gaze stayed on her brother as he joked with Witt and his other friends. How would he react when she told him she was leaving? Her eyes flicked to Makeo across the fire. And would Tekoa and his clan forgive her if she didn't answer the call to defend their people? She wanted to help after all, but she knew in her gut, this wasn't the way to do it.

She took a bite from the hunk of bread in her hand and sighed. Perhaps if she wished it hard enough, she could just melt into the shadow of the trees, and they wouldn't even realize she was gone. A mellow flute broke through her thoughts as one of the Greens struck up a familiar tune. It was an old song, but not an ancient one, and they all knew the words. It only took a moment for a deep voice to start the first verse.

Nifras, the demon,
Raised the dead,
So Odriel, the blessed,
Raised the Heirs in his stead.

He set the brave alight,

Covered the sly with a pall,
Letting the gentle heal,
To battle the demon and save us all.

They put the demon down,
And for eons he slept,
Till the world forgot,
And from his grave he leapt.

Okarria's finest answered our plea,
Led by a girl and a wolf,
And a man walking unseen,
They charged to death's arms,

Through fire and steel,
The necromancer failed,
Burned with his Lost,
Now, we sing their tale.

The Greens clapped and whooped at the song, patting her brother on the back, as if touching an Heir would get them just a little closer to the fresh legend. Aza's lips twisted into a wry grin. Her mother hated that telling. She hated how it painted the battle as if it had been some grand victory, rather than a desperate scrabble for survival. And how it left out the human necromancer who had almost killed them. Especially now that his son, Valente Conrad, was campaigning to revive the monarchy. And she especially hated how it didn't mention the death of their third counterpart, the healing Time Heir, and everyone else who'd fallen.

Aza's gut twisted. Her mother would skin her alive if she knew that she planned to abandon the Maldibor in their time of need. She stepped back from the fire and gathered the shadows around her, hiding herself from sight. If she was going to go off on her own, she had to be sure. She stopped, hesitating. The drain on her muscles would make the ride miserable for the next couple days.

"Azzaaaaaaaaaaaaaaaaaaa."

But she had to see it again. Her skin practically itched with the need for the shadows. She tensed her muscles and pulled.

In a dizzying rush of draining yanaa, the honey-colored boughs of the evergolds disappeared and the plunge into the darkness wrapped her in its rapturous arms. The Shadow Plane was empty once again, fields of gray stretching beyond her sight.

Impatient, Aza yelled into the black, "Well! You called me! What do you want?"

31

The wind swooped around her in an angry gust, and Aza braced herself for the screams. But instead, snatches of her parents' voices whispered on the wind.

"…too many…" her father said.

"…too fast for flames…" her mother called back.

"…we have to run…"

"…it's too late…"

"No." Aza shook her head. "That's not real. They just left last week."

The keen of the Lost answered her cry, chased by the crackle of fire and the burning scent of charred flesh.

Aza ground her teeth together, her muscles trembling. "Why is this all happening?"

A gust of the Shadow Plane's last command, sharp and final, pierced through Aza. *"Find us."*

Aza released the shadows and fell to her knees in the dark wood. She tried to quiet her heaving chest, but Shad's strangely luminescent eye skewered her in the dark.

"Now, why would a Shadow Heir go disappearing into the dark on a quiet night like this?"

Ignoring him, Aza came to her feet. She rolled out her shoulders one by one and then shook out her legs, her parents' voices on the Shadow Plane echoing in the cavern of her mind.

He cocked his small black head. "It wouldn't be that mysterious Shadow Plane your brother was talking about, would it?"

Aza sighed and wiped her damp brow. "You're really nosy for a cat. Did you know that?"

She walked past him into the camp, her gaze finding her brother. Zephyr sat close together with Hoku, while Luna stretched out at their feet. His head bent next to Hoku's as she told him something with a smile.

Aza crouched on his other side, waiting for him to look up. Luna snuffled at her pockets, and Aza absently fed her the bit of dried meat she'd saved for her. Makeo nudged Hoku and nodded at Aza.

Hoku cut her sentence short with a furrowed brow. "Aza, are you okay?"

Aza nodded with a tight smile. "I just need to borrow my brother for a moment."

"What, Aza?" Zephyr frowned as she pulled him deeper into the trees.

Aza ran a thumb along the scar on her sweat-slicked cheek, trying to look for the right words so he didn't explode with anger. "I…"

But she didn't get further than that before his eyes widened with furious understanding. "You crossed over to the Shadow Plane, didn't you?" He didn't wait for her answer. "Now, how long will it be before you can Shadow Step again? What happens if we get attacked—"

"I heard Mother and Father," Aza cut in, her voice quiet under his

32

bubbling outrage. "They sounded like they were in trouble."

Zephyr crossed his arms. "Oh? And does the Shadow Plane give you the ability to hear leagues away now?"

"I don't know, but—"

"This sounds like you had some kind of waking nightmare." He raised a skeptical eyebrow. "How do you know it's real and not your mind playing tricks on you?"

Aza gritted her teeth. "Even if it wasn't real. I think it was a warning." She gestured around them. "All this can't be a coincidence, Zephyr. Maybe the Shadow Plane is tied to it somehow." She paused, her voice low and urgent. "I have to find out."

"No." The muscle in his jaw bulged, and he jerked a hand toward the camp. "We can't abandon the Maldibor. They're practically like our second family."

"But you don't need me, Zephyr," she reasoned, hoping to appeal to his vanity. "You've got a dozen Greens you've trained yourself and *fire* at your fingertips."

"You've heard the Maldibor's stories, Aza. Not everything can be killed with fire and steel." His eyes glinted in the dark. "Especially not in Carceroc."

Aza held his gaze, hunting for the words he needed to hear. "The sooner I leave, the sooner I can return."

He stabbed a finger into her collar. "You're not going."

Aza stared, her thoughts running away with her. Why was he being so stubborn? Was the courageous Dragon Heir scared? For her safety? Or for his own? In the end, it didn't really matter. She wanted him to understand, but she didn't need his permission.

"The Dragon and Shadow butting heads?" Shad padded toward them on silent paws. "Now, why does this look familiar?"

Zephyr's gaze branded Aza with one last scorching look before turning to Shad. "Just a heart-to-heart between siblings." He shrugged and started back to the fire. "Nothing to worry about."

Aza stayed where she was, her gaze drifting up to the stars peeking between the evergold branches.

"The Shadow Plane worries you?" Shad's one remaining pupil narrowed to a slice of black.

She ironed her features to neutral and turned toward the laughter still buzzing around the fire. "Worrying brings no answers."

That's why she had to go find them for herself.

Aza let herself doze against a tree while she waited for the camp to fall asleep. Her eyes flicked open while the waxing moon still hovered high in the constellations. A Green kept watch on the other side of the still-bright fire. Her muscles ached from her time in the Shadow Plane, but she didn't need to Shadow Step to avoid one person's eyes. She rose silently and crept through the night.

Hoku's Dalteek's ears flicked toward Aza as she approached it, but didn't startle as she slipped the letter she'd written into one of the saddle bags, making sure it stuck out enough to be easily noticed. She resisted the urge to run her fingers through its thick black and white fur and bury her face in its shaggy mane. Hopefully, the ink would explain her absence better than her tongue had. Hoku had to understand. But if she didn't... Aza would just have to ask forgiveness later.

Sighing, she padded over to where Oakhoof dozed standing up. She was far enough away now that the Green wouldn't notice her, but she wouldn't take any chances. Aza ran a gentle hand over Oakhoof's soft nose, and the mare's eyes flicked open. Aza hushed her and, pulling gently on her halter, led her to the dirt road.

As she walked away from the camp, Aza took one last look at the glowing fire, a stab of regret twisting her gut. Sneaking off into the night felt cowardly, but she couldn't have her brother making another scene either. She didn't want to alarm or rattle the Greens. So, she would do what she did best. She would disappear, and her brother would explain it away like it had been the plan all along. His pride demanded it so.

The path curved around the ridge, and the fire faded from sight. A soft gust ruffled her hair. Savoring the quiet of the night, it felt good to be out on her own at last. Free to go where she wished without anyone else's ridiculous opinions. She could move fast and didn't have to waste time putting her decisions up for committee. No matter what the others thought, she knew this was the right thing to do. Someone was calling her, and she had to figure out who.

She was leading Oakhoof down a sinuous mountain path when a faint whinny broke through the silence from below. In a heartbeat, Aza dropped to a crouch with a long dagger in each hand. Who could be on the mountain in the middle of the night? Aza looked down the switchback curving through the rocky mountainside and could just make out a familiar silhouette against the moonlit night.

Makeo.

A thousand curses rattled through Aza's thoughts, but only one option. With a sigh, Aza sheathed her daggers and guided Oakhoof down the last bends in the path. It had been easy enough to avoid one Green's eyes, but a Maldibor's nose and ears were a different matter.

Aza stopped three paces from where Makeo blocked the path, his Dalteek calmly grazing in the trees beside him. The familiar musk of a Maldibor drifted through the air between them. Her gaze flicked to the black cat perched on the Dalteek's saddle. *And Shadmundar too?* She rubbed the back of her neck, still sore from the Shadow Plane. Were they here to try to stop her? What would she do if they were?

Makeo turned his long muzzle to Shad. "I told you her mind was already made up."

Shadmundar's one-eyed stare glided from Aza to Makeo and back. "Well, I'm glad I haven't been robbed of a night's sleep for nothing."

"What are you doing here?" Aza asked softly, fiddling with the hilt of one of her many blades.

"Coming with you, obviously," Shad said.

Aza's shoulders relaxed ever so slightly. "What about your people in Carceroc, Makeo?"

"Carceroc has been quiet for centuries," Makeo rumbled. "If the Shadow Plane is causing the unrest, we need to know how to stop it."

Aza flicked a knife in and out of its sheath. "But my brother thinks it's just in my head, you know."

"That's not what I think." He took a step closer to her, his forest green gaze taking her back to a different night when those same eyes had stared out of a fourteen-year-old boy, his features still soft with childhood.

She skipped backward, teasing with a smile. "You'll have to keep up if you want to help me find the Dolobra."

"Just try me, shadow-girl," he said as he followed her, his cracking, boyish laugh ringing through the dark.

Of course, they'd found blood instead.

She shook her head, coming back to the shaggy beast in front of her. He had changed so much; it was hard to believe he was only a year older than her, as if the curse had aged him as well.

"I don't need—"

"Stop." Shad sighed. "Spare us your lone warrior's speech. You don't know what you're walking into, so how can you know if you'll need our help?"

Aza's mouth shut with a click. She twirled her dagger and studied her companions for a moment. Makeo's strength was undeniable. He towered over her with shoulders twice as broad as a barrel-chested man. But with a Maldibor at her side, it would be practically impossible to pass unnoticed—definitely not her style. His green eyes crinkled with a smile that didn't reach his gaping jaws.

Her gaze slid to Shad. While she didn't much care for another voice telling her what to do, Shadmundar had traveled with Everard for almost a century, and his eyes glittered with a lifetime of knowledge.

Aza lifted her chin to where the trail branched to the east. "Come if you must. But we'll have to move fast, I—"

Scrabbling rocks ricocheted through the night from somewhere on the incline. Makeo's wolf-like ears stood at attention, and he turned back the way they'd come. Aza could almost make out the twitching of his wet canine nose in the darkness.

Someone was rushing haphazardly down the path, pulling a horse behind them. *Odriel's teeth. Another one?* The figure caught sight of them and waved. He left the path and half-slid down the slope while his horse continued its more sensible descent without him. Finally at the bottom, he leaned over with his hands on his knees, panting heavily before continuing on.

Makeo's face cracked into a sharp-toothed smile, and Aza squinted to try to make out who was leaping through the long grass.

"Aza!" the figure called in a voice she was sure the whole mountain could hear.

Aza narrowed her eyes at Makeo. "You invited *Witt Corser?*"

Makeo chuckled deep in his throat. "Not me." He held his huge bear paws up in surrender.

"Aza!" Witt called again as he drew near. "Zeph sent me."

Aza squeezed her temples with a hand and gritted her teeth. "*Why?*"

Still panting, Witt shrugged. "He wanted you to be safe, of course."

Odriel take him. Was this her brother's punishment for running off? She gestured to Shad and Makeo. "Well, as you can see, I already have plenty of—"

"Supplies," Makeo finished for her. "Glad you'll be coming along."

Aza glared at him.

Witt practically glowed. "To be honest, I'm flattered that Zeph asked." He turned to Aza with a mischievous smirk. "But you know, Aza, the Greens will probably assume we ran off together."

Aza didn't try to rein in the horror she was sure ran rampant on her face, and Makeo barked with laughter.

Witt's horse snuffled his neck, and Witt winked at Aza. "Zephyr's always trying to play matchmaker."

Aza's horror dripped into disgust. She crossed her arms to stop herself from stabbing Witt and making a run for it. But she couldn't give him the satisfaction when he was just trying to goad her. Maybe she could lose him on the way, when she was far enough not to have to worry about Zephyr chasing after them.

"Fine." Aza turned on her heel and stalked down the trail. "But you have to keep up. I'm not waiting for your sorry hide."

Witt whooped as he followed her. "This is so much better than a dance."

"Quiet, sheep-brain! You'll wake up the mountain!"

"Right, right," Witt said, unphased by Aza's acid words. "But Aza—"

"Stop talking, Witt."

For a brief moment, they walked in silence, following the mountain foothills to the east. As they crested a rise, Aza looked out into the heartland of Okarria. The full moon bathed the fields and forests in a silver glow. Tucked higher up in the peaks, a distant lantern twinkled in a window from her mother's childhood town of Arimoke.

"Aza?" Witt whispered again.

Aza sighed. "What?"

"Where are we actually going?"

Aza's eyes rolled so hard it almost hurt. Makeo rumbled with barely suppressed laughter, his green eyes twinkling in the moonlight. Only Shad seemed to share her distaste.

She could just barely make out his grumble. "I can't believe I'm doing this again."

Well, no one asked you to. Aza swallowed the caustic thought.

The freedom that had lightened her steps only an hour before flittered off into the night. It was one thing to run off on a possible fool's errand on her own, it was a different thing to drag the others into who knew what. The three liabilities weighed on her like a heavy steel yoke chafing at her shoulders.

But at least she was moving in the right direction.

6
MORE THAN LOST

The sun had come and gone again before Aza finally allowed them to stop for the night. Though there was a town only a few miles ahead, she preferred to shelter in the quiet of the wood, away from prying eyes and nosy questions. Witt collected some herbs and roots to add to a brace of hedge hens Aza had managed to bring down, and the aroma of meat and spice bubbled in the air. Stirring the pot of bubbling soup hanging over the glowing coals, Witt filled every threat of silence with his constant prattle of the various seasons for prime ingredients.

"I'm beginning to think I preferred traveling with Conrad's soldiers," Shad grumbled. "At least they were quiet."

Makeo rose and walked back to the road. His ears and nose twitched as his gaze swiveled up and down the forest lane. Aza stood and walked to his side.

Aza crossed her heavy arms and sagged against the rough trunk of a nearby crimson oak. "Don't tell me we have yet another annoying tail?"

"Perhaps. There's a strange smell in the air."

Aza straightened, her gaze sweeping the empty dirt road cutting between the trees. "I guess you still have that same strange way of knowing things then?"

"My uncle says it's a side-effect of the yanaa that taints our veins—it gives us a heightened sense of foreboding." He shrugged his huge, shaggy shoulders. "Or perhaps it is just an unusually powerful nose." Makeo nodded his head toward the fire and held out a clawed hand.

"Stew is served!" Witt called, as if on cue.

Aza raised her eyebrows and turned toward the camp. "Almost like one of Odriel's Blessed."

Makeo made a noise somewhere between a scoff and a growl. "More like Ivanora's silver lining."

"Who's Ivanora?" Witt asked, looking up from the stew.

Makeo settled by the fire and accepted a bowl. "The lady magus my ancestor spurned. So, she cursed him and his offspring with the smell, voice, and form of the beast." He gestured to himself.

"Except for the night of the dark moon," Aza added, remembering the short smiling boy Makeo had been. She took a bowl from Witt and settled next to the warmth of the flames. What did Makeo look like on his human nights now?

"Yes. A man for one day in twenty-one." Makeo's eyes crinkled at her with something akin to wistfulness. "Always a day to look forward to."

No sooner was his bowl empty, than Witt snored loudly at the fire's edge next to the tightly curled ball of Shad. Aza sagged against her pack, her leaden eyelids drooping toward her cheeks. She had barely slept in two days, and her restoring yanaa still sapped her strength. Makeo sat on a log across the fire from her, but his eyes were still trained toward the road.

"Go ahead and sleep, Aze," he rumbled. "I'll take first watch."

Aza opened her mouth to object, but her words slipped from her mind like water through a sieve. Her eyelids dipped again, and this time, she let them fall closed.

The headless child faced her once again, pointing at her, with the screams of the Shadow Plane swirling around them in a vortex of darkness. She strained against the spinning shadows that pushed her back, but it was useless. Falling to her hands and knees, she reached into the expanse. She edged forward just enough to catch a glimpse of her parents, surrounded by bloodied warriors with black-filled eyes.

Aza lost her footing and the shadows ripped her backward like a leaf in the rapids. She slammed onto her back, the air knocked from her lungs. As she gasped for breath, the bulbous eye in the chest of the headless child peered over her.

When it opened its neck wound of a mouth, it was the whispers of the Shadow Plane that echoed out. "Azzzzzzaaaaa." The creature grabbed her by the shirt and pulled her inches away from its night-black eye. "Find us." Aza leaned away from the grotesque creature.

"Azzzzzzzzzzzzzaaa. Aza. Aza!"

The voice morphed from the eerie keen of the Shadow Plane to a low growl. It took Aza a moment to bob up from the depths of sleep and realize someone was actually calling her name. Aza's heavy eyelids fluttered open to see the bright green eyes of a beast looking down on her in the darkness. She tensed, her hand flying to the dagger at her hip. Shaking herself free from the clutches of the dream, she tried to remember where she was through the surreal fog still clouding her mind.

"Wake up!" Makeo rumbled.

Makeo? Oh right, on the road. "Is it my watch?" Aza tried to rub the images that stained the backs of her eyelids. The horses shifted and whickered nervously on the edge of camp, but the moon still glowed high in the sky. They couldn't have been sleeping more than an hour.

"No," Makeo whispered, his voice like distant thunder. "But the smell of death draws near."

Aza pulled a dagger and sprang to her feet, her head swiveling around their camp. The fire was low but still burning. Witt snored away in blissful ignorance, but Shad perked up beside him.

Aza tapped the flat of her blade against her thigh. "The Lost? How close?" One of Makeo's ears flicked to the side. "I don't know..."

"But we should leave before we have to find out." Shad crossed to where Witt lay and batted him on the cheek with his sharp claws

"Ow," Witt whined, raising a hand to his face. Sitting up, he glanced around through slitted eyes, his voice still slurred with sleep. "S'happenin'?"

"Deminen, the riverport, isn't far from here," Shad continued. "We'll be safer on the water."

The hair on the back of Aza's neck came alive. Her eyes scanned the darkness that glued the trees together into an impenetrable web of shadow around their camp. She spun her dagger around her wrist, adrenaline already shooting through her.

"We should stay and fight," she countered sharply. "If the Lost trail us, we'll be leading them straight to Deminen."

"We're vulnerable—" Shad didn't finish his sentence before steel flashed behind him.

"Get down!" Aza lunged toward Shad, swinging her blade up to meet the glinting edge arcing down on him. As she moved, the whistling air of a near miss tickled the back of her neck. Shad darted to the side to avoid the clash. The clang of metal on metal echoed through the still night as Aza deflected the blow. The face of her towering attacker looked on her with the black-filled eyes of her nightmares.

The Lost.

Makeo bellowed a beastly roar from behind her, and out of the corner of her eye, assailants rushed their campsite from all sides. Their shaved heads, powerful bodies, and scarred faces flickered in the fire, and a coil of cold dread wound in Aza's belly. *Rastgol.* Or at least they used to be not long ago. Their bodies seemed oddly... fresh.

"It's an ambush!" Makeo roared, parrying the blade of one, and throwing a massive paw to backhand another.

Aza took a step back as her attacker lunged forward. His heavy blows jarred her arms as she parried them. Another man charged Aza from her right. She rolled toward him and came to her feet inches before his boots, bringing her blade across his face. Bone cracked as his jaw broke away from his skull, but the man hardly even slowed. Aza dodged his ax handle, whirling in time to parry a cut from the first brute.

What were these things? The Rastgol were almost as tall as Makeo with white scars crawling up their shaved heads and down their heavily muscled arms. But even in death, they didn't fight like the Lost. And they were dead, weren't they?

"We need to get out of here!" Witt dodged behind a tree trunk before an ax blade sank into it.

"Get to the horses!" Shad shouted as he weaved between the feet of the attackers.

At Shad's call, one of the ambushers grabbed a burning brand from the fire and whipped the mounts with it. The poor beasts screamed and reared, pulling free of their loose ties. Witt's horse fled immediately, Oakhoof looked ready to fly, and Makeo's Dalteek aimed his sharp hooves at the attacker's head.

"Windtorn!" Makeo barked. With another buck, the stag crossed the fire to answer Makeo's call. Makeo leapt over the stag's flanks and into the saddle while the stag was still moving. "Shadmundar!"

Darting away from a flash of steel, Shad bolted from the fire. He only made it two leaps before another of the brutes blocked his path. Shad tried to dodge the club hurtling toward him, but the weapon caught the middle of his body, and he hit the ground like a downed bird. Aza rushed toward Shad while the Rastgol turned to swing his club at Windtorn, leaving his back unprotected.

Aza buried her dagger in the man's neck again and again, until his nearly decapitated head slumped onto his shoulder. Wrenching her dagger free, she scooped up Shad's limp body in one hand. Makeo reached down from Windtorn and grabbed the unconscious cat from her arms.

"Ride to Deminen!" she shouted.

Holding onto Shad with one hand and slashing at an attacker with the other, Makeo growled and locked eyes with Aza. "Not without you."

Aza ran her dagger across the throat of the Rastgol assailant. "We'll be right behind you." With that, she slapped Windtorn's flanks with the flat of her blade, and the stag sprang toward the road into the darkness.

Shad and Makeo safely away, Aza faced the three remaining Lost. She mustered her reserves of energy and dredged up the shadows. Oakhoof's excited whinny shattered her concentration as Witt ran the mare into the clearing.

"Aza!" Witt reached out as Oakhoof cantered by her.

With two quick steps, Aza grabbed his hand and swung up onto Oakhoof behind Witt. She could practically feel their pursuer's breath on her neck.

Witt spurred Oakhoof toward the road. "Ya!"

Oakhoof leapt through the underbrush and hit the road at a gallop. Aza clutched Witt's skinny ribcage, his heart thrumming like a rabbit's under her fingers. She craned her neck to watch the shadows in the night fade from view as the winding road turned sharply around the hilly landscape. Her eyes strained in the moonlit night as the distant thunder of hooves caught her ears.

"How many are there?" Witt yelled.

"I can't tell." Aza stared down the sinuous road behind them. "With the road winding like this, they'll be on our heels before we see them."

The beating of the hooves grew louder and louder until Aza was sure the horses would be nipping at Oakhoof's flanks any second. The twisting road finally straightened, and Aza caught sight of the riders in the dark. There were at least six of them, great hulking brutes on draft horses that devoured the road like starved demons.

Aza shifted on Oakhoof's slick flanks. "They'll be on us in a moment."

Witt's head whipped around to catch a glimpse of their pursuers, and Aza smacked him on the shoulder. "Turn around, you idiot! Oakhoof will run off a ledge in this dark if you're not looking."

"How are we going to lose them?"

"Don't be stupid. It's dark and we don't even know where we're going." Aza took inventory of her weapons. She had four knives, two daggers, and a sword and bow on her saddle. With Witt on the horse, she wouldn't have enough room to draw the bow. Her mind raced through the options. "Don't move!" Aza commanded as she shifted her grip around Witt's middle and hooked her right leg around his waist.

"What are you—"

"Just hold on!" She swung herself around Witt until she was in his lap, their noses only inches apart.

"Aza!" Witt spluttered, his voice thick with embarrassment.

"Watch the road!" Aza reached for one of the throwing knives, and focusing on the frothing horse's rider only two lengths behind, she lifted the blade. "Lean right."

"W-what?"

Aza pushed him aside with her free hand and let the knife fly. The blade buried itself into the rider's shoulder, but nothing happened. The rider flinched slightly, but he didn't slow or even cry out.

"Bleeding skies." Aza grabbed another knife.

She shoved Witt aside once again and heaved the short blade as hard as she could. This time the knife found its mark in the man's throat, an obvious death blow. The rider's head whipped back, and his horse stumbled, slowing. Blood oozed from the wound, but the man slapped the horse's flanks, and the beast lunged forward once again.

Aza's eyes narrowed. Only fire or decapitation would kill the Lost, but her blows weren't even slowing these things down. She growled in frustration. This was her brother's strong suit.

Poor Oakhoof was blowing now as she strained to keep up the breakneck speed. Aza swung back behind Witt to ease the load on Oakhoof's neck.

Witt turned Oakhoof sharply around another steep bend as they crested the hill. "Did you hit one?"

For a moment, Aza had no words. "These aren't the Lost..." But the rushing wind stole away her whisper.

"Earth below," Witt swore.

"What now?" Aza looked over Witt's shoulder. "Odriel's teeth."

Orange flames, screams, and smoke twisted together and rose from the river town below them. Townsfolk ran aimlessly about in the streets, and globs of people fled up the hill toward them.

Deminen was on fire. They didn't have to worry about leading these things to town. They'd already been there.

"We can't ride into that!" Witt shifted his grip on the reins to slow Oakhoof.

She slapped him on the shoulder again. "Keep riding! We have to find Makeo and Shad."

Oakhoof charged down the hill, weaving between the refugees scattered before her. The riders following them didn't bother to avoid anyone, running down any unfortunate soul in their path. As they entered the city, the smoke and heat from the burning buildings assaulted Aza's senses. Packs of the hulking Rastgol went from door to door, cutting down anyone or anything that stood before them. They'd been chased by the bees straight into the hive.

Witt had started to shake in Aza's arms. "They're everywhere!"

Aza's eyes watered from the smoke as they flicked from shadow to menacing shadow, and the shrill screams of the townsfolk pierced the air. A mesmerizing howl rose above it all. The voice emanating from the river was not human but sounded eerily familiar.

"Makeo's on the river, Witt! Keep on toward the water!"

Two of the riders had pulled up alongside them now, the spitting conflagration of the burning town reflecting off the naked steel of their blades. Aza drew her own sword just in time to block a slash to Witt's head. With her free hand, she drew one of her daggers from the holster on her thigh and parried a thrust from their right. Rasping out a hoarse scream, she brought her blade down on one of the riders.

Witt ducked low. "There they are!"

Out of the haze, Aza could make out Makeo's form on a small keelboat already drifting away from the dock. He lifted his snout and howled again.

Witt choked on the smoke. "They're leaving without us!"

Aza blocked another blow from the rider on her right. "Take Oakhoof to the bank; she'll swim it." *Hopefully.*

Witt yelped as Oakhoof leapt from the bank into the river. The punch of the icy mountain water knocked the air from Aza's lungs. The riders charged into the river behind them, but Oakhoof stopped when the water came up to her chest.

"She won't go any farther!" Witt cried.

"Then swim, you idiot!" Aza pushed off from Oakhoof toward the center of the river. The icy snowmelt water stiffened her limbs as she swam furiously toward the boat. She looked over her shoulder to see Witt flailing around, just keeping his head above water. Oakhoof had already swum back to shore, but the dark-eyed horses were running in too, and the river boat was passing swiftly with the current.

Indecision tore at Aza. Did she have time to save him? Could she risk it? The thump of a wet, heavy weight saved her from the choice. A rope! She threw the end to the sinking Witt. "Grab hold!"

Witt clutched the lifeline desperately, his arms still frantically splashing. Aza waved to the keelboat and the rope tightened under her fingers, pulling them through the water and away from their pursuers.

When they reached the boat, Makeo lifted them over the side and deposited them unceremoniously on the deck before unfurling the small, ragged sail. As Aza trembled on the rough wood, she glanced back toward the burning town. Amidst the swirl and chaos of the killers and their victims, she could just make out one figure standing rigid among the carnage. His hood fell back, and two hateful eyes met her stare from a slumped, rotting face still grinning 28 years after his death—his decomposition slowed by the dark yanaa coursing through him, the green haze of it curling around his limbs.

Mogens.

The Heir killer.

He slowly lifted a hand to his face, and then snapped his gloved fingers with a crack that cut through the chaos. The Rastgol froze in place, turning to face Aza as one, their eyes all glowing with that same flickering jade.

At last catching the wind, the keelboat charged away from the swimming horses, their unnatural riders, and the destruction they wrought. But the screams echoed down the river for miles.

7

AQUILOND

Makeo grabbed an old blanket wadded in the corner of the deck and draped it over Aza's shoulders. "Are you all right?"

Aza dried her face and tossed the blanket to Witt trembling next to her—from shock or cold, she wasn't sure. "I'm fine, I just..." She wrung out her sopping hair with shaking fingers, adrenaline still singing through her. "What were those things?"

Adjusting the tiller, Makeo guided their narrow vessel to the center of the stream. "Were they not the Lost?"

"The Lost I've seen were never that strong. They're clumsy and not very intelligent. Usually, they're only really dangerous if there are a lot of them." She wrapped her arms around herself as if to try to hold on to what little warmth she had left. "These seemed almost... alive."

Makeo nodded, his thick fur gleaming in the moonlight. "These were Hunters."

"A living body would be stronger than a dead one if it could be controlled," Shad muttered weakly from where he lay curled against the mast. "Why didn't you use your gift?"

Aza grimaced. "I'm still drained from entering the Shadow Plane."

"You need to rest and restore your energy," Makeo rumbled, concern reflecting in his large emerald eyes.

A sudden thought flashed through Aza, and her gut sank like a stone. "Where's Windtorn?"

"Don't worry for Windtorn," Makeo reassured her. "I sent him back to my kin in Carceroc. Without a rider, nothing will catch him. Not even those creatures."

Aza wished she could say the same for Oakhoof. Hopefully those creatures hadn't… She shuddered and tried to rub the chill from her arms. "Do you think those Lost could have been the same that burned Direfent?"

"The stories match. But Direfent is weeks away." Shad's ears flicked with a wince. "How could they be here already?"

For a moment, she was still, an odd certainty coming over her. "Idriel's Children."

Witt sat up, the blanket swaddled around him. "Whose children?"

"Idriel is the true name of Nifras, the demon necromancer my parents defeated all those years ago." Aza licked her lips. "Before he died, he told my mother his children would avenge him."

Witt frowned. "The demon necromancer has children?"

"No." Aza got to her feet, trying to stamp warmth back into them. "We don't know what he meant, but much of his dead army disappeared, and I could've sworn I saw Mogens back there… pulling their strings."

Makeo stiffened, his eyes meeting hers. "Yes. That was the scent. I knew I recognized it."

Witt looked from one to the other. "Mogens?"

"The Heir killer. He murdered Aza's grandfather and the generation of Heirs before him," Shad muttered, his eye half-closed. "Among many others."

"He's survived the dragon rage twice now." Aza ran a finger down the scar in her cheek. "Some even say he's unkillable."

She didn't have to ask to know it was Mogens' face that haunted her mother's dreams. He was the reason Aza's grandfather had tried to hide her mother away, the same reason the Time Heirs had gone into hiding, and the reason her parents had trained them so intensely. Like the Heirs' personal demon, forever haunting them.

Witt swallowed. "Well, that's reassuring."

Aza nodded absently. If Mogens was hunting them with these creatures, what did that mean for her brother and parents? Her heart stuttered. Surely they would be safe. Her parents' skill in battle was unmatched, and her brother had trained his whole life for this. She squeezed her hands together. If she could survive these things, then so could they. She had to believe it.

"Mogens is connected. Just like everything else. I need Dorinar to help me put it together." Aza rolled her neck with a crack. "There are many ships that sail from Aquilond to Austerden. I just have to convince one to make a stop in Tazgar."

"You mean *we* need to convince them," Makeo said with a chuckle.

Aza shrugged. *Or I could stow away on one.*

"I know someone who can get us a clipper to Tazgar," Shad said, blinking slowly.

Aza picked up the long river pole from the deck and dug it into the dark waters. "Good. We'll need to move fast with those things following us."

Aza bit the inside of her cheek. Part of her wanted to turn around and hunt down Mogens right then, but she shoved the thought away. That could come later. He was just another symptom of the disease that threatened Okarria. A distraction. She had to speak to Dorinar first.

Witt pulled the blanket tighter around his shoulders. "But the Lost can't swim, right? They won't be able to reach us on the boat."

Aza dug the pole into the river bottom, a slippery, cold feeling sliding around in her gut.

"Perhaps," Makeo rumbled. "But these aren't the Lost."

At dawn, Witt awoke, and Aza surrendered her pole to him to let herself doze. She rose at midday with yanaa once again swimming through her veins and found the small tributary had merged into the wider Koth river. By dusk, the Koth widened into the rocky bay that was Aquilond. Soaring pillars of natural stone rose out of the bay with roads and houses spiraling around them. Rope bridges swung between some of the spires, and people bustled from tower to tower without one glance toward the long drop to the calm water below.

Lanterns dotted the rocks, bathing the stone and water around them with their warm glow while all manner of voices echoed across the bay. Calls from one watercraft to another, laughter trickling out a window, and the indistinct barks of a heated conversation bobbed along the calm bay. The sun had already set, but the waterways were still crowded with short slender canoes as well as the keelboats that carried supplies and livestock.

Shad directed them through the maze of pillars to a shadowy tavern tucked into the bottom of a squat island on the edge of the city. The battered sign swinging from the door read *The Scorched Tooth* in faded blue letters. While a lantern glowed from the window, none of the talk and laughter of Aquilond's heart reached this far rock. Makeo pulled their small vessel up onto a creaking, uneven dock, and Witt hopped out to tie them fast.

Aza stepped out after him and wrinkled her nose at the inn, hunched and rickety as a doddering old man. "Well, this looks… cozy."

"So quick to judge, Shadow." Shad's left ear twitched. "You three stay here while I make the arrangements."

But when Shad padded up the steps to the old doorway, Aza followed.

"I said stay with the boat," he said over his shoulder, his fur puffing in annoyance. "The owner can be a bit… paranoid."

"All the more reason to bring insurance."

"They won't let you in."

"Have a little faith, Shadmundar." Aza smiled, gathering the shadows as she disappeared. "Besides, who's going to open the door for you?"

She reached out and twisted the tarnished brass handle before pushing open the squealing door.

Shad fixed her with a pointed glare before slipping past the doorjamb. "Rivka?"

Aza peeked in behind Shad to see a dusty, old tavern looking back. Circular tables and chairs cluttered the small room, while a low fire sputtered to one side. An empty bar crossed the back wall, and the staircase slumped up to a shadowy second floor. It was deserted. Aza wondered again how long it had been since Shad had last visited this place. Maybe the owners were long gone.

"Rivka," Shad called out again, louder.

Stepping in the doorway, Aza gently pushed him forward with her boot. He glowered at her with twitching whiskers. She only had one foot in the tavern before the whistle of a weapon had her dodging for cover. A hatchet whooshed by her to clatter on the stone floor. Shad bolted away with a yowl.

"Shadmundar, whoever's with you best go ahead and show themselves," said a husky feminine voice from above. A bald, muscular woman in a patchwork robe took a step down the staircase, another hatchet gripped in her meaty hand. "A magus? Or a Shadow Heir perhaps?"

"Peace," Aza said hurriedly. She released the shadows, and color flooded the world again as she blinked into view. "I meant no harm."

Shad sat on his haunches, his ears flattened into a peevish *I-told-you-so*.

"No harm?" Rivka took another step down the stairs. "You're Odriel's Assassin. You're full of harm, whether you mean it or not."

Aza opened her mouth to respond, but Shad cleared his throat. "Rivka, we've come on Everard's business."

"Ah." Rivka's squinty eyes shifted from Shad to Aza. "Then why isn't he with you?" Taking another slow step down, she raised the thin line of an eyebrow. "And why do you look like a battered stray? You used to be such a handsome cat."

Shad sighed. "Both an unfortunate sign of the times."

Rivka grunted and tapped her hatchet thoughtfully on the dull wooden banister, her shoulders relaxing. "Shame to misplace the last sane magus."

"Only temporarily I'm sure," Shad said dismissively. "Regardless of his whereabouts, I assume his accounts are still good here?"

"Of course." Rivka straightened with indignation, taking the last few steps quickly. "You won't find me crossing a magus here, there, or anywhere. Just be quick about your business and take your trouble with you." Bustling off toward the bar, she beckoned to Aza with a hand jangling with bracelets. "Come in then, Shadow, no use letting the night in. And the Maldibor and the other can come in, as well." She jerked a thumb toward the batwing doors that no doubt led to the kitchen. "Fausta's already preparing dinner."

Aza closed the door with a soft click and let the tension ease out of her in a slow breath. "Sharp ears, then?"

Rivka smiled, showing off a gleaming gold tooth. "Oh dear, we keep everything sharp here."

Aza's lips curved. She could like this woman.

Producing a bottle and a tall stein, Rivka poured herself a drink, and then lifted her chin at the nearest table. "C'mon then, cat. You know I hate small talk. What's your business?"

"I need to cash in a few favors." Shad padded over and leapt onto one of the tables. "We need an Austerden bound clipper that will drop us in Tazgar."

"Easy enough." Rivka took a swig from her mug. "Are you taking that Maldibor with you?"

Shad nodded.

"Well, that might make things more interesting." Her gaze slid to Aza. "But I suppose with a Shadow Heir on your side, you can look after yourselves just fine. I'll send Merryn to arrange it."

Shad nodded. "Much appreciated, as always."

Aza resisted the urge to fiddle with her knives. "Have you heard of any violence in the north of late? Gangs? Cutthroats?" She paused. "The Lost?"

Rivka rested her solid forearms on the bar. "Your clothes smell like the smoke that's been in the eastern breeze these last two days." She set her mug down with a *thunk*. "But you're the first to walk through with that brand of trouble."

The door creaked open, and Makeo paused at the threshold. "The girl, Merryn, sent us in."

Rivka nodded to him, her long fingernails clicking on her mug. Makeo ducked in through the doorway with Witt close on his tail, just as a tall, rangy woman walked in from the batwing doors on the other side.

She carried a tray of four steaming bowls of stew, earthen mugs, and two large loaves of bread. Setting the tray down on Shad's table, she retreated back to the kitchen.

Rivka gestured to the food. "I'll add dinner to Everard's tab. Take any rooms you like upstairs when you're ready." She pointed a long white nail at Shadmundar. "But come find me before you retire, cat. I want your ears." With that, she turned and followed the other woman out.

Shad's ragged ears twitched.

"Finally." Witt rushed the round table and fell upon a bowl. He'd scarcely put the fat spoon to his mouth, when his face contorted in pain. "Hot, hot, hot! Why did they serve it so hot?"

Aza shook her head as she sat next to him, still feeling strange in the empty room. She passed one of the bowls to Shad. "What kind of tavern is this?"

Shad bent to lap at the milky broth with his pink tongue. "A tavern with only a select clientele. Specifically those looking for privacy, or who have a lot of money to change hands."

Ah, well that would explain Rivka's… edge.

Makeo put a log on the fire before he pulled up a chair. "And which are you?"

Shad didn't look up. "Both. Everard has coin and enemies in every city. As his servant, so do I."

"I've never been in a tavern before." Makeo tore off a hunk of bread and took in the room. "Is this not normal?"

"The food's good, the fire's warm, and the beds are empty." Witt shrugged his bony shoulders. "That's all that really matters."

Aza drank from the bowl, letting the creamy stew coat her tongue. "That and catching the first clipper out tomorrow." She sipped dark cider from her cup. "You think she'll be able to make it happen?"

Shad nodded. "If Rivka says it will be done, it will be done."

"Why did she ask if Makeo was coming?" Aza asked.

Shad paused, his gaze meeting Makeo's. Makeo shifted in his seat as he answered. "Probably because there are many who still believe the Maldibor to be child-snatchers."

Aza snorted. "Because you take in runaways?"

Makeo shook his long muzzle. "They need no better reason than the teeth and claws."

"But the Maldibor were heroes in the last war," Witt said through stuffed cheeks.

Makeo's ears flattened. "As I'm sure the elder Heirs can tell you, most people remember the last war differently than we do."

Aza's lips twitched. The Heirs and the Maldibor had that in common. Since her mother had killed Valente Conrad's father in the Battle of Gyatus, the man had dedicated his life to spreading lies about the Heirs. While some understood the Heirs were sworn to protect them, others feared their power. She scowled. Let the Lost take them. After all her family and the Maldibor had sacrificed to keep Okarria safe, the pissers deserved it.

Witt swallowed his mouthful of food, unfazed by the heaviness that had settled over their table. "So, what's your village like?"

Makeo stared at his empty bowl as if hoping more food would magically spring from the ceramic. "Not so different from Catalede, just smaller."

Not meeting his gaze, Aza tossed Makeo half of her loaf of bread, and he nodded to her.

"And just the Maldibor live there?" Witt asked.

"No, our village acts as a sort of refuge for orphans and runaways." Makeo swabbed his bread around his empty bowl. "Some eventually make their way in the world, but many stay and make their home in the village."

"Hmm…" Witt's brow furrowed, and he looked at Aza. "But didn't your mom say most of the Maldibor got killed in the battle with Idriel?"

Aza glared at him, her fist tightening as she resisted the urge to hit him.

Makeo's ears flattened again. "Yes, there were many more orphans than usual," he murmured. "After the battle, there were only a few cursed Maldibor men remaining. But even if all had died, our sisters still carry the curse to their children."

"Well, that's interesting," Witt went on, oblivious to Makeo's visible discomfort. "That'd be incredible to have a Maldibor at Catalede. Might finally give Aza a challenge." He winked at her, and Aza punched his arm.

Makeo chuckled softly. "I'm not sure about that. Aza and I used to tussle when we were children, but I'm afraid I only bored her."

Aza frowned as the image of the Maldibor village wrapped its nostalgic arms around her. For a moment, she was skipping once again through the cabins in the forest of huge-trunked trees. The grassy town square, the fires, the music. And there was Makeo, laughing as he fended off her mock attacks with a sturdy stick.

"Well, don't feel so bad; it seems like no one can hold a Shadow's interest for too long. That's what makes their selective company so delightful," Witt said with an obnoxious smile.

Aza sniffed, pushing the bowl away. "I prefer my own company."

Shad's tongue darted over his dark nose, his voice seeming soft next to Witt's loudness. "But the students seem to like you a great deal."

Witt nodded, his eyes shining with mischievous snark. "She maintains a mysterious aura many are drawn to."

"Sheep scat." Aza set her spoon down on the table with a clack. "It's not me; it's our title they flock to. I'm just a passing curiosity." Greens asking for help, braggarts wanting to fight, Zephyr's flirtatious friends. She pressed her lips together, and her eyes found Makeo's once more, her voice softening. "But I always enjoyed visiting the Maldibor as a girl. I loved to dance on the dark moon nights."

The music, the laughter, the food, and the stories… the glow of her best memories quirked her mouth with a bittersweet curve.

Witt feigned a look of hurt. "But you never dance at Catalede!"

Ignoring Witt, Makeo leaned forward ever so slightly. "So, why did you stop coming?" His casual words belied the intensity of his gaze.

Aza's smile melted away. She missed that girl she had been. Back when the shadows were just a fun trick to make Makeo laugh. Now the shadows seemed to be all she was. Just darkness lined with good intentions.

"I wasn't a girl anymore." She rose from her seat with a shrug, fleeing the dull ache of memories long gone and the echo of her mother's voice reciting *The Heir's Way*.

And forever more, the Shadow Heir only danced with death.

8
TO THE SEA

By the time they got to the oceanside docks the next morning, the water markets crowded the bay like a teeming anthill with people stepping from boat to boat to glance at the wares. The salty scent of fish coated the stiff breeze as the mariners haggled and hawked their goods in booming voices roughened by the sea. The city swayed with the waves below it as sharp-beaked storm eagles watched carefully with gold-ringed eyes from their perches on the towering stone pillars.

Following Rivka's instructions, Shad led them to an immense whaler with three thick masts and a spiderweb of ropes connecting them. Two small whaleboats hung from each side of its impressive length, and a few passengers strolled the deck with wide smiles.

Its three-dozen crewmates lumbered to-and-fro, carrying the last crates, barrels, and sacks of cargo into the hold. Shad instructed Makeo, Aza, and Witt to wait with the supply packs Rivka had gathered for them and approached a man in a wide-brimmed hat reading over some kind of paper. Shad nodded to where Aza looked on with the others, and the man crossed his arms.

Witt eyed the massive vessel. "So, how long does it take a thing like that to sail to Austerden?"

Watching Shad closely, Aza's fingers moved to fiddle with her knives before remembering she had buried them all in the Hunters. The shipman's sunburnt nose wrinkled as he looked at Makeo and Aza, and his voice rose, but the sea breeze snatched away his words.

"My father says it depends on the weather, but it usually takes about six days," she said absently.

Makeo's short muzzle twisted this way and that in the salty fish-scented air. "Have you been on a ship before?"

Another man with a beard and fine leather jacket joined the man in the hat, a smile on his round rosy cheeks. Aza shook her head. "I've never been as far south as Austerden, but my father and I have discussed going one day. It would take weeks by horse."

Voices rose again, and the hair on Shad's back rose, his teeth bared in a hiss. The man leaned forward with a sneer and feigned as if to kick him. Aza's patience slipped, and she strode toward the group.

Shad's snarl drifted to her ears. "We've already paid twice the passage fare, what does our business matter to you?"

Aza joined them, her gaze piercing the man in the hat. "Is there a problem?"

People were always glad to talk to her father when they had a need. When they wanted protection. When they were scared. But on calm, peaceful days like this, they had a way of forgetting their manners.

"Cap'n Sonlyn and Mate Perrow at your service, Miss." The man with the beard—Sonlyn—smiled apologetically. "The beast may make our other passengers a little nervous is all. S'bad for business."

Sonlyn had said beast, but Perrow's gaze hadn't wavered from hers. Aza straightened. "You may refer to me as Guardian Thane." Technically she didn't inherit the title until her father passed, but she was sure they didn't know that. She rested her hand on the hilt of her dagger in a dangerous pause, before speaking just loud enough to be heard above the bustle of the shore. "We're on Odriel's business to protect Okarria from the Lost burning the north, so unless you want your dead wife plucking out your bloody eyes, your children's limbs torn from their screaming bodies, and your bowels spread across the town... I suggest you let us aboard."

Perrow's ruddy cheeks paled, and Sonlyn's plump lips parted.

"T-t-the w-what? L-l-lost?" Sonlyn bobbed his head, his trembling hands plucking at his beard. "M-my apologies. Come r-r-right aboard. We'll be on our way w-within the hour."

With the crew still peeking over at them, Aza smothered the triumphant smirk toying at her lips while the captain and his stiff first mate shuffled away, wide eyes darting over their shoulders.

Shad's tail whipped from side to side. "Was that really necessary?"

"I don't have time for mincing words around petty prejudice." Aza shrugged. "It got the job done."

"And now you get to spend four days with their prejudice on a floating piece of wood. Congratulations. I'm sure they feel so much better about it now."

Makeo edged up to her side carrying two of their packs. "Everything all right then?"

"Perfectly sunny," Aza said.

He grunted noncommittally and dug something out of one of the bags before handing it to her. "Here."

"What is it?" Aza asked, reluctantly accepting the leather-wrapped parcel.

"Something just in case things become…" He flashed his wolfish smile. "Less than sunny." Before she could open it, he threw his bag over his shoulder and walked up the plank onto the ship.

Aza unwrapped the leather to see a host of throwing knives glinting within. Her fingers moved to the empty sheaths along the belt that crossed her chest. Makeo must've been to the markets early that morning.

She wrinkled her nose at the gift. She didn't want to owe Makeo anything more than she already did. But—she ran a finger along the shining blades with a wry grin—she couldn't fault his choice in steel. The crew whispered to each other as they snuck glances at her. She tucked the throwing knives into her sash and hoped she wouldn't have to use them on this voyage.

But Odriel's Assassin would be ready, just in case.

True to the captain's word, the clipper raised its puffy white sails, and they pushed away from the dock within the hour. They dropped their bags in their claustrophobic cabin, a simple wooden box with four sagging hammocks and a port window. Shad leapt into the nearest hammock and curled into a small black ball, looking content to sleep the whole voyage away, while Witt went in search of the kitchen.

Aza spent the day in an out-of-the-way corner of the stern observing the crew. While she meant to go unnoticed, she couldn't stop Makeo from tagging along and drawing every pair of eyes on the ship. The wide deck swayed under their feet, and the bustle of Aquilond faded on the breeze as they cut through the waves farther out to sea.

The shore shrank into a dim outline, and a strange nervousness roiled through Aza. She unsheathed one of her new knives and twirled it in her palm, finding its balance. For the next four days, they'd be trapped on this drifting cork, stewing in the suspicions of the sailors.

But despite her unease, the days passed uneventfully, the dark shoreline crawling along their starboard. Aza exercised on the deck with Makeo as her ever-silent companion. Witt bobbed among the crew until they at last put him to work, showing him how to tie off the lines and adjust the sails. And Shad emerged from his hammock for mealtimes, padding along the deck like any other ship's cat.

On the third day, Aza leaned against the rail while Makeo perched on a crate next to her. Together they watched in silence as Witt scampered up and down the masts and rigging with the sailors, turning and pulling the three tiers of canvas this way and that. While the crew went about their work, a scattering of passengers meandered in long circles along the ship's rail, giving Makeo's bulky form and Aza's scowl a wide berth.

Three sandy-haired children, probably between the ages of six and twelve, sauntered right up to him, staring unabashedly at his paws and muzzle. Makeo returned their stares with crinkled eyes, and they whispered amongst themselves in awed wonder.

"Do you think it's a bear?"

"No, it looks like a wolf."

"Then why is it wearing breeches and boots?"

"Why does it stink so much?"

"It won't eat us, will it?"

Aza opened her mouth to tell them to clear off, when Makeo reached out a paw, the dark pads facing up.

"I'm actually a Maldibor." He chuckled deeply. "And no, we don't bite."

"Wow!" The youngest girl reached out and brushed her fingers along his paw. "And you can talk too?"

The middle girl with short, curly hair edged forward. "Are you a person or an animal?"

Makeo bared his teeth in the Maldibor smile. "We're people cursed to look, smell, and sound like animals."

The oldest girl's face twisted. "My teacher said the magi and curses are just pretend."

Aza started at that. With only three Heirs—one of whom was missing—and eleven hermitic magi, she knew there were people who didn't believe in such things, but it still always surprised her when she encountered it. No one ever saw Odriel either, and yet most still believed he would guide them safely to the afterlife.

"Not at all." Makeo shook his head. "Just because you don't see them, doesn't mean they're not there."

"I knew it." The girl's chest puffed up. "I told him so, but he still didn't believe me."

"Girls!" A pink-cheeked woman in a flowing, white dress huffed as she ran after them. "My goodness, you can't just run away like that." Her eyebrows rose when she got a glimpse of Makeo, but to her credit, if she was afraid, she didn't let it show. "I'm so sorry. I hope they weren't bothering you."

Makeo let his paw drop to his side. "Not at all."

"It's a Maldibor, Mama," the youngest said.

Her mother nodded with a knowing smile, and she held out an arm. "I'm Lacenda."

"Makeo." He gripped her arm gingerly in his large paw. "You don't seem particularly surprised to see me."

"My mother and I sought refuge with your tribe for a time when I was young." Lacenda put her hands on her curvy hips. "But what're you doing on a ship during a dark moon night?"

Aza frowned and tried to remember the moon's shape the previous night. Was it really a dark moon night? How could she have forgotten that?

Makeo chuckled. "You look away for a moment and find yourself drifting out to sea."

"I can understand that, but I know it's such a special night for you..." She tapped her chin. "Oh!" She brightened, tossing her long brown hair behind her shoulder. "I have my guitaretta with me; perhaps we could have a dance tonight to celebrate?"

The little girls practically glowed at the suggestion.

Makeo put up a paw. "Much appreciated, but I don't need—"

"Nonsense. It's tradition." She leaned forward. "And I would just love for my girls to see the magic of the Maldibor." She winked at him. "If they can manage to stay up till midnight, that is."

"Oh yes! Please! Please!" The girls reached out to pull on Makeo's paws.

"All right, I suppose." He turned his muzzle to Aza with a chuckle. "But only if Lady Aza here dances with us."

The girls turned to Aza as if seeing her for the first time. They paused for a moment before reaching out with small fingers to yank on her hands too. "Yes! You must! We can teach you how!"

She flinched back, trying to keep her knife out of their sticky fingers. "Okay, okay." She glared at Makeo with gritted teeth, the guilt of forgetting about the dark moon sticking in her belly. "Just one."

Makeo's mouth widened into a full-fledged beast smile, and the children cheered.

Lacenda clapped her hands together. "Wonderful." She wagged a stern finger at her children. "But you must rest if you want to wake for midnight. Come along." She waved as she herded them away below deck. "We'll be back."

Makeo leaned against the railing as he watched them go, a smile still lingering on his wolfish face.

Aza's knife resumed its twirl, and she returned a sailor's belligerent stare. "Sorry you're stuck here on this ship with us for the dark moon."

"Your concern is appreciated." He flashed his teeth at her. "But you can stop apologizing for my presence when I chose to be here."

Aza's brow creased. She normally wasn't *this* bad with words. Why did it seem like she was always on the verge of insulting Makeo these days? She was just trying to... well, she didn't really know what she was trying to do. But she wasn't trying to be mean.

"The sea breeze on my bare face will be festive enough, but you don't have to worry. I won't hold you to a dance." He pointed his nose into the wind with a smile. "I'm just looking forward to seeing the crew when they find I'm, in fact, a man, and not some monster their grannies warned them about."

Aza winced. "Do the questions bother you? I'm not sure I can do much about the sailors, but I think I'm at least capable of shooing away three little girls."

"No, no." He chuckled in his gravelly voice again. "I much prefer the open questions and curiosity to the unspoken fear."

Aza nodded, her lips twisting. "If it makes you feel better, I don't think the crew likes me much either."

"You mean after you threatened them to gain passage aboard?"

"I didn't threaten." She shrugged. "I can't help if the truth is ugly."

"You're as sharp as your knives, Aza."

She tossed the spinning knife to her other hand. "Is that a bad thing?"

"I'll let you know when I catch the edge."

The memory of fourteen-year-old Makeo covered in blood seared across Aza's thoughts, stealing her breath away. "That's why I prefer to be alone," she whispered.

Makeo straightened with a long sigh. "No Shadow is ever alone, Aze." With that, he walked away, the other passengers parting at his approach.

Aza shoved her knife into its sheath and looked to the sky. She and Makeo used to talk for hours, and now she couldn't go five minutes without acting like a complete ass. What was *wrong* with her?

9

DARK MOON

The sun had already burrowed into the horizon when Lacenda reappeared on the deck, petite guitaretta in hand and her three sleepy-eyed girls in tow. Aza followed them to the bow where Makeo had his nose to the dark blanket of sky. The creaking ship complained against the constant waves, and the sails snapped fitfully above.

Aza sighed and looked up at the overcast night. Odriel's Guiding Star peeked at her from the swirling black. Midnight couldn't be far off. She watched from the shadows as Lacenda exchanged pleasantries with Makeo, laughing and smiling easily together, with the now-quiet girls sinking sleepily down against the crates on the dock.

Something twisted in Aza's gut. While she certainly preferred her own company to that of others, she envied the talent some seemed to have for companionship. Interacting with others made her feel so stilted and impatient, but people like Lacenda and Witt made it seem effortless.

Makeo's tall ear flicked toward her, and Aza realized he already knew she was there.

She stepped forward into the lantern light of the bow, and Lacenda brightened. "Oh, I'm so glad you decided to join us." She gestured toward her dozing girls. "I'm afraid my other dance partners couldn't quite keep their eyes open."

Makeo opened his mouth to say something, but Aza cut him off. "Of course." She shifted her weight from one foot to the other, rubbing her arm self-consciously. "I said I would, after all."

Lacenda shook her daughters awake, and they blinked sleepily at one another like fledgling owls. She breathed in the gusting breeze, her eyes on the dark sky as if she could see the stars hidden behind the clouds. "Almost time now."

They stood for a moment more, maybe two, before the sonorous clang of the ship's bell marked the hour.

"Now," Lacenda whispered.

Aza vaguely remembered her first dark moon in Carceroc so many years ago. She couldn't have been older than Lacenda's youngest, but she could still remember Makeo's small, soft body leaning into her shoulder, his pudgy hand finding hers and squeezing it tightly as though to keep the enchantment from tearing him away.

The girls' eyes widened as a green shimmer flashed across Makeo's body—so fast Aza almost missed it. With a sound like the rustling of fabric, the transformative veil swept across Makeo. His claws receded into his skin, his fur melted away, and his wolfish muzzle disappeared into the face of a young man. The man he would've been without the curse.

In only a few seconds, he was completely unrecognizable. Even the Maldibor stench had been whisked away on the sea breeze. She drew in a sharp breath, the wonder of it freezing her in place yet again, like it had done that first time.

With a sigh of relief, Makeo tightened the belt around his now loose breeches, his chest bare. He ran his broad hands across his bare arms, running them up his shoulders to his neck. Aza knew she was staring, but she couldn't quite absorb this incongruous being before her. He was familiar to her now, and yet so different from the short, laughing adolescent she had chased after years ago. Though he was smaller than his Maldibor form, he still towered above her, his body lean and muscular. His smooth jaw still looked freshly shaven, a common habit of the Maldibor men on their human days, and a mop of dirty blond hair fell into green eyes crinkled in a sheepish smile, the only thing connecting this man to that boy of her memories.

For a moment, a smile stretched across her face in recognition, and she took a step forward. She longed to run to him, to tease and tussle his hair as she once had. To hear his ringing, contagious laugh untainted by the curse.

But then her eyes caught on the ragged scar stretching diagonally across his chest—right over his heart. The one *she* had caused.

Yes. Now *that* she would never forget. She quickly took a step back, guilt bleeding through her nostalgia.

Sleepy eyes widening, the little girls cheered and clapped while Lacenda rapidly strummed her guitaretta in applause. "To the irrepressible Maldibor." With that, she played a volley of chords that vibrated across the deck, launching into the first verse of a jaunty tune.

Fully awake now, the girls rushed to him, grabbing at his hands to spin him round and round. Aza caught the sailors on watch staring at them, mouths agape, and she had to smile. Makeo was right. It really was worth it just to see their dumbstruck faces. This was no man-eater, no childhood nightmare. Just a tribe who had run across the wrong magus.

Makeo laughed and traded steps with each of the children. He swung them into the air while they giggled and cheered. They hooked elbows and danced with each other, singing along to their mother's lively tunes in enthusiastic voices. But they only lasted a few tunes before they started to slow, their heads nodding once more to the slosh of the sea.

Then as quickly as the frolic began, the girls drooped and their smiles faded into yawns, like matches already spent. With a smile and a tip of an invisible hat, Lacenda gathered up her children to shepherd them below deck once more.

"Happy dark moon, Makeo," she murmured.

Makeo gave her a short bow. "Thank you for the song, Lacenda. It was nice to hear a piece of home." They shuffled away, and Makeo's eyes flicked to Aza's, still hiding in the shadows. "Well, was it worth staying up for?" Unlike his gravelly Maldibor voice, this one flowed as smooth as dark honey.

"I didn't stay up for that." Aza tapped the toe of her boot on the deck, not meeting his gaze while her emotions churned into a gray muddle she couldn't sift through. "I agreed to the dance, but it seems our music has wandered off."

He put a hand to his ear, the voice of the wind and the rhythm of the waves filling the silence. "You mean you can't hear it?"

She sighed, a war waging within her, as she remembered the last time they'd shared a dance. How they'd whirled hand in hand around a cheery fire. How they'd snuck away into the shadows. And how she'd even been so bold as to steal a quick teasing kiss before running off laughing into the forest. She resisted the urge to touch her lips at the memory—how his mouth had seemed to spark against hers.

Her eyes flicked back to the thick mottled scar snaking down across his chest. He had followed her into the darkness, of course. And he had come out half-dead.

But tonight was different. She breathed in the bitter, salty taste of the ocean while the lantern's gold brush of light washed the deck in its glow. Makeo leaned against the rail, and the deck swayed beneath them, as if pushing her toward him. How many times had she thought about doing this again? Her lips twisted in indecision. She shouldn't...

But then again, her mother *would* certainly skin her if she didn't keep a Maldibor company on a dark moon night.

With a small shrug, she gave a little bow and held out her hand. "Well, it *is* tradition."

His grin broadened, a wide smile of even teeth stretching across his wheaten skin, but his eyes dropped to the deck. "I guess I can't say no to a Shadow Heir."

He stepped forward, suddenly close, taking her hand in one of his and resting the other on her waist. She set her tentative fingers on his bare shoulder, hyper-aware of the flat planes of his smooth chest inches from her cheek—and the raised, pink scar that ran across it. The brother to the cut that marred her own cheek. She wondered if his still ached sometimes as hers did.

Humming softly in a deep familiar tune, he guided her in time to the music, moving her smoothly through the steps. His hand was firm under hers, and he radiated warmth and joy in the cool breeze, his calming song melting the tension from her shoulders and the uncertainty from her brow.

She grinned as he spun her around with a confident hand. "You've definitely had practice since we last did this."

"Of course." He pulled her back to him, dipped her low, and smiled. "And if I didn't know better, I'd say you're enjoying this."

"Don't congratulate yourself too much—it's a low bar." Aza swayed to the familiar Maldibor tune that had worked its way from the air into her thoughts. The thrill of his closeness buzzed on her skin. "But whatever you do, don't tell Witt."

In the circle of his broad arms, Aza breathed in his human scent of pine and earth. Her gaze moved from his grinning eyes down to his wide pink lips she had kissed once. She'd thought it was just another game they could play, but how many times had she imagined a second kiss? Had it crossed his mind too? She looked away and shoved down the heat that threatened her cheeks. Her emotions weaved into impossible words tingling on her tongue—all the things she'd thought a thousand times but dared not say. Could not say.

They turned with the haunting melody of their invisible music, and Aza was met with the sharp reminder that they weren't alone on the open deck. Even from afar, the stares of the crew seemed to fall heavier on them from the darkness. In the distance, a glow tangled in the clouds, and a deep rumble growled beneath it.

Makeo paused, and Aza glanced up at his face. Another distant flash of lightning illuminated his green eyes and broad jaw. Aza squinted in the cloudy veil of darkness that had fallen over the sky.

"Should we go in?" she asked reluctantly.

Makeo slowly turned to the crewmen watching them. One up in the crow's nest, another at the helm, one leaning against the captain's cabin, and three against either rail. More than there had been only an hour ago. Many more than there should be on the deck at midnight. Was it because of the storm?

"I hadn't planned on it." Makeo stepped away, rubbing a hand along the goosebumps that dotted his arms.

The ache of regret nipped at Aza where his skin had touched hers, but she let the ocean wind fill the space between them once more.

He closed his eyes and lifted his face to the sky. "But something's not quite right here."

Aza turned her back to the bow, unease rattling through her as her gaze sifted through each of the sailors, her traitorous emotions returning to their usual stone.

Her fingers twitched on the hilt of the dagger at her hip. Short cutlasses hung from the sailors' belts to defend against pirates, but she doubted they had any real training. Still, Makeo was unarmed, and they needed these men to get them back to shore. Surely the tension in the air was just some kind of misunderstanding. But what was she supposed to do now? She suddenly wished Witt were here to talk them down. Lightning flashed again, glinting almost green in the sailor's eyes.

She snuck another glance at Makeo. He was still, his face wary but placid, his muscular arms relaxed at his side. It'd be up to her to smooth this over before it came to blows.

"Evening." She nodded tensely.

One lifted his chin at her. A slow, measured movement. "S'late."

"Going to be a rough night?" Aza gestured to the cloud-choked sky, and it responded with a grumble of thunder.

The sailor shrugged. "Never can tell on the water."

They didn't make any move toward them. And their faces didn't hold their usual fear, just a strange sort of blank stare. Odd. Definitely. But aggressive? Dangerous? No.

Without any more words to throw at them, she really only had one recourse. She grabbed Makeo's wide hand, still wondering at the smoothness of the skin. "Well, we wish you calm seas." She tugged Makeo to the ladder leading below, her eyes raking across the still crewmen. "Until tomorrow."

She towed Makeo down the narrow passage to their cabin, pulling him in. His blond hair still brushed the top of the doorway as he followed her. Aza shut and latched the door behind him, her heart beating faster than it should have been. But if that was because of Makeo or the sailors… she couldn't say. Witt's soft snores buzzed through the near blackness.

"What was that?" Aza whispered.

"I'm not sure." Makeo shook his head, his full lips flattening in a frown. "Perhaps nothing?"

"It was *not* normal."

"Well, we were on the deck in the middle of the night. That's not exactly normal either."

Shad's soft whisper emanated from his hammock. "They saw you transform?"

Makeo was close enough in the cramped quarters she could feel his warm breath as he nodded. "They did."

"Hm." Shad's one eye blinked in the darkness. "Sailors can be extremely superstitious about yanaa aboard one of their vessels. It's one of the reasons

I'd imagine the captain was so reluctant to take you and Aza aboard."

"Ah." Makeo's weight shifted, the planks creaking beneath him. "Perhaps I should've just stayed down here then."

"What nonsense," Aza scoffed.

Hearing the remorse in Makeo's voice made Aza want to shake each and every one of those ridiculous backward-minded sailors. Makeo got such little time to be free of his curse, from one midnight to the next, and they'd summarily ruined it. But still... "There was something off though, Shad. They didn't seem frightened or angry, they were just... staring."

"Doesn't everyone stare at a Maldibor the first time they see them shift?"

Aza's cheeks warmed in the dark. Had Makeo caught *her* staring? She crossed her arms. It didn't matter. But what did they do now? Taking another breath, Aza could feel the shadows still roiling in her belly. She opened her mouth and then closed it again.

There was another place she could take her questions. Her skin itched for the thick sheen of the Shadow Plane to swallow her up. She could almost hear the Plane calling for her across the waves. What would it say now?

Makeo shifted in the dark, bending his body into a sagging hammock. "Whatever the reason, I don't have a good feeling." He reached out as if to squeeze her hand, but then paused. Her fingers twitched, wanting to close that small space, but then he withdrew into the dark. "We should try to keep our eyes and ears sharp. Stay armed and stay together."

Aza dipped into her own curved hammock, resolve crystallizing in her. "Yes, I'll let you know what I see."

10
HUNTED

Aza awoke gasping for air in the pitch black, heart racing as she twisted in the drooping hammock. When had she even fallen asleep? After a beat, she remembered where she was. Still on the ship. Safe in their cabin. But her tense muscles refused to unwind.

The blank stares of the crew skewered her thoughts. If they were really safe here, why did her skin prickle with warning? Why did she feel so trapped?

She lay back into the rough fabric of the hammock once more, listening for the even breathing of her companions. All still asleep, and their small porthole showed no signs of dawn. The shadows curled in her center. She had to go back to the Plane. Her skin crawled, yearning for the call of the raspy wind. Perhaps the shadow dwellers would know something she didn't.

She took a breath. It would drain her, of course. But surely even Witt could handle a gaggle of peevish, half-trained sailors. It was worth the risk. And by the time they went ashore at Tazgar, she would be recovered.

Not wanting to risk second-guessing herself, Aza's body tensed as she drew in the shadows. She wrapped them around her like a cloak and plunged into the heart of the darkness. Aza opened her eyes to the gray sky of the Plane, her muscles burning as the shadows drank in her yanaa. Sitting up, she found herself face to face with a shadow dweller. A hundred onyx eyes peered at her with mandibles quivering inches from her jaw. But it wasn't alone. A half-dozen more of the dog-sized ant creatures surrounded Aza, crowding in on her.

"*Come closer, Aza,*" the wind whispered.

Had they been waiting for her? Her fingers rested on the pommels of her daggers, not that she'd ever needed them here. She wasn't even sure if she could kill these things with steel. "There is a new breed of evil in our land."

Aza swallowed. "What do you know of it?"

The mandibles all clicked in unison as if they shared one mind. "They crave you." Another click. "And they are here. All around you."

"That's not possible." Aza shook her head through gritted teeth. "I've seen everyone on the ship. There are no Rastgol aboard."

"Their heart beats, but they do not die. Their master controls them." The onyx eyes blinked, all six pairs at once. "And they are coming." With that, the creatures scuttled away on spindly legs, one after the other, moving in unison like a many-headed centipede.

The wind swirled around Aza, toying with her hair. *"Come to me, Aza."*

Sweat prickling her scalp, Aza fisted her hands in tight, frustrated balls. "Come where? Why are you calling me?"

A chuckle rattled in her ears, and Aza released the shadows, letting herself crash back into the tangible world.

The boat rocked beneath her and a lighted lantern swung from a figure looming over her bed. Aza's hand flew to her knife before she recognized Makeo's tense human face staring at her, with a loose shirt hanging from his broad shoulders, and his huge sword strapped across his back.

"You're back." He sagged with a relieved sigh, running a hand over his square jaw. "I was sure I would've heard you leave, but there was no sign of you."

Shad glared at her as he pressed his small triangular ear to the door. "When you visit the Shadow Plane, please be sure to inform us peasants so we don't assume you went overboard."

Even Witt looked worried where he perched on the far hammock behind Makeo. "Good timing though; it sounds like something's not right on deck."

"We need to get out of here as soon as possible," Makeo said, the muscle in his jaw flexing.

"Odriel's teeth." Aza blinked as if waking up from a dream, beads of sweat sliding down her temple. "And go where?"

A thumping from above drew their eyes upward.

"Two options," Shad whispered. "Take control of the ship or get in a whaleboat and try for shore."

"Is it really all that bad?" Witt scratched at his mousy curls. "We don't know how to sail a ship. Maybe it's just because of the storm."

Someone screamed.

Aza nodded and rose to her feet. The boat rocked harshly, knocking her into Makeo. He righted her with a steady hand, and she met his eyes. "I've had worse options. Let's get out of here before we get trapped." They grabbed their packs and edged into the hall.

Other passengers watched them from cracked doors, eyes wide with fear as they took in their weapons and bags. Makeo paused for a moment, staring at them, before Aza pushed him along from behind.

"They'll be fine," she said.

He frowned but let her shepherd him down the pitching hall.

Shouts and the distinct clang of sword on sword rang above them. Shad stopped before the ladder to the top deck and looked back at Aza.

She moved past Makeo and Witt to go first. "If it's a mutiny, we'll suppress it. If it's the Rastgol Lost, we break for a whaleboat."

"What about the other passengers?" Makeo asked, a roll of thunder underscoring his words.

Aza shifted, her muscles shaky and aching. "There are other whaleboats. They'll find their own way."

Not looking at him, she scaled the rungs and pushed open the hatch. And into chaos. The crew of forty had turned on one another. Ocean waves slopped over the sides, sloshing through the blood and bodies littering the deck.

The helm swung listlessly as the captain fought alongside his men. "Don't let them get to the passengers!"

But whatever mutiny had gone on here, he was vastly outnumbered. He and three shaking sailors faced down the other thirty, led by the blank-eyed first mate, his shirt darkened with blood. Too much blood. The shadow dwellers had been right. These weren't the Rastgol, but the hunting Lost had found them all the same.

Abandon ship it was.

Before she could say anything, Makeo pushed past her. "What's going on here?"

All eyes turned on them. If Makeo knew he had made a mistake, he didn't show it. He drew his long broadsword from his back, and they rushed him.

Aza swore and pulled her daggers from their sheaths. "Witt, get to the helm. Try to get us closer to shore. These things are here for me."

With that, the first Hunters were on her. She parried and stepped in, running her blade through the chest of the first. It didn't even flinch. Shad raced away with Witt, slipping and sliding on the deck as he made his way to the freely spinning helm. Aza gritted her teeth and blocked the next blow while Makeo battled three on her right, obviously aiming to wound, not to kill.

But they couldn't afford that luxury. Alive or not, if these things were going to act like the Lost, she would have to treat them like Lost. Throwing her weight into the swing, she hacked through one's neck, and it crumpled to the deck. Lightning flashed and thunder cracked its whip right on the bolt's snaking tail. Two rushed her at once, and Aza rolled away, her body creaking in protest.

"You have to behead them," she shouted to Makeo. "Otherwise, they won't stop."

Someone screamed, and Aza became distantly aware that the captain and his men had fallen. Thunder crashed again, and the boat pitched, throwing Aza to the deck. Deafening thunder boomed above. Even if they could kill these things, they wouldn't be able to manage this ship in the storm.

Aza kicked the legs out from another and brought her dagger down across its neck. A pair lunged for her but found Makeo's swinging broadsword instead. He grabbed her arm and hauled her to her feet. "What's the matter? Are you okay?"

She shook her head to try to ease the exhaustion that threatened to drown her. "I'm fine."

With their backs to the captain's cabin, she cut through another with Makeo at her side. Her gaze scraped across the deck. Under the dark sky, the mob of at least twenty sailors churned furiously across the ship. Though Makeo hacked at them with huge whirling strokes, they ignored him. Thirsting only for her yanaa, they surged toward her. Sweat slicked her face as her daggers worked. Block, thrust, parry, dodge, forward, back. She could do this.

No sooner had the thought crossed her mind, than the smell of smoke tickled her nose.

"Fire in the cabins!" someone cried.

Feet pounded across wooden planks as the passengers bobbed to the deck, coughing and spluttering, adding to the chaos. In Aza's distraction, she missed a step, and a blade cut across her forearm. She leapt back with a hiss of pain, ducking another slash before burying her dagger in the creature's eye.

"I need to find the children." Makeo swung his blade close by. "Witt!"

"Just go." Aza's chest heaved. "I'll be fine."

Witt slid across the slick deck, and Aza rolled in front of him to block the sword coming down on his head. She dispatched the possessed sailor.

"What about the helm?" she yelled.

Drawing his sword, Witt hacked at the legs of another advancing attacker. "I did the best I could, but it's no use."

"One of the whaleboats is already gone!" someone shouted.

Aza's limbs grew heavier with every swing, the weight of her body pressing down on her. Witt scrambled to his feet, face blotchy and blood streaming from a cut across his forehead. Twenty on two was a lot to ask of anyone. Witt wouldn't last long here.

"Can you see the shore, Witt?" The whipping wind nearly stole Aza's words away.

He locked blades with a sailor and pushed him back. "Yes," he puffed. "We're still half a league out."

Lightning flashed, and Aza got a glimpse of Makeo running across the smoke-filled deck with two of the girls in his arms, while Lacenda and the third followed behind dragging a bag. Relief flooded through Aza even as a sailor backed her against the wall of the captain's cabin. He sank his blade into the wood, and she cut him down.

The fire crackled audibly now, and Aza could almost imagine it licking at their boots. She pushed Witt toward the landward side. "Where's Shad? We need to get off this ship." A splash announced the departure of another whaleboat. Aza hoped Makeo had the sense to go with them. She looked toward the helm where Shad ran toward them, his claws scratching against the deck. "Shad, let's—"

The crunch of wood rent the air, and the boat jarred to an immediate stop, the deck tilting up. Together, Aza and Witt slid down the slick wood of the floundering ship. They scrabbled at the railing to keep themselves from falling overboard, but the waves crashed into them, threatening to tear them away.

"Aza!"

Aza looked up to see Makeo aboard one of the empty whaleboats bobbing in the waves a safe distance away. Not close enough to jump, but maybe close enough to swim. She could make it.

Another wave washed over them, and Witt spluttered. *Odriel's teeth.* He couldn't even splash across a stream. And what had happened to Shad? Her eyes scanned the waves by the stern. A black ball of fur gripped the railing with frantic claws, and Shad's dark head dipped below the waves as he struggled to hold fast to the ship.

She swallowed. The boat shifted, and smoke curled above them, precious seconds ticking away. She had to make a choice. Shad or Witt? Her mind ran through a set of cold calculations. Witt was good enough with a sword, but she needed Shad to get to Tazgar.

She pointed at a crate floating just out of reach. "Jump for the crate and kick toward Makeo."

Witt shook his head. "I won't make it."

"You have to." She swallowed, her chest tightening at his wide eyes. "I'll get Shad, and we'll meet you at the whaleboat." With that, she turned and climbed toward the sodden cat.

"Aza!" Witt called from behind her, his voice cracking with fear.

But she didn't hesitate. Her fingers squeezed the railing to keep herself upright, resisting the ocean's cold tug. The first splatter of raindrops drove into her shoulders, a cursory warning before the skies opened up and dumped their overdue burden. Water assaulting her from above and below, Aza's muscles went numb as she moved. Fingers, toes, and muscles all lost feeling, but still she crept along.

Finally, she reached where Shad clutched the edge of the sinking ship, scrabbling furiously. The ship shifted again in the waves, sinking in earnest now.

She bent down. "Can you swim?"

He retched in response. Aza looked back to where Witt clung, only to find that he had disappeared, and the furious sea had smashed the floating crate against the hull. *Bleeding skies.*

"We've got to get away from the ship before it pulls us down with it." Aza kicked at the cracked railing until a plank splintered off in her fingers, and then grabbed Shad by the scruff. "Just try to hold on."

Aza jumped into the water, holding the plank to her chest with one arm and the cat with the other. Kicking desperately, saltwater rushed into her eyes and mouth. They were only two oar lengths away, a distance she could swim half asleep. But the Shadow Plane had nearly drained her dry, and with the gasping Shad weighing her down, they crawled through the surf. Another wave ducked them under, and Aza fought to surface.

"Aza, here!" Makeo yelled.

Aza reached out blindly, and found a slick, grasping hand. Makeo was in the water with them, a rope securing him to the boat. Aza pushed Shad toward him, the water choking any words she had.

She started to follow when the ship at last slid off the rocks that held it. Groaning as it flopped over in the water, the masts snapped off, and the suck of the current ripped Aza away from Makeo. Something hard slammed into the back of her head, and then the dark, stormy world melted away.

She was in Carceroc, the tremendous trees rising up around her, their trunks as wide as cottages, their branches scraping the clouds. And there was Makeo, round-cheeked and young, chasing after her into the darkness. With her parents away with the Time Heir, Yolie, at the western border, Aza brimmed with daring, drunk on freedom. Feet lighter than air, she raced through the trees away from where Zephyr entertained the much smaller Time Heir, Yolie's precocious five-year-old, Ioni.

"Dolobra," she called with a laugh. "Keo wants to meet youuuu." She ducked around a tree and disappeared, smothering another giggle.

She waited for him to panic at her absence, to worry that she'd left him, but instead he stopped right in front of her. "You can't hide from me," he said in his boyish voice, smiling wide. "I can smell you from a mile away." He leaned closer, his shining eyes only a finger's breadth from hers.

"And what do I smell like?" she whispered, blinking into view.

He didn't flinch at her closeness. "That starclover you pick for Windtorn," he said, his eyes as soft as his voice. "And rain-washed night air."

She kissed him then. Just a light press of her cold lips on his warm smile. His eyes widened, and she laughed at his shocked grin before bounding away. "Come find me then, Keo."

Time spun forward, and a blade was at her throat. The rotting mangled flesh of the man's face pressed against her cheek.

"And here I thought I would have to come to you," Mogens' gravelly voice rasped from

his lipless mouth. His fingers dug into her neck. "I'm going to enjoy this." He slowly dragged the dagger from her jaw to her cheekbone, the pain screaming through her face. "How about we start with an eye?"

"Aza!" Makeo rammed into Mogens with nothing but the knife from his belt, burying it into the maggoty flesh.

The distraction was just enough. Aza wrenched free, but no sooner was she away than Mogens' dagger tore through Makeo's chest. Mogens laughed in a shrill screech, and the Lost closed in all around them with bony, reaching fingers.

Then, Zephyr was there in a gush of flames, and the Maldibor warriors, and even Ioni's father, determined to protect her. And then it was over. Mogens disappeared in a wash of bloody darkness, Ioni's father was dead along with a handful of the Maldibor, and Makeo lay dying.

And in this nightmare, Ioni couldn't save him.

Heart heavy and throbbing, Aza woke to the sound of rain tapping on wood, a splitting headache, and something warm pressed up against her back. Her eyes fluttered open to find herself in a shelter cobbled together from a wooden door wedged against a leaning tree trunk. The ocean waves shushed her from somewhere close in the near-dawn twilight, and a shiver ran through her damp body. Her numb fingers moved to the back of her head to probe the tender, fist-sized lump that had grown out of it. She had made it back to shore. But how? Where were the others?

She winced and noticed someone had bound the cut along her forearm with strips of fabric. Turning in the sand, she found the still-human Makeo curled behind her, his breaths even against her back. One of his sleeves had been torn off at the shoulder, which explained the binding on her arm. A warm rush of hysterical relief tingled from the crown of her head to her fingertips. Makeo was alive. Makeo was here.

Had he done all this? Her mouth curved into a wistful half-smile. This was definitely not the way he would've wanted to spend a dark moon night. But where were Shad and Witt?

Makeo rolled away, taking his blessed warmth with him, and Aza had to force herself not to scoot closer. His bleary eyes half opened, and then, on seeing her awake, snapped wide.

"Aza, you're awake." Relief melted the tightness behind his gaze, and he wiped a hand across his face. "Thank Odriel."

"How'd we get here?" Aza tensed her muscles to sit up, muffling a groan.

He put a hand on her shoulder. "Rest for now. There's no use moving until the rain has stopped."

Aza sighed but couldn't deny the weariness that sat on her chest like a stubborn mule. "I was in the water when I got hit in the head." She pressed her fingers to her temples as if she could squeeze out the lost memory. "What happened?"

"When the boat fell, I looped the rope around Shad so Witt could pull him in, and then I swam after you." Makeo crossed his arms, goosebumps raising the fair hair on his bare skin.

"What hit me?"

"It was actually the last whaleboat." He smiled. "It was overturned, but I was able to push us onto it."

Aza's lips parted. In a stormy sea, he had dragged her unconscious body up onto a boat. That took some otherworldly strength. "How'd we get to shore?"

"We were fairly close to land, so it didn't take too long for us to wash up with all the other debris."

Aza nodded her leaden head, reluctant to ask the next question, the guilt already welling up within her. "What about Witt and Shad?"

"They were safe in the whaleboat when I last saw them."

The relief stole her breath away. *Thank bloody Odriel.*

He gestured out to the beach. "I assume they're also waiting out the rain on the shore somewhere."

That was a big assumption. Their whaleboat could've easily overturned, and they could've just as easily drowned last night. Aza's hands clenched. "This is why I wanted to do this by myself. You're putting your lives at risk for no reason."

Makeo met her hard words with his soft ones. "We want to protect Okarria just as much as you do. We're putting our lives at risk because we believe in you, Aza."

Aza sucked in a breath, picturing her father's furious face and Zephyr's skeptical one. Were they okay? Had Mogens' Hunters found them too? Thinking of her mother, a sharp pang wrenched her gut, and she squeezed her eyes shut. "But what if I'm wrong? And this is all for nothing?"

"Then we'll try something else."

"Ugh." Aza pressed her still-clammy palms to her face. "There's a reason the Shadow Heirs work alone."

Makeo chuckled with a deep rumbling in his chest, reminding her the curse of the Maldibor still hid somewhere deep inside him. "As I recall, the Shadow Heirs of legend always had the two other Heirs by their side. And your father has at least one."

He didn't understand. The Shadow was the cold one. The calculating one. The assassin. She ran a finger across the scar along her cheek. Friends were just liabilities. Makeo thought he knew her from their bright childhood memories. He hadn't yet accepted that the little girl Aza used to be was gone—snuffed out by the shadows. And he had a right to know who he was dealing with. That he couldn't depend on her.

"Witt was terrified out there, and I abandoned him." She swallowed, the confession sizzling in her throat. "He would've drowned if it weren't for you." Maybe he still had.

"There was no right choice." Fatigue lined Makeo's face, and he lay back down beside her—close but not touching. "You did what you thought was right."

Too tired to keep them in, Aza's thoughts flowed from her tongue. "But I wasn't thinking of it like that. I decided based on who'd be the most"—she choked on the word—"*useful.*"

Makeo's warm hand found her icy one, and she couldn't bring herself to pull away. She had spent three years trying not to miss him, and in this moment, she was too tired to fight it anymore. Instead, her fingers laced between his, the completeness of their knitted hands making her heart ache. She shouldn't be doing this. He had to stay away from her.

"It sounds heartless…" Though Makeo's voice was gentle, Aza flinched at the word. "But the fact that you're worrying about it now says otherwise."

"I want to believe that, Keo." His childhood nickname slipped out before she could stop it, and she sighed, his words soothing her in a way she wished they didn't. The thoughts slid through her exhaustion-slicked mind, and a shiver ran through her. "But sometimes I'm afraid the shadows have stained me."

"In the face of pain and fear, a heart will raise walls to protect itself." He scooted closer to her, and she leaned into his heat, her pulse stuttering. "But that doesn't mean it's not a good heart."

Exhaustion and vigilance warred within Aza, but exhaustion won out. She let her eyelids fall shut just for a moment. "There's a thin line between a walled heart and a stone one." Aza almost imagined she could still feel the sway of the boat. "You can't know which one it is until you see inside."

"I see you, Aza Thane," he whispered in her ear. "And I will remind you as many times as you need to hear it. You don't have to be alone."

On the edge of unconsciousness, Aza wasn't sure if he'd really said that, or if she'd dreamed it.

11

TAZGAR

"Aza!" Witt's voice ripped through Aza's dreamless slumber. For a panicked moment, she pictured him on the edge of the sea, pleading with her not to leave him. Then, she forced her eyes open and returned to the present.

The rain had stopped, and the weak morning sunlight peeked through their lean-to shelter. Sometime in her sleep, her cheek had found the crook of Makeo's bare shoulder, and their bodies touched from their chests all the way down to their twined ankles. Her eyes widened, and her face burned hot. Careful not to make any sudden moves, she lifted her hand from his chest and rolled away from his warm, human form.

How mortifying. What if he'd woken up before her and found her like that? It was just because she'd been cold. She'd needed his body heat. Nothing more. She tried to scrub the embarrassment from her face before ducking out of the shelter.

"Aza!" Witt yelled again.

She spotted Witt lumbering down the beach with a bag over his shoulder and Makeo's huge sword strapped to his back. It took her another heart-stopping second before she spotted Shad's small dark form padding next to him. A thick knot loosened in her chest. Two of them. Thank the skies, they'd made it. Aza waved at Witt from the tree line but didn't have it in her to shout his name. Behind her, Makeo shifted with the groans of awakening.

It took a moment before Witt caught sight of her. "Hey!"

He said something to Shad and pointed in her direction before taking off running.

Aza found herself smiling at his enthusiasm. Sure, Witt was annoying most of the time, but his perpetual ebullience was hard to totally ignore. She stiffened as he threw his arms around her, the guilt of abandoning him still prickling her enough to let him do so. Even after she had left him to drown, he still embraced her with open arms. He had a forgiveness in him she was sure she could never muster.

"Thank Odriel, you're okay." He lifted her off her feet for a brief moment before releasing her. "I knew you'd be all right, of course, but Shad was worried."

Aza retreated a step. "I'm fine."

Shad sat on his haunches behind Witt, but his gaze stayed on the bits of wreckage scattered in the sand. "I'm glad to be wrong."

Makeo emerged from their lean-to. "What about the other whaleboat? Did they make it?"

Witt nodded. "Yeah, we ran into them farther north. The passengers were a little shaken, but okay. They're going up shore to the next town to regroup."

A shadow lifted from Makeo's brow, and the guilt in Aza thickened. She hadn't even thought about the others.

"And here's this." Witt unstrapped the broadsword on his back and tossed it to Makeo. "Something tells me you may need it again before too long."

"Where are we?" Aza shifted her gaze to the shoreline.

"The fates seem to be on our side," Shad said, starting down the beach. "We are on the northern edge of Tazgar. If we follow the beach to the river, it should take us almost directly to Dorinar's dwelling."

Makeo strapped on his sword. "How long?"

"Without horses?" Shad's ragged ear flicked. "Four days, maybe three if we move fast."

Aza turned south. "Let's move fast then."

"Now, wait a minute." Witt strode after her. "Don't we want to talk about how those things got on the boat first?" His gaze slid to Makeo and Shad following behind them. "Because they weren't like that when we started. I worked with those sailors for days. They were just normal people." He shook his head in disbelief. "Maybe a little on the salty side, but definitely not possessed."

Aza bent her head to one side and then to the other with a crack. She tried not to remember the faces of the sailors she had left on the deck. She didn't want to think of them as normal people. They were people who had tried to kill them.

"Whatever changed them must be the same dark yanaa that raises the Lost," Shad said.

"Only more powerful," Makeo added.

Aza thought of the green glinting in their eyes. It was the same green as the smokey veil that clung to the bones of the Lost. "I think they're drawn to my yanaa like the Lost are." She swallowed, her mind weaving through the spiderweb of connections. She flexed her fingers, the void of yanaa still aching within her. "It takes an enormous amount of yanaa to enter the Shadow Plane, and twice now, they've attacked on the same night as I've spoken with the shadow dwellers."

Witt's brow wrinkled. "But even so, what would have changed them? One of Odriel's Blessed, a magus, a necromancer…?" He threw up a hand. "I don't know about you, but I think I would've seen a necromancer in the mess."

Shad shook his head. "You would not be able to identify a human necromancer unless you saw them using their yanaa."

Aza looked at Makeo. "Did you sense anything aboard the ship?"

"I felt much ill will, as I'm sure you did. But among the sailors' suspicion, it didn't seem out of place." Makeo's brow furrowed, and he ran a hand along his bare arm. "But there was a whaleboat missing before the fire even started."

Witt rubbed his pale, angular jaw. "Some of the crew could've escaped."

"Or the necromancer could have changed them before saving his own skin," Aza said darkly. It had to have been Mogens. He was the unnatural thread weaving the Lost together from one generation to the next. But how had they not noticed him on the ship? Makeo should've been able to sense him, or at the very least, smell him.

Shad nodded, his gaze staring off into the swamp of moss sprawling across the beach. "A necromancer who can turn the living into mindless killers."

"Not mindless." Aza's teeth ground together. "Those things are strong, capable, and murderous."

"But what if it's not their fault? If the necromancer released the sailors, maybe they would have gone back to themselves," Witt said.

"That's a big 'what if' when there's a blade at your throat," Aza replied. "Ifs make you hesitate, and hesitating gets you killed."

Those were the simple terms her father had taught her as a girl. A heartbeat could mean the difference between life and death. Don't look at their face, look at their blade. No faces. No emotions. No hesitation.

Aza kicked a rock into the waves. "So, I'm going to leave that 'if' with you so I can keep us both alive."

Frowning, Witt looked away, but Makeo met her gaze. "You're a protector, Aza, not a killer," he said, just loud enough for her ears.

Aza wrinkled her nose, her tense muscles unwinding under his soft eyes— a gentleness she had to keep reminding herself she couldn't afford.

"Draw your line in the sand, Keo, but don't be surprised when it washes away," she murmured.

Witt kicked at a rock, unfazed by Aza's heavy words. "On the bright side, they probably think we're dead now."

"Yes." Shad agreed, his thin, dark pupil narrowing on Aza. "So if they are drawn by your strolls on the Shadow Plane, let's not tempt them again."

It made sense, but Aza stiffened anyway. Had the Shadow Plane warned her, or had it led them straight to her? The Shadow Plane was a strange place, but surely it wasn't… evil. Even thinking about it made her want to dive in again. She shook her head, and irritation bubbled under her skin. *Leave it alone.* Why did the thought of not going to the Shadow Plane bother her so? She could go a few days without walking its gray fields, couldn't she?

Makeo placed a hand on her shoulder. "Don't worry, in a few hours, I'll be back to my big-eared, sharp-nosed self." His smile didn't reach his eyes. "And a Maldibor doesn't miss much."

Aza had a sudden urge to press her cheek into the warmth of his knuckles. His touch was strangely reassuring, even if his words weren't. A Maldibor's ears were all well and good, but she preferred her own. Even so… without the Shadow Plane, the world seemed strangely quiet.

Though Aza still yearned for the draw of the shadows, its whispers fell blessedly quiet in the swamps of Tazgar, and the fresh memory of the mindless sailors kept the temptation at bay. Aza pushed forward as hard as she dared, but it still took four days of wet feet and Witt's senseless babble before Shad pointed them to a moss-covered ramshackle of a dwelling growing up between the swamp's tangle of roots and branches. Hidden in its coat of green, the cottage seemed to lean to one side, hiding sullenly in the strange silence of the bog. Green and brown vines snaked over the roof and around the stone walls as if to strangle this strange intruder. A thin curl of gray smoke swirled out of the squat chimney stack in the lone sign of life.

Witt threw his hands up in the air. "Finally."

Makeo's huge body—bear-like once more—exuded a sigh of relief, and even the bedraggled Shad seemed to pick up the pace. But an unwelcome nervousness needled Aza's belly. After they'd risked their lives and come all this way, would Dorinar even have the answers she sought? Or would he brush her off too?

She pressed her lips together and waded through the ankle-deep bog. Steeling herself, she knocked on the door. Her nerves vibrated with anticipation. She'd only ever met one magus, Everard, and that had been over a decade ago. He'd been a surly, stern sort who didn't take well to children or nonsense. He'd sentenced Shad to a century of servitude and didn't even have the courtesy to lift the curse on time, and he was supposed to be the *kindest* of the magi. What if Dorinar was—

She didn't get to a third knock before the door swung open.

Though Aza had never met Dorinar, she was fairly certain the petite, short-haired, young woman standing before her was not him.

"I'm sorry..." the woman trailed off. Her eyes skipped between Witt, Makeo, and Shad and then returned to Aza, her apologetic wince fading away to curiosity. "Oh." Retreating a step, she opened the door wider and looked over her shoulder into the shadowy parlor. "Aza Thane and Shadmundar are here with a Maldibor."

Aza's brow rose. Did she know this woman? Aza didn't wait to be invited before she brushed past her onto the stone floor.

Two more figures stood across from each other in the spacious room, a fire crackling between them and a plush rug connecting a broad desk and collection of deep red armchairs. The young man stood near the far wall, his hands crossed tightly across his thin chest, and a deep frown creasing his face below his muss of brown curls. *Dorinar.* Exactly how she had pictured him from her parents' stories.

Aza's eyes slid to the gorgeous woman across from him, her yanaa almost palpable as it radiated from her in thick, powerful waves. She stood tall and slender, her caramel hair falling to her waist. Distaste pulled at the corners of her plump mouth while her onyx gaze flicked from Aza's muddy boots to her dirt-streaked face.

"I thought I could smell a dog." The honed edges of her melodious voice cut through the silence. "Make sure you tell it to stay outside. Beasts don't belong in the house."

The short-haired woman retreated a step to lean against the wall, her dark blue eyes wary, but she didn't move to close the door.

Aza's muscles tightened. The sharp-tongued one had meant for Makeo to hear her. But unlike the sailors, it wasn't fear that filled the bitter words. This woman was a different creature entirely. Dangerous, and powerful. Aza's instincts screamed in warning, and she fought to keep herself from drawing her weapons.

Shad padded through the open door beside her and then jerked to a stop. "Ivanora."

Shock raced through Aza, and she had to force herself not to look at Makeo waiting outside. This was the woman responsible for his curse. The magus who reveled in the Maldibor's eternal humiliation.

Ivanora flashed a glittering smile at Shad. "Ah yes. Hello, pet." She tutted. "Did Everard tire of you already?"

Shadmundar brushed against Aza's leg in a silent warning. "Seems like he's tired of just about everything these days."

Aza nodded to him in understanding. Everard's favor had always granted them a certain amount of protection from his bitter siblings. If Ivanora didn't know he had abandoned them, they certainly wouldn't tell her.

But from the tension that stretched between Dorinar and Ivanora, Aza got the distinct impression the two magi had already been fighting about something before they'd arrived. Something neither of them wanted to keep on about with strangers in the room. But that was normal for the secretive magi. For all Aza knew, Makeo's ancestor, Elika, may have been the last human to see Ivanora when she cursed him for not loving her.

Ivanora's glittering black eyes lingered on Shad. "You could always come with me, Shadmundar. I like cats too."

"I appreciate the offer, but I think a century is quite enough."

"Suit yourself. But why the Shadow Heir of all people?" She wrinkled her dainty nose. "They've always been so… stiff." Her saccharine smile dripped with sticky disdain.

Aza snorted. "When was the last time you even met a Shadow Heir?"

"Just because you do not see me, does not mean I do not see you, Aza Thane." Her lips twisted. "Although I am disappointed I never got the chance to meet your father."

Aza's stomach dropped, her ears buzzing. Her eyes darted around the room. Dorinar's face darkened, but he said nothing. The woman by the door paled beneath her freckles, and even Shad seemed to shrink an inch.

Keeping her countenance smooth, Aza cleared her throat. "I'm afraid you're mistaken." She clasped her hands behind her so they wouldn't betray the shuddering emotions that threatened to rattle her bones. "My father is alive and well."

Ivanora's mouth opened, false shock widening her eyes. "Oh, you haven't heard?" She put a long-fingered hand to her cheek. "Your parents died in an ambush not two weeks ago." She shook her head in mock sorrow. "They think it was Idriel's horde come back for revenge, but no one knows for sure."

Aza's whole body froze over. She thought of their cries on the Shadow Plane, and her heart spasmed with a wild panic. Had they been calling out for her? Shocked static fizzed in her ears. Perhaps if she had gone to them instead of embarking on her own selfish mission, they would still be alive. She swallowed the nausea that rose in her throat in bubbling, burning acid, her faraway stare focusing on Ivanora's barely concealed mirth.

No.

She didn't believe this woman with her snarling smile and hollow eyes. Aza's gaze slid to Dorinar, leaning against the corner. He'd saved her parents' lives more than once. Though he was still dangerous, he was certainly a more reliable source than Ivanora. Aza's silent regard asked the unspoken question.

Dorinar's face did not break from its hard mask, but his tight nod knocked the breath from her lungs.

Aza fought to keep her expression neutral as she slowly sucked in air. *No.* Ivanora was lying. This was a woman of jealousy and secrets and bitterness. She could not be trusted. Aza wouldn't let herself be baited. Her parents were the two strongest people in the land. They'd defeated a demon necromancer and his army nearly single-handedly. They'd taken the powerful Dracour clan with them, and her mother had suspected something. They wouldn't have been caught unaware. They wouldn't have fallen to some mere ambush.

No. Aza shredded through the icy flood of shock and panic and sorrow that threatened to drown her, to suffocate her, to destroy her. Not here. Not now. She could not—she would not show weakness. Not in front of this viper coiled to strike.

She would mourn *no one* until she saw their graves herself. Straightening under the eyes pinned on her, she lifted her chin. "If I'm the Shadow Heir now, then you may refer to me as Guardian Thane."

For a moment, the room stilled. Ivanora stiffened, the mocking glee in her countenance replaced by a stony mask of rage. Then remembering herself, she bared her teeth once more. "As you wish, *Guardian* Thane." She adjusted the collar of her cloak and picked up a pair of slim volumes from the desk. "And I will be borrowing these, Dorinar," she said, daring him to contradict her as their matching glares locked.

The air sizzled, the yanaa sparking between them, thick and electric. Ivanora looked away first, punctuating her retreat with a haughty sniff. "You wouldn't begrudge your sister a little light reading. We are family after all."

With that, she whisked past Aza, out the door into the darkening swamp. She paused only a moment before Makeo's broad chest, bringing a hand to her nose. "Even more repulsive than I remembered."

Witt crossed his arms. "Rude, lady."

An unexpected swell of affection rushed through Aza. Witt might've been an idiot, but he was no coward.

Ivanora's eyes narrowed at him, her fingers twitching in a way that made Aza's hand jerk for the hilt of her dagger. Shad curled his tail around her ankle, his eye widening with a silent "no." Makeo shifted ever so slightly to angle his huge shoulder in front of Witt, and Dorinar strode to the doorway, his thin frame not filling it by half.

Ivanora smirked and pushed her long, shining hair behind one shoulder. "My dear, you have no idea." She spun on her heel, and in three steps, she had disappeared amongst the trees.

12
DORINAR

"Well, that's that." The freckled woman clapped her hands together as if to snap them all free from the net of tension Ivanora had cast over them. She waved to Makeo and Witt. "Come in before the draft does."

Dorinar stalked to the plump armchair in the corner of the room, and Makeo and Witt stepped in.

"I'm Marloa. I help Dorinar with his research and make sure he survives out here." She gestured to the cushioned seats gathered around the fire. "Please, rest yourselves while I get a bite to eat."

Aza's tongue lay dry and heavy in her mouth. A sudden exhaustion seeped through her, as if fending off Ivanora's claims had taken some actual feat of strength. The horrified grief she had pushed down threatened to rise again, but she buried it once more with a brute force of will. *My parents are not dead.* Makeo sagged into the closest armchair, the seat nearly threadbare, his muzzle turned to the floor, while Witt watched her with glistening eyes of concern.

Only Shad seemed unfazed by the strange encounter as he crossed the room to the glowering magus. Dorinar gripped the arms of his chair as if bracing for attack.

"Well, Dorinar?" Shad began, the two words weighted with unsaid questions.

Dorinar didn't give. "Well, cat?"

Marloa came back in with three steaming mugs gripped in her hands and passed them to Witt, Aza, and Makeo. "Had some crallusk chowder on the fire." She put her hands on her hips. "Thought it might warm you up."

Aza nodded her thanks, but something else stuck to her thoughts. "Have we met?" Something about the cloud of dark freckles on Marloa's fawn skin seemed familiar. "How'd you know who I was?"

"I'd be shocked if you remembered." Marloa's face softened in a smile. "You could barely put four words together when I first met you at Catalede, and I was but a girl myself." She rubbed at her ink-stained fingers. "But you look so much like your father; you're impossible to mistake."

"Ah." Aza tried for a weak smile, but it seemed to catch in her throat at the mention of her father. She swallowed it thickly, a pressure building in her forehead—all the thoughts she could not let herself think demanding to be released. But she could master them. She had to.

Across the room, Shad still worked at Dorinar. "Are you going to tell us why Ivanora was here?"

"What business is it of yours?" Dorinar crossed his arms as if to shield himself from the wet cat.

Shad pressed on, his voice low but urgent. "What about the news of the Heirs? Is it true?"

"What do I care?" Dorinar shrugged, but an old sorrow tugged at his eyes that belied his flat tone. "If you've come for gossip, find it elsewhere."

"Oh stop, Dorn." Marloa rolled her eyes. "Ivanora showed up yesterday demanding texts on curses, yanai barriers, talismans… everything. But you know how possessive Dorn is about his spell books. She was quite nasty about it. Even more than usual."

"What about Guardian Dashul and Guardian Thane?" Witt asked, staring into the fire.

"There's been talk in the village of trouble up north, but that was the first news I'd heard of the Heirs' passing." Marloa brushed a hand against Aza's arm, her face soft with kindness. "I'm so sorry. It's been a while since I've seen them, but they were always so kind to me."

Aza ground her teeth together to stop herself from slapping Marloa's hand away. Ivanora had been lying. Couldn't the rest of them see that? She sucked in a breath, but her voice still came out rough. "What about Zephyr? Is he…"

Marloa shook her head. "She said nothing of your brother."

"And if something had happened, she would know," Shad said, his gaze strangely soft. "She would have mentioned it."

Of course she would have, if only to twist the knife. Aza nodded, holding her breath to keep the treacherous sob in her throat—of relief, or sorrow, or fury—she wasn't sure.

"I would ask what brings an Heir trespassing into my home… again," Dorinar grumbled, squeezing the bridge of his nose. "But I simply do not have the energy for whatever pathetic human troubles you're bringing with you this evening." He stood and made his slow escape through the hall with shuffling steps.

"We'll be here tomorrow, Dorn." Shad turned his long dark whiskers to the fire. "You know we won't leave that easily."

Dorinar adjusted his robe with a huff. "You never do."

After four days of sleeping in the wet and chill of the Tazgar marsh, the dusty room and lumpy mattress of Dorinar's sprawling house should have been a pleasant reprieve. With fatigue clinging to her bones from weeks on the road, she should have fallen asleep as soon as her scarred cheek met the flat pillows. But with thoughts of her parents and Ivanora's infuriating smile twisting through her mind, she couldn't let her guard down in the slightest. If she did, the unthinkable possibility would seep into her. Maybe her parents really were dead.

They are not, she rebuffed herself furiously, fists clenching as if to batter down the encroaching sorrow. Ivanora had lied to get under her skin for some reason. But why? A predawn bird released a single questioning trill, and Aza couldn't lay there a second longer. She rose from the bed and made her way out the door into the near darkness. The damp air chirruped with ribbed frogs, mire finches, and who knew what other marsh creatures.

The hiss of Aza's blades escaping their sheathes cut through the swamp serenade, and her boots squelched as she whirled and slashed. She missed the extra weight of her training weapons in her hands and Catalede's firm cobbles under her boots. She breathed in the smell of moss and still water with every strike, willing it to purge the guilt and despair from her disobedient thoughts.

In. Out. Control your breath. Control your body. Control your mind.

With each movement she coiled the emotions that threatened to overtake her. Confusion, anger, and sorrow wrapped into a tight manageable ball she could lock away. The scent of musk invaded the air, and a large shadow edged her vision, pulling away her focus.

Aza sighed, not looking in Makeo's direction while debating whether to acknowledge him or not. She couldn't risk his kindness tearing down the shaky walls she was so desperately trying to brace. If she didn't say anything, he might just take the hint and give up. But Makeo was nothing if not patient. Perhaps if she was short with him, he would leave sooner.

"What, Keo."

"Couldn't sleep?"

She stabbed the air. "Sleep is just wasted time."

"I expected you to be storming into Dorinar's chambers this morning." He paused. "Thinking about your parents?"

She winced at the too-gentle words, the thought of her mother's warm arms around her constricting her chest. *Stop it.* She whirled and kicked out. "What's there to think about?" She slashed again, and his huge broadsword met her dagger with a clang.

"We're all hurting for you, Aza." His green eyes were soft. "I'm sorry you had to hear it from someone like Ivanora."

And he was, the pain glistening in his eyes—reaching out to her. The very sight of them stung the raw open wound she refused to acknowledge. Aza broke away and slashed twice more, his broadsword twisting to block. "I thought the Maldibor were supposed to be able to sense things. She was obviously lying."

He nodded, his blade between them. "Perhaps she was. But with what you heard on the Shadow Plane I thought you might be…"

She feinted and darted under his guard, the point of her blade tickling his unprotected side. Her breath came out in a hiss. "Don't worry about it. I've got everything under control."

He shook his head, lowering his weapon. "It's okay if you don't."

"Not really." Aza straightened, brushing her hair away from her damp forehead. Her fatigue mercifully leeching away her other emotions. "We have to move forward, Keo."

"Are you sure you wouldn't rather go to your brother?" The point of Makeo's sword dug into the spongy ground as he leaned on it. "What if he's—"

"By the time I reach him, he'll already be with your tribe." Flicking a knife from its sheath on her chest, she flung it toward the nearest trunk, spearing a leaf on its way. She latched onto the distraction to keep her from meeting the worry in Makeo's gaze. "He'll be safe with them." *Wouldn't he? Please, for the love of Odriel, let him be safe.*

Makeo hummed, a deep vibration in the back of his throat. "But you don't think he's worried mad about *you*? That with your parents gone, he might need *you* with him?"

"That's a sweet thought." Aza yanked the knife from the trunk and wiped it against her breeches, her movements slowing from the exhaustion no longer content to be ignored. "But even if he was the worrying type—which he's not—Zephyr has Hoku and his friends." She swallowed, willing it to be true. It had only been ten days since she'd seen him last. Which meant she still had at least another week before he even reached Carceroc. If she moved fast, she could still meet him there. "He'll be fine, and I'll find him as soon as I get answers about the Shadow Plane."

"Well then, what're you waiting for?" He cocked his head toward the cottage. "The magus was already at his books when I arose."

Aza sheathed her daggers, the heaviness of reluctance weighing her thoughts. With disappointment or vindication looming over her there was a part of her that wanted to stay in this moment of unknown. What if they'd come all that way for nothing, and she had to face her brother and the deaths of her parents empty-handed?

She shook her head, trying to bat away the hesitation. No matter what, she had to continue on. No matter where her path led, there was no use waiting.

Without another word, Aza strode past Makeo into the cottage. The smell of roasting fish and honey floated from the kitchen. She was only half surprised to see that Witt had taken over the kettle at the fire. He stirred the pot, and Marloa handed him a jar of spice.

She noticed them at the doorway and greeted them with a smile. "Come in and join us." She nodded at Witt. "Your boy there certainly knows his way about a kitchen. Even I'm curious to see what he comes up with."

A smile curved Aza's lips as Witt added a pinch of the dried green plant to whatever delicious experiment he was concocting. But she wasn't here for that. "We'd like to talk to Dorinar. You know where he is this morning?"

Marloa's smirk deepened. "Ah, yes. Let me go drag him out of his cave for you. He needs to eat too, after all."

"What smells so delicious?" Makeo asked, sitting on the bench next to the long table that ran the length of the kitchen. A chaotic scattering of dissimilar chairs and stools lined the other side.

Witt blew on a spoon of what looked like hearty porridge. "Marloa caught a hissing bass in the pond this morning, and I couldn't just let it go to waste." He gingerly tasted the spoon and closed his eyes with a smile. "Honeyed hissing pottage." He rustled around the open shelves for wooden bowls and spoons like he'd lived here all his life. "Good to warm bones and souls."

"Sounds like just the thing we need," Makeo said with a grin.

Aza sat across from Makeo, feeling empty but not hungry. Witt set a steaming bowl in front of Makeo and then slid onto the bench next to Aza, placing a bowl in front of her. Feeling his eyes on her, she braced herself with a steely sigh and faced him, taking in the shadows under his lashes and the red around his brown irises.

He leaned a little closer. "Aza, I'm *really* sorry about your—"

She jerked her gaze back to the burnished table, something threatening to unravel inside her. Could no one speak of anything else? "Not now, Witt."

A hubbub echoing from the hall saved her from further wretched condolences.

"Ach! Stop pushing me, woman!"

"Then move faster, old man. I don't want to have to pick your skinny bones from the floor."

"I don't have to talk to them! They're uninvited intruders!"

"Oh, don't be ridiculous. You know you're curious to see what they came all this way for."

"They're here for what they always come for. They need something."

"Well then, the sooner you hear them out, the sooner they'll leave."

Witt rose to scoop two more bowls just as Dorinar huffed into the kitchen with Marloa close at his heels. He crossed his arms indignantly, and she pressed down on his shoulders until he slouched into a chair like a pouting child. Marloa took the bowls and spoons from Witt with a nod of thanks.

"Look, this is so much better than the scorched grub I make." She smiled sweetly and took a bite, her face relaxing into an expression of bliss. "Try it. It's definitely worth a chat over breakfast."

"I don't—" Dorinar started.

Marloa pounded her spoon on the table, making Dorinar jump. Her eyes widened with warning. "Try. It."

He rolled his eyes, a long-suffering sigh rising through him. "Whatever it takes to get you to leave me alone." They all watched him in silence as he dug his spoon into the porridge and brought it to his thin lips. He inhaled suspiciously before slowly placing it in his mouth, chewing and softening. His expression didn't change, but his spoon dipped back in the bowl. "What do you want, then?"

Marloa practically glowed with triumph, and all the shoulders in the room relaxed. Makeo chuckled, and a smug grin tugged at Witt's face. But Aza didn't waste the window of opportunity. "Have you heard of Shadow Heirs leaving this world to cross into a colorless plane filled with strange creatures?"

Dorinar's third spoonful paused on the way to his mouth, and Marloa brightened. "You mean not just go unseen but go somewhere else entirely?" she asked.

Aza nodded, and Marloa leaned toward Dorinar. "Wasn't there something odd like that in the account of Silvix?"

"Yes…" Dorinar sucked on the spoon. "It does sound familiar."

"Silvix?" Makeo asked.

"A Shadow Heir two centuries past…" Marloa's fingernails tapped on the wood. "His writings were always… difficult to interpret."

Dorinar nodded. "He was—"

"I already found them," Shad said from the doorway. "It's slow with paws, but I was able to read through a few. Marloa, if you could please assist me."

Marloa cocked her head and rose from the table. "Is that what you were up all night poking around for? You could have just asked me, you know."

Aza stilled. Did no one sleep last night?

The tip of Shad's tail twitched to-and-fro. "Last time I was here, the ever-pleasant Dorinar was less than helpful. But at least the library was in better order this time."

Marloa preened in Dorinar's direction as she walked out. "See, someone appreciates my organizational system."

A few moments later, Marloa returned with a short stack of weathered volumes. She plopped them on the table in a plume of dust, and Dorinar shielded his pottage, glowering irritably.

"So, Silvix could walk the Shadow Plane?" Aza asked, trailing her fingers along the spines.

Shad pawed the book on top of the stack. "He talks of entering the Shadow Plane to hear voices from afar but…"

"He claims to speak to the dead," Dorinar cut in, his voice flat.

Aza swallowed, a cold chill prickling the back of her neck.

"But that's not in *The Heir's Way*, is it?" Witt asked, voicing her own thoughts.

Witt had sat with them at many a fireside listening to her mother recite the history of the Heirs from that very book. Her mother… Aza clawed away the thought before it could surface.

Marloa scratched her short brown hair. "Silvix is not really an Heir you'd want to remember."

"What do you mean?" Aza picked up the book Shad had indicated, another cloud of dust billowing into the air as she leafed through it.

"He eventually went mad," Marloa murmured, sliding into her seat. "Speaking to people who weren't there, violent outbursts, and then eventually, he disappeared."

"Sounds like a peach." Witt grimaced.

Aza skimmed the yellowed pages scrawled with uneven text—half-complete thoughts and nonsensical phrases scribbled across the paper in unreadable loops and curves. Finally, she found a few legible lines near the end.

The stronger he grows, the tighter the Plane holds him. He forgets himself. The wraiths are ever with him now. They call him farther. He pleads to go farther. Cries to be one with the Plane day and night. The deeper he goes, the louder his ravings become.

Impatient, Aza closed the book. "Does he say what the Shadow Plane is? Or how we're connected to it?"

"They claim it is the place between the living and the dead." Shad frowned. "But not much more than that. However, he does mention that he trained others to go there, as well."

"Other Shadow Heirs?" Makeo asked.

"No," Shad replied. "He refers to them as the Wraith-Called, but I think they're ordinary humans."

Dorinar nodded, tugging absently on one of his curls. "It's been many years since I've been there, but the Wraith-Called still train in Somisidas Abbey."

"An abbey?" Aza asked.

"They are an odd folk." Dorinar rolled his eyes. "They wouldn't even let me inside their precious little circle for the sake of research." He slurped another spoon of pottage. "But perhaps they would feel differently about a Shadow Heir."

Aza swallowed. Could they really use the Shadow Plane to speak with the dead? If so, would her parents be there waiting for her? Her stomach flipped with an aching dread.

Witt tapped his spoon on his lips. "But how is this connected to the not-Lost and the unrest in Carceroc Forest?"

"Maybe it's not," Shad said.

"If anyone knows, it would be the Wraith-Called," Marloa said, pushing her empty bowl away.

Aza slid the slim volume of nonsense back to Shad. "So where is Somisidas, and how do I get there?"

"How do *we* get there?" Shad corrected with a stern glare.

Aza shrugged. "You heard Dorinar; they probably won't even let you in." And she didn't know if she could survive their compassion chipping away at what little defense she could cobble together.

"Then we will accompany you as far as we can," Makeo rumbled.

"I'll provide a map…" Dorinar rubbed a thumb along his sharp jawline. "*If* you return with a full account of Somisidas for my records."

"My, my, Dorinar," Shad said, the tip of his tail twitching on the table. "You're practically amenable now. You must have had quite the change of heart these last few decades." Shad's gaze slid to where Marloa's elbow touched Dorinar's.

Smiling, Marloa poked Dorinar in the shoulder. "Perhaps it's the pottage."

The magus scoffed and rose from his seat, his pale cheeks coloring ever so slightly. "You can never please humans," he grumbled as he shuffled into the hall. Shad leapt from the table, silently following after him like a fond housecat.

Aza took a bite of her pottage. Even tepid, the delectable flavors of honey, fish, and herbs washed through her. She oozed a sigh of tense relief. There were others who knew of the Shadow Plane. They could teach her. This wouldn't be for nothing. A cautious flame of hope warmed her belly. "We'll leave as soon as possible."

"How exciting." Marloa beamed in a sunny smile. "Take whatever supplies you need. Dorinar keeps all kinds of odds and ends out in the barn."

"Thank you for your kindness." Makeo rose from the table. "C'mon, Witty, let's see what we can find."

Setting his bowl and spoon next to the wash basin, Witt turned to Aza. "If you like the pottage, there's more by the fire."

Aza's gaze slid to the large kettle. "Only if you promise not to get a big head about it."

"Too late," he laughed as he followed Makeo out.

Marloa shifted to sit across from Aza. She peered up at her from beneath long lashes. "Those boys care about you a great deal."

Aza rolled her eyes, debating how rude it would be to excuse herself and flee. She stuffed another spoonful of pottage in her mouth. "It's not me they follow."

"Oh?"

"Shad is eternally loyal to my... to my parents. Witt's been my brother's left hand since they could walk, and Makeo..." Aza paused. "Makeo is trying to find answers for his own family."

"That may be true." Marloa took Aza's bowl to the kettle and spooned her another helping. "But it's not the only truth." She replaced the full bowl on the table, her eyes softened with a pity that made Aza swallow a scowl. "They worry about you, and they believe in you. I wouldn't let such friendship go idly."

Aza nodded to appease the woman and spooned out a chunk of honeyed fish. She did nothing idly. If her parents were truly dead, there was only one person who was capable of killing them. And when Mogens came for her, she would make sure no one else was around. Friendship or not.

13
WRAITH-CALLED

The mud of the swamp squelched beneath Aza's feet as they made their way through the marsh once more. A spongy moss coated every surface in fuzzy shades of deep green, thickening the air with the stinking rot of mildew. The tiny silk toads belched irritably at the rude sloshing of Aza's feet, and the occasional hard-shelled otterillo snuffled in her direction with dark shining eyes. Every weed, branch, and leaf dripped with the thick mist that hovered stubbornly over the soggy ground, turning the air to a gluey soup long gone cold.

She glanced at the weathered map in her hands where Dorinar had scrawled a meandering line from Tazgar into the steep cliffs on the morning side of the Naerami.

Witt peered over her shoulder. "Are we close to escaping this bog before it swallows us?"

"The faster you walk, the faster we get out of the wet." *And onto the icy rocks,* she added silently with a frown. "If you pick up the pace, we might even be able to make camp in the foothills."

Witt sighed. "Surely we could've spared one more night with a dry bed and a decent pantry."

Aza stepped around a puddle in the path. "No one stopped you from staying, Witty."

"But you'd miss me."

He reached out to put an arm around her shoulder, and she ducked. "Witt Corser, I have yet to miss you—ever."

"Oh c'mon, you can admit it. I know you like my cooking."

"I don't have to admit anything."

Even while she groused with Witt, she angled an ear to catch Makeo's question to Shad. "Did Dorinar ever explain why Ivanora took those spell books?"

"He did not." Shad picked his way delicately from dry spot to dry spot. "Even though he seemed more restless than usual when I asked him."

"I always imagined confronting her and making her break the curse, but I never thought I'd actually come face to face with her." He paused, his boots making huge footprints in the muck. "Do you think I'll get another chance?"

"Ivanora walks among men often, but rarely does she reveal herself. I haven't seen her in thirty years." He shook the moisture from his whiskers. "Not that it aggrieved me."

"There has to be some way I can get her attention. Some kind of deal I can make with her."

Shad's breath escaped in a hiss. "Ivanora has always been mercurial at the best of times, but after her sister magus, Bellaphia, was murdered a century ago, her cruelty has festered with each passing decade. She wields her yanaa like a club, and the Maldibor are neither the first nor the last to bear her ire." He shook a cloud of water droplets from his fur. "I pity whatever poor soul she plans to turn Dorinar's spells on next. Frankly, I'm relieved she departed as quickly as she did."

"Still, I'm already cursed. What have I to lose?" Makeo's rumbling voice lowered even further. "It'd be worth the risk to ask her. I won't hesitate next time."

"Just remember, were it not for Everard's bargain, the Maldibor would not even exist." Warning weighed on Shad's words. "More damage can always be done."

Aza blinked rapidly, only half-listening to Witt as he rattled off the ingredients to his favorite recipe. She thought back to Ivanora's snarl of disgust when she looked at Makeo. Her hate for the Maldibor had almost been palpable, and her power had been... overwhelming. Was she the one stirring up Carceroc? Trying to take away their home or erase them from Okarria completely? But why now after all these years?

Aza pressed her lips together. Surely it was just a coincidence they'd met Ivanora at Dorinar's abode. Her fingers touched the dagger hilt at her thigh. But with every shadow sharpening its knife, she couldn't trust chance to play nice. In this game, a coincidence was just a riddle she had yet to solve. But time wasn't on her side.

Aza's boots slid on the slick rock as she pulled herself up the incline with her bloodied fingers. Her breath clouded, while the cold rain mixed with her sweat, dripping down from her chin. The sun had already sunk below the mountain, and the clouds turned to charcoal gray in the fading light. After three days in the marsh and another six on the trailless rocks of the Naerami bluffs, frustration ached through her every joint. But they had to be close.

With one last heave, she pushed herself onto the narrow ledge of the peak to find dots of distant light peppering the canyon wall in front of her. She nearly wilted in relief. Squinting in the dusk, she could just make out the wood buildings balanced atop stone landings carved into the mountain. If not for the lights, she wouldn't have been able to distinguish them from the jagged stone at all. The low-hanging clouds misted over the canyon, and her gaze followed the snaking structure along the cliff until she found the ledge that served as a trail leading to it. It was actually below where they were now, but if they didn't hurry it would be too dark to find it.

"Anything?" Witt shouted from below.

Not bothering to answer, Aza lowered herself off the ledge. Hand over hand, she felt her way back down to where the others waited. With his thick fur damp with rain, Makeo's beastly odor was more pungent than ever. Shad cringed away from the wet beneath the meager shelter of a boulder, and even Witt's scratched face had lost its usual annoying glow.

Aza wiped the rain from her face with a soaked sleeve, tucking her dripping dark hair behind her ear. "It's just down to the next valley." Her mind ran over the trail again, carving it into her memory. "We're a few hours away, nothing more."

Witt looked up into the dark sky. "I suppose we can't make it there tonight."

Aza sighed, wanting to contradict him and press on. But even she wouldn't take that risk on a foreign mountain in the dark. She shook her abnormally heavy head.

Makeo nodded. "In that case, I saw a rock shelf not too far back that should keep us out of the wet for the night."

"Backward?" Shad groaned. "If you're going to kill me, Maldibor, please just do it quickly instead of running me to death on these godforsaken rocks." Shad's small legs shook as he rose to his feet. Although Makeo had carried him from time to time, Shad's still-healing body was in no shape for the kind of climbing they'd been forced to surmount in the past couple days. Aza had spent most of her life training Greens to strengthen their bodies on the cliffs near Catalede, and even *she* felt spent.

He stumbled, and Aza reached out to lift him into her arms. "How many times have you crossed the land in the last century?" She tried a stiff smile. "Surely, you can make it one more day."

He growled in annoyance, his dark fur plastered to his thin body. "The difference between dead and alive is one day."

"So it is." Makeo chuckled. "But it's not this day." He pointed to a pathetically small outcropping in the path, a scrub of a tree reaching out to one side. "Not big enough for a fire, but it should keep us dry."

Shad leapt from Aza's arms and curled into a tight ball in the driest corner, his ears peevishly pressed against his head.

Witt tucked in next to him and dug into his bag for the remnants of the supplies they'd brought with them. He held up strips of meat and a soggy lump of hardtack. "For dinner we'll be having two succulent entrees, accompanied with the clearest of mountain rainwater to wash it down."

Aza mentally measured out three even portions and a smaller one for Shad before grabbing her meager rations. If she wasn't careful, they would let her eat more than her share. Though her belly ached, if someone was going to collapse from hunger, she knew she'd be the last one.

His paws tucked under him, Shad sullenly gnawed on a strip of meat and looked Aza's way. "We should properly greet you as the Shadow Heir before we go to Somisidas tomorrow."

Witt tossed a brick of bread to Makeo. "What does that mean?"

"Traditionally, when an Heir ascends, a passage is chosen from *The Heir's Way*, and the Heir formally swears to grant Okarria their protection."

Makeo nodded. "I've never seen one, but I heard the Heirs describe it as both a farewell to the last generation and a blessing of the next. Perhaps we could—"

"No," Aza cut him off. Her wounds had only just scabbed over, and she refused to let them break open once more. "There will be no greeting of any kind until my parents' fate is more than just a rumor."

Shoulder-to-shoulder they chewed their bread and listened to the rain tapping its cold nails on the ledge above them.

Finally, Shad swallowed the last of his paltry meal and sighed. "Well, I'm too tired to argue." He curled his tail tightly around himself in the corner of the shallow cove. "Don't wake me until you're ready to carry me the rest of the way." With that, he closed his good eye and tucked his small head against his haunches.

Aza looked down the path to where the abbey carved into the side of the cliff awaited them. Would she find the secret of the Shadow Plane somewhere in those walls? Would she even be able to cross over without drawing the Lost to them? And if the Plane were a place for the dead, would she find her parents wandering the gray grass with the grotesque shadow dwellers? She could already see the disappointment etched onto her parents' faces.

She squeezed her brow to dispel the somber image, her arm brushing Witt's in the close space. Makeo breathed in and out slowly on the other side, the pulse of his life rising and falling against her shoulder. Fatigue looped around them all, but Aza couldn't even begin to imagine sleeping in this crevice.

She let her hands fall to her lap. "You can rest. I'll take first watch," she said to no one in particular.

Witt fidgeted beside her. Discomfort obvious in his tense shoulders. "I'm sorry about your parents, Aza. They were heroes of Okarria." His hands clenched the loose canvas of his bag. "And they were always good to me."

Aza's arms tightened around her knees, but she didn't reply, and he didn't press. She almost wished he would. That he'd go into one of his pointless, long-winded tales. That he'd go down some rabbit hole that made him laugh at his own stupidity or ask her for something silly. Because that would be the normal she needed.

Eventually, Witt's body loosened with sleep, and his mop of curls fell onto her shoulder, breaths slow and deep. Aza's fingers closed around a weed growing up in the sandy rock under her. She pulled it up and twirled it between her fingers. Had her parents been surprised by the Rastgol Lost? How many did it take to overwhelm two people who had faced down a demon necromancer's army? Had anyone witnessed it?

She stiffened. And if on the off chance they were dead... what had happened to the bodies? Unless they were burned or beheaded, whatever necromancer was responsible for the hunting Lost could raise her parents as part of their army. Sweat beaded on her temple as she pictured the ravaged corpse of her mother spinning a tornado of fire toward her. Her fingers flew to her neck at the thought of her father's unseen black blade at her throat.

Makeo leaned into her. "Are you okay?"

The words flew out of her mouth in a tense whisper. "My parents aren't dead, my parents aren't dead, my parents aren't dead."

Or was she just incapable of accepting a world in which they were?

"It's okay to grieve the possibility, Aza." Hesitantly, he placed a large paw on her shaking hand. "Sometimes our grief doesn't care for the facts." His shaggy shoulder was warm beside her clammy skin. "That doesn't mean we shouldn't feel it."

Two silent tears escaped Aza's eyelashes and trailed down her cheeks. *Odriel take it.* She wanted to scream and rage. She wanted to storm back to Ivanora and demand the truth. She wanted to fly across the mountain to warn her brother. She wanted to cross to the Shadow Plane and plead for answers. But she was stuck here in the rain with a wet Maldibor, a kitchen boy, and an irritable cat.

She wiped at her eyes with a fist. "Can we talk about something else?"

Makeo's ears twitched. "Like what?"

"Anything. I don't care." She turned her face to the ledge above them. "Why don't you talk about you? Isn't that something people like to do?"

Makeo's chest shook in silent laughter. "I don't think most care to hear about a reeking Maldibor."

"Well, I do." She sniffed. "Were you trying to find Ivanora to break the curse? Why risk that?"

He scoffed. "I would think that would be obvious."

"I thought the Maldibor were a happy people." She shrugged. "Besides, you'd have to be pretty desperate to seek out Ivanora after the way she looked at you the first time." *Like you weren't even human.* Aza shook her head. "She even makes Dorinar nervous."

Makeo lifted his paw from hers, folding it in his lap. Water dripped from the lip of the ledge onto his boots, and for a moment she thought he wouldn't answer her. His chest rose and fell in a silent sigh, and his voice vibrated through the night air. "You remember the Maldibor boys are born human?"

"Of course, I remember." Aza snorted. She had spent years running around with him when they were younger. How could he even ask such a thing?

"We don't change into a beast until we're nine, ten, eleven… depends on the child." His paws flexed and loosened. "And every generation, we wonder if perhaps the line is too diluted to hold the curse. Maybe at last, these brand new, beautiful children will be free of Ivanora's hatred."

Aza swallowed, turning toward his bulky silhouette.

"My mother is a fourth-generation Maldibor, and I was the first of Elika's twice-great-grandsons. The village waited on the tips of their claws as I turned eleven, then twelve, then thirteen." A rueful grin flashed across his face. "I walked on air thinking I was free. That Odriel had chosen *me* to shed the curse." The grin faded. "Then, when I was fourteen, shortly after…"

Makeo's story faltered, and Aza nodded. There was only one thing that split their lives into before and after. She put a hand to her scarred cheek.

"I changed, just like the rest of my cousins and uncles."

Aza flinched, her fingernails digging into her scar, and she thought about its matching brother that crossed Makeo's chest. The memory of Mogens' bony smile and the knife flashing in his hand sent a stab of guilt through her. The tiny Time Heir almost hadn't been able to keep him alive… and he had been the lucky one that night. Was it that trauma that had caused the change somehow?

"My human father couldn't bear the disappointment and left soon after."

Aza racked her brain for the image of his father. It wasn't hard when Makeo looked just like him—large shoulders and thick blond hair, with a quiet way about him. How could he just run off?

"That wasn't your fault," Aza whispered.

"I feel like that's one of those things we can't really know." He paused, turning his muzzle to her. "But our emotions don't care for facts either way."

"The facts matter, Makeo. There's nothing wrong with becoming a Maldibor." Her hand balled into a fist. "There's a lot wrong with someone abandoning their family."

Even as she said it, the words made her sick. Hadn't she abandoned her family? She swallowed the thought. No. She had left to protect her family. It was different. Of course it was.

He went on as if she hadn't spoken. "So, I decided even if I wasn't the chosen one, maybe I could choose to do something about it."

To free his people? Or to bring his father back? Aza's eyebrows rose as another piece fell into place. "So, when you heard I was set on visiting Dorinar, you were going to ask him about Ivanora?"

"No." His emerald gaze met hers. "I left because I couldn't let you go alone." He shrugged, a sheepish grin revealing his white fangs once more. "But it might have occurred to me later. Though I wasn't exactly expecting to meet the delightful magus in the flesh. Got a bit tongue-tied in the moment by her *charming* presence."

Aza put a hand to her mouth, stifling the strangled giggle that threatened to burst out of her.

"Really, that's the saddest story I have, and you're going to laugh?"

But Aza could feel his shoulders shaking in the dark too, even as fresh tears of silent mirth streamed down her face. "No. I'm glad, really." She wiped the tears away once more. "I'm glad you got a chance to see what you're really up against. And that you held your tongue." She blew out a breath of emotion, sorrow, and laughter all tangled up in one exhalation of lightening. "Shad's right. Who knows what she would've done if you'd actually challenged her."

"When I see her again, I won't lose my nerve," he said quietly, serious once more.

A deep unease roiled through Aza's gut, but she said nothing. She didn't have to tell him the danger of crossing a magus with Shadmundar murmuring in his sleep not two paces to her left. And the odds of him ever seeing Ivanora again were nearly nonexistent.

"Even if you don't..." She swallowed, resisting the urge to grab his hand. "You're enough the way you are, Keo."

"No." His unwavering gaze met hers as if trying to communicate something she couldn't quite read. "I'm not enough for the things I want, and I refuse to pass on the curse. It'll die with me."

"Don't say that," she whispered, her sorrow trembling in her fingers once more. She couldn't think of Makeo dying. Not right now.

For a moment, they fell silent. The rain still beating its steady rhythm into the stolid, unmoving mountain, wearing it down drop by drop.

"Is it wrong to want more?" he asked, his big voice so quiet she almost couldn't hear him.

She snorted softly. "If it is, then I'm afraid we're both in trouble." Aza flexed her numb fingers in her gloves. "But... my father says that's how we grow."

Witt snuffled against her shoulder, and Makeo leaned in closer. "Aza, I—"

A loud thump crashed through the night.

Aza snapped to her feet, daggers out, peering into six pairs of golden eyes a hand's breadth from her face, the creature's breath hot on her cheeks. The dim light of the moon reflected off two long black beaks protruding from heads of naked red flesh. A goat-like body anchored the two swaying necks, and its giant wingspan spread out before them like a cloak billowing in the wind.

Immediately awake, Witt scrabbled on the sandy ledge. "What is that?"

The creature snapped its beaks, and Aza's muscles tensed, ready to sever the first neck that lurched her way.

"Easy, Aze," Makeo said, stepping close to her side.

"No way," Aza whispered. "That thing could run you through with one of its beaks and pluck out your heart."

Another crash and then another, and more gold eyes lit the darkness. The clacking of beaks punctuated the still night.

Aza glanced at Shad, blinking owlishly from his corner, exhaustion still glazing his sapphire eye. "Care to weigh in, Shadmundar?" The necks swirled and swayed together like a pair of snapcobras. "How close to death are we standing right now?"

"I've never seen one before," Shad said, his words thick with sleep.

Aza clamped down on a swear. Why had they dragged him up here again?

"But..." he continued, "it looks like a grizzard flock."

"So, are these things here to eat us or what?" Witt gripped his bag to his chest with pale hands, pressing his back to the cliff wall.

The grizzard in front of Aza opened its long black beak in a hoarse squawk. "Follow."

The scratchy voice raised the hair on Aza's neck. "They can speak?"

"Yes, but they're just imitators." Shad rose to his paws with a small groan. "It's repeating something it's heard someone say."

The bird nipped at Aza's arm, its sharp beak cutting through her sleeve. "Follow."

Aza flinched back. "I'll pass, thanks."

In a violent movement, the strange birds shook out their wings at once, clacking their beaks in fervent rejection. "Come now, or not at all."

"You think the Wraith-Called sent them?" Witt whispered.

Impatience tightened Aza's grip on her daggers, her eyes not moving from the grizzard's. "You want us to go down the rocks in the dark?"

"Eyes deceive." The grizzard's head bobbed and twisted. "Feel your way." The wings all snapped closed. "Follow."

Soundlessly, the grizzards leapt into the air, one by one, until just the creature in front of Aza remained. Aza hadn't moved as her mind calculated, trying to weigh her options. The rain had subsided into a thick mist, but going down the sheer cliffs in the dark was madness. Was this some kind of test? But why?

They could just ignore the creature and find their own way in the morning. She doubted these Wraith-Called or their grizzard pets could really do anything to stop her. But would they answer her questions if she had to bust down their door?

Shad hobbled on stiff legs out from under their pathetic ledge. "Well, this is what you wanted right? What are you waiting for?"

"Really, *you're* going?" Aza slowly lowered her daggers. "You'll be the first one to fall off this cliff."

"Then at least that could put an end to these blistered paws." Shad's puffy tail belied his calm words. "Come then, Grizzard, lead the way."

But the creature didn't flinch, its yellow eyes still on Aza. Expectant. Challenging, almost.

"Oh, all right." Aza wrinkled her nose and sheathed her blades. "Don't get your necks in a twist." The birds clacked their beaks with satisfaction and turned away, one head facing her to make sure she was coming. "But I'm going first." She turned to Makeo. "Try to make sure no one falls off the cliff."

Witt bobbed up beside her. "And me?"

Aza's lips twitched, and she lowered her voice. "Keep an eye to our backs." She scanned the rocks around them. "This is the perfect set-up for a trap."

Witt nodded, his eyes lighting up with the responsibility. She resisted the urge to smack her palm to her head. Had she really sunk so low as to depend on *Witt Corser* of all people?

The grizzard strode away on its strange legs—the front two flush with hawk talons and the back two equipped with neat goat hooves. Its rat tail whipped behind it, beckoning her. She leveled her arms out to her sides, eyes straining in the almost-dark to find her footing. Shad's weak legs scrabbled on the slippery rock shelf, and she turned to see Makeo scoop him up into the crook of his arm. Under different circumstances, the sight of the huge Maldibor with the huffy cat in his arms might've made her smile.

Instead, a knot tightened in Aza's throat. If one of them fell, they could end up pulling each other down with them. The grizzard daintily tripped down a slope of stone, its gold eyes taunting her as it pressed on. She pressed her lips together. When she got there, these Wraith-Called had better have some answers. Her foot slipped, and her arm lurched out to the rock wall beside her.

"Careful, Aza," Makeo rumbled from above.

"This is madness." The rocks cut into her as she slid on her backside down the incline, hoping it didn't lead to a drop off. "I can't see jack-all."

But they couldn't stop. Not after coming all this way. She skidded and crawled on the precipice. Her toes found nothing but air more than once, and her heart jolted with every misstep. The creature wound up and down the cliff like a lazy river, but whether it knew where it was going, she couldn't tell. She cursed every cloud that obscured the moon's weak light and urged the sun to rise faster. But it didn't seem to help.

She tried to look ahead for any hint of the abbey and the lanterns she had seen at sunset. Surely, they should be seeing it by now. She edged around yet another corner after the glowing eyes, fatigue and impatience mixing into a cold fury. Two grizzards awaited her now. One on a path that led slightly up, and one that led down. She swore.

"Now which way?" She turned to where Makeo still held Shad behind her. "What if these things aren't leading us anywhere?"

"Why in Odriel's name would it do that?" Shad asked, his tone sharp with annoyance.

"Because it's a demon bird?" Aza threw her hands up. "I don't know."

"Didn't the grizzard say our eyes would deceive us?" Witt asked, peeking around the cliffside.

Aza squeezed the bridge of her nose. "Then how else are we supposed to find this place?"

"Didn't it tell you to feel your way?" Makeo scratched at his floppy ear. "Would the Shadow Plane show you the way?"

A coldness welled in Aza. Yes, she had thought of asking the shadow dwellers for help. But she didn't like the idea of being left helpless with the grizzards leering at them. And then of course... what if her parents were there?

"But surely not every person that comes here can enter the Shadow Plane." She shook her head, thinking aloud. "It's difficult even for me, and I've been training in yanaa my whole life." She folded her arms and glanced at the two grizzards with their many matching eyes waiting in the dark.

"Then perhaps you're supposed to be feeling something else?" Witt said, his brow creased with confusion.

Like what? With a sigh, Aza let her heavy eyelids fall reluctantly closed. She breathed in the cool, soggy mountain air—the scent of Maldibor mixing with stone and petrichor wafting on the gentle kiss of the breeze. She listened to the breaths of her companions: Shad's ragged, Makeo's slow, and Witt's quick. Talons scratched on stone and wings fluttered somewhere farther away.

But feel? She flexed her toes in her damp boots, the mountain steady under her leather soles. Her eyes flicked open with a growl of frustration.

Witt cocked his head. "Anything?"

"No, I'm just wasting time because I like it." Aza steadied herself on the side of the mountain. "Let's just try the higher path and see where it goes."

She turned on her heel, a prickle of guilt needling her. Had she brought them all this way for nothing? The narrow path crumbled beneath her foot and her hands lunged out toward the cliff wall, looking for holds on the sheer face.

"Aza!" Makeo barked. "Are you all right?"

Hanging on by little more than her fingernails, fear clogged her throat. With numb fingers, she inched her body back to solid ground, her heart pounding. "I'm okay." She risked a peek at the drop below and queasiness rolled through her belly. This was a fool's errand.

"Should..." Witt's nervous eyes darted to Makeo and Shad. "Should we turn around?"

"Go ahead." Aza felt for her next handhold, and to her surprise, found a deep groove in the stone. The inside was smooth, as if many hands had touched it. Interesting. Gripping it firmly, she stretched out her other hand as far as it would go. The groove continued like a smooth snake etched into the jagged wall. She looked back at the others with a hard smile of gritted teeth. "I've found the bloody trail."

Aza dropped from the final handhold onto a polished stone landing just as the sky lightened with the first signs of dawn. One by one, the others descended the cliff to stand beside her.

The landing cut into the cliffside was broader than it would appear from above or below. On their left, a three-story wooden building grew up alongside the cliff. Past that, she could make out other narrow structures of various shapes and sizes crawling up the mountain in a chain. On their right side, the green roofs of yet more buildings crawled down toward a narrow valley floor far below. Polished stone landings, like the one they were on, separated the structures, with spindly stairs winding from one to the other.

Shadmundar growled as Makeo put him down on the smooth white stone. "So, this is the place we've crossed the land to see. It looks just *lovely*," he said, the words coated in thick sarcasm.

A grizzard's beak clacked from the nearest roof, and Aza's focus snapped to the figures in front of her. A woman with golden skin and deep-set eyes stood before her. A long black braid ran down one side of her head, while the other side was shaved short, and she hid her hands in the wide sleeves of her robes. Behind her, two muscular young men stood, long hair tied into knots atop their heads and staffs in hand.

"Somisidas Abbey welcomes you, Aza Thane." The woman's silky voice slid through the mountain silence.

Aza froze, her ears buzzing. Was this the whisperer from the Shadow Plane?

The woman continued on, "We're pleased to see you found your way. However..." Her narrow chin dipped at the others. "I'm afraid your companions will have to depart. They don't belong here with the Called."

Aza's eyes skimmed over Witt, Shad, and Makeo. Dirty. Exhausted. Hungry. And now defeated. They'd traveled hundreds of miles to be here with her, and she wouldn't let this woman dismiss that for no reason other than haughty indifference.

"They belong with me." She crossed her arms. "If they aren't welcome, then I'll leave with them."

It was... mostly true. She wouldn't stay without them. But she wasn't leaving without answers, even if she had to wring it from this woman's long neck. Another grizzard landed with the clack of talons on wood.

The woman said nothing. Still and expressionless, she waited. Was she expecting Aza to change her mind? To come up with a different answer? Aza mirrored her stiff posture. After pushing hard for weeks, she could stand here for as long as they wanted.

Two more grizzards landed somewhere in Aza's peripheral. Their black bodies lined the spines of the buildings, big wings tucked behind their backs like they, too, were waiting. Makeo took a step closer to her, whether in solidarity or in concern for her well-being, she wasn't sure.

Aza's shadows coiled in her center. She was ready to disappear in a moment if they decided to attack. Her body might be tired, but her yanaa was brimming with disuse. She could take on a flock of ugly bald birds.

Finally, without a word or a nod, the woman turned her back on them and glided toward the staircase. Aza's patience slipped away.

"Why did you call me here?" she shouted across the landing.

The two warriors moved to protect the woman, and Aza flung herself into the Shadow Step, the yanaa embracing her like an old friend. She swept the feet out from under the first, then rolled away from the other's staff crashing down on her. Jumping to her feet, she blocked the surprisingly accurate blow to her face and delivered a kick to the man's jaw. With two more swift punches, she ran past the downed bodyguards.

She put her invisible body between the stair and the woman. "Why are there screams on the Shadow Plane?"

Although she couldn't see Aza, the woman's dark gaze pierced through her. She cocked her head ever so slightly. "Why don't we get properly acquainted, shall we?" She pressed her hands together, then slid them apart with a sharp jerk—and disappeared.

Aza's shock only lasted a single heartbeat, her parents flashing before her eyes as she deepened the shadows around herself. The euphoric surge of the crossing flooded her mind, submerging her senses in its familiar, tantalizing power. Breathing deep, she opened her eyes in the gray fields of the Shadow Plane. Her head whipped around, but the Somisidas woman was the only person there. No parents, no shadow dwellers, and no wind whispering her name.

Aza's eyes narrowed, her muscles tense. "Who are you?"

"My name is Seela, the Master of Somisidas." She took long, even breaths as though it didn't tax her at all to be there. As if the Shadow Plane were the most natural thing in the world. With smooth steps, she began to walk through the long gray grass.

Aza followed her, every step an effort while her yanaa flittered away. "How are you here?"

"The same way you are. My yanaa takes me here." Her voice was soft but matter-of-fact. "It's impressive that you found the Shadow Plane on your own. For many of our novices it takes years of training."

"Well, I'm not exactly a novice, but thanks for asking," Aza said through gritted teeth.

Seela considered her beneath long lashes. "And yet, you seem to find it difficult to control yourself here."

Aza swallowed. Had Seela purposefully lured her here to weaken her? Cool sweat beaded on her temple. Is that why they'd tried to get Makeo and the others to leave?

"Why have you been calling me?"

"The Plane can be a dangerous place." A frown curved Seela's thin lips. "Silvix asked us to find you."

Aza shook her head, her breaths coming harder now. How was this woman so calm? "Silvix is dead."

Her arched eyebrows rose. "So you truly don't know what this place is."

"I know it's tied to the Lost and Carceroc and maybe even my parents." Pain wrenched through her limbs. She had to leave, but she couldn't let this woman best her. "And I want to know why."

Seela watched her struggle, her face still.

A slight breeze ruffled the air, but it wasn't Seela's voice this time. "*Teach her.*"

Seela's lips parted, and an emotion Aza couldn't quite recognize flashed across her face. She pressed her mouth firmly closed. "So be it."

With that, Aza's last strand of yanaa slipped through her fingers, and she passed out.

Aza's eyes snapped open back on the cliffside, her head pounding. Dawn's gentle fingers played over the polished stone of the landing, but a shadow fell over her. She looked up to see Makeo's hulking form standing between her and a knot of the Wraith-Called in their gray robes. He held his huge broadsword out in front of him and bared his teeth, growling fiercely. Gone was the gentle Keo of her childhood, and before her stood the snarling Maldibor the villagers feared.

Witt stood on his right side, his sword also drawn, but with nervousness

101

pulling at his jaw and brow. Shad peeked out behind Witt's ankle, fur on end, hissing something to placate the Wraith-Called and their sturdy wooden staffs. Aza squeezed her temples and tried to focus on his words.

"We're just here to ask a few questions."

"This is a sacred place," one of the robed men replied, his hands folded behind him. "Not one for the gawking of bored minds."

Shad laughed dryly. "Is that so? Do you get many bored minds willing to crawl over bare wet rock in the dark to be in your esteemed presence?"

One of the other stockier men stepped forward, his hands tightening around his staff. He opened his mouth when Seela reappeared like a ghost in the half-light. Her eyes flicked from Makeo to Shad to Witt to Aza on the ground behind them.

"The visitors will stay."

The stocky man's eyes widened. "All of them?"

"All." She straightened and slid her hands into her deep sleeves. "But you will adhere to our rules. You will learn our ways. And you will keep our secrets." She lifted her chin. "Understood?"

Aza sat up with a hiss, and Makeo looked over his shoulder at her, his eyes still half-wild. She nodded, and he turned back.

"Fine," he growled. "But we're keeping our weapons." Makeo offered his paw and helped Aza to her feet.

She winced. "And we want answers."

14

SOMISIDAS

Hours later, bathed, fed, and clothed in the simple gray robes of the Wraith-Called, Aza knelt on a circular cushion across from Seela in an otherwise bare room. The stone floor and cliffside that comprised one wall chilled the air in a way that raised goosebumps on Aza's arms. Talons clicked above them, announcing the presence of the grizzards that perpetually lined the rooftops.

Aza shifted on the cushion, her muscles creaking beneath her. Outside the window, the gray-robed novices crossed the landing in near silence. She could've easily slept the day away like the others, but then her thoughts churned to Zephyr across the mountain, maybe fighting off the same Lost that had killed her parents. And she knew she couldn't waste time on sleep. She needed to learn what was going on in the Shadow Plane and find a way to stop it.

And even though Seela had agreed to let them stay, an undercurrent of tension pulled taut in her gaze. Their tenure here was probationary at best. She'd have to prove to this woman that she was worth the answers she needed. That she was worthy of trust—worthy of the Shadow Plane. Seela wouldn't give her a word without it. The task towered over her like the mountain itself. Where did she begin?

"All of our novices start in the lowest building in Somisidas," Seela said as if reading Aza's thoughts. She gestured to the room around them. "As your skill in the Plane progresses, you will ascend the mountain."

"But I can already walk the Shadow Plane. Doesn't that mean I should start higher?"

A smile curved the edge of Seela's mouth. "Could you cross to the Plane at this moment?"

"Of course not. It takes days to recover after using that much yanaa."

"Oh, does it?" Seela's smirk deepened, and she disappeared.

Aza's eyebrows shot up. Seela had walked the Plane for even longer than she had. How was that possible?

Seela reappeared with a smug grin. "After you, most advanced Shadow Heir."

Carefully smothering her irritation, Aza looked away to the rough wall of rock. "I already told you. I can't."

"That is because you're going about it the wrong way. Like calling yourself a swimmer when you are merely floundering to survive. Your mind is weak."

"It isn't weak." Aza's jaw tightened, her words slow and deliberate. "Tell me what to do, and I'll do it."

"As the Shadow Heir, you have a great deal of power. And you have used that power to force your way into the Plane with brute strength."

"So, what would you have me do instead?"

"The Plane is found through the mind. If you lead with your mind, then your body will follow."

"So you want me to think my way into the Shadow Plane?" Aza slouched back onto her hands, the stone cold under her skin. "Are you saying anyone can enter into the Plane then?"

"Not at all." Seela's thin eyebrows tilted with disdain. "The wraiths allow only a chosen few, and the physical crossing still requires a small amount of yanaa." The ghost of a hard smile glittered in her eyes. "But it takes much less yanaa to open a door than to break it down."

Aza ran her tongue across her teeth. It was more than obvious this woman had no love for her or her companions. So why had she called her in the first place? She inhaled deeply, her impatience swollen and red with irritation. It didn't matter. As long as she was willing to teach her, Seela's reasons didn't matter. She shifted on her flat cushion. "All right, then. How do I open the door?"

"If you wish to open a door, you must first know the door you wish to open."

Aza pressed her lips together. Why was this so difficult? "I want to open the door to the Shadow Plane."

"Why?"

"Does it matter?"

"Of course."

Standing, Aza paced the floor. "Dead-eyed Rastgol hunt me, Carceroc rebels, and the Plane screams." She flicked a knife out from its sheath and twirled it between her fingers. "It's connected. And I need to know why."

"Perhaps," Seela mused idly, as if pondering when the star blooms might flower. "The Shadow Plane is the space between the living and the dead. Here, we strive to follow in Odriel's footsteps as he guides souls from one to the other, and we seek wisdom from those who have already passed."

Aza stopped, a buzzing filling her ears. *The space between the living and the dead.* So, Dorinar's books had been right.

"It is possible," Seela continued, "that something in the Plane could be affecting the living, or the living could be affecting the Plane."

Suddenly cold, Aza crossed her arms and leaned against the smooth wooden wall opposite the mountain. "But for the living to affect the Plane, they'd have to be connected to it somehow, right? They'd have to be from Somisidas?"

"Yes, the person would have to be a Wraith-Called, but not all of the Called are here at Somisidas." She laced her small hands in her lap, blue veins visible through her nearly translucent skin. "Some ignore the call, and others do not stay."

"How do I figure out who it is, then?"

"By taking the first step." Seela gestured to the cushion Aza had abandoned.

With a sigh, Aza sheathed her knife. She crossed the room on silent feet and sank down in front of Seela, mimicking her posture—legs folded, hands in lap, face blank.

"Close your eyes and breathe deep. Empty your mind, Shadow Heir. Think nothing. Feel nothing."

In the silence, Seela's words echoed through Aza's thoughts, dredging up an old memory of her mother and brother doing this very thing when he coaxed fire to his fingertips for the first time. Aza had never needed instruction. The shadows had come to her as easily as breathing. Even now they pulsed in her with every heartbeat, weak from her last foray into the Plane, yes, but always present. Cool and soothing like the air in her lungs.

"Now, think of the Plane," Seela said, her voice soft. "Focus on it, but do not try to enter."

In her mind, Aza found herself in the gray fields. The dark sky above her. The wind through her hair. The unnatural silence. A prickling of dread as she wondered once more if she would meet her parents there. Or if the Hunters would crawl down the cliffs to find her instead.

"Your mind is wandering," Seela said. "Leave the emotions behind. Think only of the Plane. The grass between your fingers, the soft ground under your feet, the quiet in your ears, the scent of dust and ancients."

The picture was so clear in Aza's mind now, she wondered if she had slipped into the peacefulness of the dream. It felt like the Shadow Plane, but she wasn't struggling. She was just... there. But she wasn't.

"Now, see the door."

In her mind, Aza scanned the field, and there behind her, was a door. Obsidian black but without the shine, like it swallowed all light—a hole in the air with a curved handle.

"Reach out and grasp the handle."

Aza curled her fingers around the cool black handle and pulled. But the door wouldn't open. She tugged again. This was all in her head. So why wouldn't it open? The little yanaa she had left bunched within her. Not even enough to Shadow Step, much less cross into the Plane.

"Let your yanaa trickle into your mind. Let it drip from you into the door. It is the key that will open the door." Seela's words were hypnotic and monotone now. Almost as if it was Aza's own voice, instead of someone else's. "But remember. Here, you are a mind. Not a body."

Aza let her reserves of yanaa flow into the door, the handle smooth under her fingers. She pulled again. Still stuck. Not enough yanaa? She scraped more from her core, her muscles tensing.

"*No.*" Seela's voice jarred her thoughts. "*Not* your body. That is the Heir's way, not the wraith's. The key is in the lock. Open it with the strength of your mind."

Aza pulled harder. It didn't budge. This was stupid. You couldn't just think your way somewhere completely different. This woman just wanted to make a fool out of her—waste her time with impossible nonsense.

As if Aza had spoken aloud, Seela's words cut through her thoughts. "To enter, you must first accept that the door is already open. The real barrier is the one you are creating in your mind." Aza took a deep breath. "Every thought you have. Every untamed emotion is another plank in the door. To weaken the door, you must strengthen your mind."

I am not weak. Aza wiped the thought away as soon it popped up. She was strong enough. She could do this. Don't feel. Don't think. It is possible. Just open the door. Aza focused on the long grass swaying against her waist, the hard metal under her fingers, the scent of age and soil. She was a part of the Shadow Plane. She belonged there. The intoxicating draw of the shadows itched at her skin, begging her to enter. Fingers on the handle, her gaze bored into the darkness of the door.

For a moment, she thought of nothing, the shadows and her heart pulsing together in rhythm. Then, with certainty, she opened the door. It swung ajar with aching slowness, and she stepped into the other side. In that one step, the Shadow Plane's power poured into her, not with the uncontrolled rush of before, but in a steady stream of strength. As if, instead of fighting to dive to the bottom of the ocean, here she was already on the ocean floor, the weight balanced evenly on her shoulders.

And there was Seela before her. For a moment, Aza could've sworn Seela smiled, maybe even in approval, but then her brows lowered in an expression Aza couldn't decipher. "Perhaps you will be teachable after all, Shadow Heir."

A flash of frustration whipped through Aza, shattering her focus, and suddenly the Shadow Plane was gone. Her muscles screamed as she landed back in the spartan room of Somisidas. Flat on the floor, a splitting pain pierced through her head in thousands of torturous bolts of light.

Seela appeared before her again. "Spoke too soon, I suppose."

Aza tried to form a thought, but the words slipped through her mind. She groaned with the stabbing spikes of pain.

"You must depart through the door you entered, or you will experience the pain of breaking through it." Seela rose to her bare feet. "That's enough for today. We'll start again tomorrow."

"No," Aza growled through gritted teeth. "I can do more."

Seela paused, her pale lips pursed. "Do what you will." She walked to the doorway and slid the panel open. "When you enter and exit the Plane with ease, I will show you the next step."

15
SCREAMS

A gentle hand on Aza's shoulder brought her out of the blackness. Something cold and smooth pressed against her cheek, and her head throbbed against it. Where was she?

"Aza," Makeo said softly.

"What happened to her?" Witt asked in the background. "She doesn't look so good."

Aza's eyes fluttered open to Makeo and Witt hovering above her in the dim room. What were they doing here?

Witt leaned in closer. "Are you okay?"

Aza sat up in a wave of dizzied pain, her vision blurry through her sleep-smudged eyes. She rubbed her fists into them. When had she fallen asleep? "I'm fine," she managed, her voice hoarse.

Makeo offered her his paw-like hand and helped her to her feet. "We came looking when you didn't show up to the evening meal."

"We saved you a plate." Witt wrinkled his nose. "But don't get too excited, it's just boiled rice and eggs."

Aza took in Makeo's gray robes and Witt's white ones. "So have you been officially initiated?"

"Maybe Makeo has, but they just had me doing chores all day, and they didn't even let me talk." Witt grimaced in mock horror. "On the bright side, maybe I'll be able to commandeer breakfast and cook something halfway edible while I'm in the kitchen."

Witt's words flowed past her as Makeo pulled her into the swiftly approaching night. Silence had fallen over Somisidas once again with a heavy dusk, and the only lanterns flickered from the buildings highest on the cliff.

"We found the library though, so perhaps we'll be able to find something useful in there," Makeo added.

Aza nodded, but the words wouldn't soak in. What'd he just said again? Why couldn't she think straight?

"No one will say a word to us though." Witt scowled, a strange expression at odds with his usual open-mouthed grin. "It's a good thing Makeo has a strong nose, or we may not have found you."

Aza blinked, trying to get her bearings as they led her down a narrow wooden stair. "Where are we going?"

"Well, we thought you might not want to sleep on the stone floor." Witt's words rushed out as though he were nervous. "Not that the pathetic bedrolls here are much better, but at least you could have a blanket against the cold."

A cloud passed across the gibbous moon, and Aza stumbled over a missed step. The long fall to the rocks below swam in Aza's vision, and Makeo's hand tightened on her elbow, pulling her closer to him.

"Of course, if you prefer the floor, don't let us stop you," Makeo said, his voice tighter than usual.

He slid open a wooden door to where four long bedrolls lined the edges of another minimalistic room. Shad had already curled up on the one closest to the door, the even rhythm of his small chest suggesting he hadn't quite recovered from their journey. Makeo let her slide onto the one across from Shad's and handed her a waiting wooden bowl.

She shoveled the cold food into her mouth, but Makeo and Witt's worried eyes stayed on her in the near dark.

"Aza, this place smells... different, and you're obviously not yourself. I'm not sure I trust these people." Makeo looked at her expectantly, but she just blinked, eyelids lazily falling closed and then opening. "What happened today?" he pressed.

Aza scraped the last bit of food into her mouth and put the bowl down. She had made it into the Plane twice more that she could remember, but neither exit had been graceful. Though she didn't have the muscular soreness of her usual visits to the Plane, it was almost as if her mind had taken the load instead. She could barely connect her thoughts to words.

She swallowed, the exhaustion weighing down on her. "I went into the Shadow Plane."

"And did you find anything?" Witt asked, his voice tense.

"Not yet." Aza licked her lips. "But I will. I just need to work harder."

Makeo's emerald eyes bored into hers. "Somehow, I doubt that's the problem."

Aza found Seela the next afternoon. The woman balanced on one foot on a gusty outcropping, inches between her and a fall to her death. She held her open palms to either side with her eyes closed while a smattering of students imitated her from along a craggy staircase. Aza crossed her arms and leaned against the edge of the wooden building hugging the cliffside. At first, she thought they were standing still, but as she watched she could make out the slowest of movements, like a flower turning to face the sun. Their arms and legs slowly rotated with their bodies. And what's more, they were in near-perfect unison. But how could they be when their eyes were closed?

Seela brought her other bare foot to the ground and opened her eyes, her gaze cutting straight to Aza. Her students didn't heed her though as she weaved between them to the landing where Aza shifted against the wall. How had Seela known she was waiting?

Opening the sliding door, Seela jerked her head for Aza to follow. Aza padded in after her and snapped the door shut behind them.

Seela gestured to the two cushions already laid out on the floor. "So, you can take the first step now?"

"I did, and it didn't even take years of training."

Seela laughed humorlessly, her brown eyes narrowing. "Speed has little to do with it. It's the depth of understanding that will feed your ability. Try as you might, it will not be something you can achieve by force. But our novices do often struggle with the concept."

Aza wanted to strangle this woman with her edged words. If she did, would Seela even be able to put up a fight? Seela was tall but lean and carried no weapons. She'd last thirty seconds—at most.

"The more time it takes me to understand, the more time the Lost have to ravage Okarria." Aza dipped down onto her mat, crossing her legs beneath her. "But I could see how a hermit would struggle with the concept." A line of frustration between Seela's brows brought a victorious smirk to Aza's lips. "Meet you on the other side."

Straightening, Aza closed her eyes. The visual came quickly. She had been in and out of the Plane so much in the last day, her mind seemed to return to the Shadow Plane even when she wasn't trying. When she was just walking around, or talking to the others, or eating her flavorless food. In all the little spaces between her thoughts, between breaths, in those slight pauses that peppered her every day, she was in the Shadow Plane.

For all her talk though, for all her single-mindedness, she really wasn't fast at all yet. Especially not like Seela. It took time for her thoughts to bleed out between them. Minutes for her to forget the cool air on her cheeks, the murmuring of voices outside, and the lump of cushion separating her from the cold floor. Finally, she reached out for the door, yanaa spilling from her fingers, mind straining to bridge the gap. Then, with an almost audible click, she was among the swaying gray grass, and Seela waited with her hands folded behind her back.

Aza grinned triumphantly. "How's *that* for a novice?"

But Seela didn't so much as smile. If anything, she sighed, as if resigned to the chore of Aza's training. "This way then." Seela strode away with long, slow steps.

Aza took a deep breath and picked up her foot to follow. In her repeated attempts yesterday, she'd realized that just like when entering the Shadow Plane, she'd been trying to use her body to move through it. Which was about as useful as throwing a punch to fight off a nightmare. Using her thoughts to move her body let her go much farther, but it wasn't easy. Every movement that came automatically in the sunlit world—bending her knees and toes, swinging her arms—took intense concentration here. Everything had to be deliberate. It took her a few moments to acclimate enough to go anywhere. But by the way Seela moved with her usual long-limbed grace, it seemed that it was something she could learn with more training.

Aza's gaze swept the Plane as she tried to keep up with Seela's practiced gait. The emptiness calmed her. Of course, her parents wouldn't be here. Even if they were dead. The very thought was ridiculous. Did she really believe this was the space between the living and the dead? She'd never seen any dead people here, had she?

A cloud of little batlike creatures fluttered around them. No faces, just bony wings attached to the dark inkblot of a body. Aza swallowed. Were these the dead spirits? She pointed to one. "So, if we're between the living and the dead right now, what are these things?"

"Wraiths." Seela lifted a finger, and one of the bats landed on it, clutching her with the sharp fingers on its wings.

"So they're dead?"

"No, the wraiths belong here." She tossed it up and away and it fluttered around her face. "They are neither living nor dead."

One landed on Aza's arm, and she squinted at it. "How is that possible?"

"They feed on your yanaa."

"They what?" Aza brushed away the creature. "So, they're parasites."

"Yes, it's the toll they exact for your presence, but most of them are too small to do any real damage."

A dark line in the distance drew Aza's gaze. "Most?"

"Some of the wraiths feed on yanaa, and some of them feed on other wraiths."

The dark line grew into a line of shadowy trees. Strange. Aza had just assumed the nothingness went on forever.

Seela's eyes focused on the horizon. "If you met one of those, it would be... unpleasant."

"Ah." Aza's thoughts seemed to grow heavier, but still she felt a sense of relief. It seemed like luck had been with her after all. "Is that what lives in that forest?"

"The Plane can appear in many ways, but generally, the farther you get from the living world, the darker the realm will seem."

Aza's body tightened. "So, we're literally walking toward death right now?"

Seela stopped and turned to her. "Yes, we call it the Mortal Wood. I wanted to test how close you could get." Her eyes flicked up and down Aza's form. "The farther you travel from the living, the more difficult it becomes. As your mind has tired, you have started to use your body as a crutch."

Aza opened her mouth to deny it and then closed it again. She couldn't ignore the tension tightening in her muscles. She turned around. "I need to go back to the door."

"Ah, so you haven't figured that out yet." A soft chuckle escaped Seela's flat mouth. "The door is just a product of your mind. You can recreate it here if you concentrate."

A shout drifted between them on the wind—a short, punctuated cry—familiar this time. Aza sucked in a breath. *Zephyr?* "That. I've been hearing screams for months. What is it?"

Seela closed her eyes, her long waist-length braid swirling around her. "Like I said, this place connects the world of the living and of the dead. It is a place of the mind and a place of yanaa. As such, sometimes we can hear snatches of either kind here. Especially if the person is strong with yanaa." She put her long fingers to her neck. "It's one of the main reasons people seek us out. To listen for messages from beyond the grave."

Another yell echoed on the wind, this one from behind them. Definitely Zephyr. Panic chilled Aza's bones. No. He could *not* be dead.

Seela stopped and pointed the way they'd come. "In this case, though, it's coming from the land of the living."

Aza turned, her heart beating faster, painstakingly making her way toward Zephyr's voice. "Can I go closer? I want to hear more."

Seela followed along close behind. "You must mind your strength. You're not yet practiced enough to stay for long."

"I tire of telling you, I've been fighting since I could walk."

"Ah. And what does the Shadow Heir fight exactly?"

"Murderers, rapists, slavers… I scrape the scum from Okarria's hills." She flashed a cold smile at Seela. "And I send them here." They were back in the endless Plane now, the gray bordering on a blinding white.

"Here. They are close." Seela put out a hand as though to grab Aza but stopped short of touching her.

Aza scowled, her head whipping around. "I can't see anything."

"Don't see." Seela folded her arms once more. "Close your eyes and just listen."

Aza blew out a frustrated breath, her thoughts sluggish. She wouldn't admit it to Seela, but her limit was fast approaching. She pictured the door, when Zephyr's voice cut through her hazy mind.

"We can't get them out if we can't get into Carceroc to begin with." His voice was hard, strained. "We have to try harder. Who knows what's happening to them in there."

Aza squeezed her eyes shut, trying to focus. Her brother's voice sent relief shooting through her. So Zephyr had made it safely to Carceroc, but why couldn't they enter? The creatures trapped within couldn't escape of course, but everyone else was free to come and go as they pleased.

Hoku's voice answered him, though she seemed so much farther away. "It's like the Carceroc creatures are trying to keep us out." She panted as though running a distance. "But they've never attacked us—"

"Behind you!" Zephyr shouted. A rattling hiss and a crackle of fire chased his voice.

Aza's eyes flashed open. A wave of dizziness rocked her, and her muscles tensed to steady her, yanaa unspooling from them like a kite in a gale. But she'd heard all that she needed to.

She had to move faster. They were running out of time.

16
SILVIX

Aza stepped out of the building with her mind wrung out and her muscles exhausted. Unfortunately, Seela had been right; she'd leaned on her body once she became too tired to think. *Too tired to think.* She'd never thought that was possible, and now that seemed to be her normal existence.

On the landing below, she caught sight of Makeo and pairs of other novices armed with staffs. His shaggy bulk moved slowly against a novice's willowy frame. Were they sparring in slow motion? Aza stepped down the stairs. *Blindfolds wrapped around their eyes. Interesting.* Is that how the Wraith-Called strengthened their thoughts?

With soft steps, she approached from behind them. Even blindfolded, they sparred with confidence, sure and swift, the knocks of the staffs echoing against the cliff wall. Makeo moved to strike low but the novice misread and moved high. Aza winced at the impending blow, but just before impact, Makeo's staff froze a hand's breadth from the novice's knee.

Makeo straightened and turned to Aza. "You seem in better form today."

Aza cocked her head. She was sure she'd been soundless. Had he smelled her? "I've made progress."

"Have you?" Makeo removed the blindfold and stepped toward the buildings that hugged the cliff. "Then we should talk."

Aza closed her eyes and rolled her neck, trying hard not to think of lying down on her hard mat. "I don't want to interrupt."

Makeo opened the sliding door. "We're not here for this."

Instead of another empty training space, this door opened up to a low ceiling room filled with shelves of books. The smell of paper and dust wafted through the cool air. Makeo weaved through the rows of volumes until they found Witt hunched over a low crimson oak table. One fist propped up his cheek while he scratched at his head with the other, and Shad peered over his shoulder into the open book in front of them.

Witt looked up and brightened. "Finally! I thought I was going to die of boredom here."

Aza pulled out one of the cushions stacked in the corner and sank down onto it. "Why weren't you out training with Makeo?"

He shut his book and added it to the stack growing up on the table. "I know with all my many talents, this is probably shocking to you, but I have no yanaa running through me."

Though Witt smiled, Aza could see the disappointment curving his shoulders. She turned to Makeo. "And you do?"

"Apparently it's a side effect of being cursed by a magus. Their yanaa never fully leaves you." Makeo leaned against a bookshelf. "But it's not very strong."

Aza ran a finger along the whorls of the table. "But it could be enough for you to visit the Shadow Plane?"

"Maybe." Makeo shrugged with a teeth-baring grin. "Anything interesting there to see?"

"Yes." Aza straightened, fighting against the weariness weighing on her. "My brother has arrived at Carceroc, but the creatures there are preventing them from entering to move the villagers."

Makeo stilled. "You can see that?"

"The Shadow Plane connects us through our yanaa, but I could only hear them." Aza reached for a book, its binding soft and worn. "It sounded like he and Hoku were in the middle of a battle."

Makeo's tall ear twitched, and he looked west, as if trying to see through the mountain to his people on the other side.

Witt watched him with wide eyes. "So, do you think we should leave?"

"Do you really think if Zephyr and Hoku can't get through, that we'd have any better luck?" Aza shook her head. "No. If everything is connected through yanaa, I think I should be able to find out what's causing this."

"Which is what we've been looking for here," Shad said, tail whipping. "But the only interesting thing we've managed to find so far is this." He pawed a stack of paper in front of her. "Apparently, there used to be a guardian of the Shadow Plane. A monster that ate the souls of people trying to cross from life to death."

Makeo leaned over Aza's shoulder to read the spidery text. "And what happened to it?"

Aza handed the pages to Makeo, too tired to decipher the aged dialect.

"I think it says they trapped it somehow," Witt said, running a hand through his mousy curls.

"More specifically," Shad added, "it says Silvix sacrificed himself to defeat it."

Makeo turned his muzzle toward him slowly. "And what did they say this creature was called?"

Witt squinted. "Um… Dolonsa? Dolonba?"

The memory flashed through Aza's mind hard, fast, and painful. She raised a hand to the scar on her cheek and met Makeo's gaze. "Dolobra."

The nightmare of Carceroc Forest.

Aza was in the Shadow Plane again, the grass whispering against her legs. Last night, when she'd tried to let her exhausted body rest, her disobedient mind had only returned to the Shadow Plane, straining to stay longer and longer. Her headache from yesterday had yet to fade, and she'd felt no better for the wasted time of sleeping. Her patience frayed at the edges.

So she followed her mind to where it obviously needed to be. The Maldibor believed the Dolobra lived in the depths of Carceroc. But the texts said it was imprisoned in the Shadow Plane. Was that the connection she had been looking for? Had the Dolobra somehow gotten free?

To find the answer, she would need to go to the source. Seela had said they could talk to the dead after all. Silvix wouldn't mind helping out his descendant. Or… if she couldn't find him… maybe her parents would know. But which side were they on? If they were alive, wouldn't she have heard them, like she did Zephyr? Or could they be waiting for her at that dark line in the distance?

She stopped, swallowing the sudden lump in her throat. She'd heard them before. Surely, she could hear them again if she really tried. She exhaled the stale air from her lungs and closed her eyes, her mind taut with the strain of searching the Plane. *Where are you?*

Something small and sharp nudged her leg, and she knew a wraith had found her, sticking close to nibble away at her yanaa. She took another breath. *Just listen. Just listen. Just listen.* Another nudge, and she could feel the suck of yanaa on her bones.

She stomped her foot, her eyes flashing open. The little mice creatures skittered away. "Earth below, just say something already!" she yelled into the silence.

For a moment, she stood still. Then she pressed her lips together and moved away. How ridiculous to scream into the empty space. Maybe she didn't—

A whisper interrupted her thoughts, and she froze. There it was again, and her muscles eased ever so slightly. Not her parents, but familiar somehow. Raspy and cheerful in a way that sent a shiver from her neck to her toes.

"I got rid of the Shadow and Dragon, so now just the brats are left."

Aza's eyes widened. She'd only heard that voice once before, but it was one she'd never forget. Her breath came faster as she cast about for the source. Toward the dead or the living?

"So which will you choose first?" said a velvety, masculine voice. While also familiar, this one was harder to place.

"The girl, of course." Aza took off running in the direction of the voice, along the tree line, rather than toward it. Her muscles burned as her emotions surged out of her control, but she didn't care. "The boy is difficult. The Maldibor, the fire, and that stupid dog. It's hard to get close to him. But the girl…" Aza could practically see his skeletal, too-wide smile. "She'll be alone. Without her brother to save her again, she'll be easy."

Across the Plane, Aza could just make out two shadows along the tree line… no not two—three. Aza longed to reach across the distance and run her dagger across Mogens' throat. Her muscles cried out now, her focus totally lost and her yanaa tearing away from her. He seemed so close, the phantom scent of rot and death burned her nose. Though some part of her knew she wouldn't be able to find him, she whipped around all the same, desperate to close her hands around his neck, blackness edging her vision.

"Then once we have her, the boy will come without trouble," the smooth voice replied.

It took Aza a moment to place it, before the memory of the blond noble crystallized in her mind. *Valente Conrad.*

The shock of recognition nearly knocked her over. Conrad and Mogens were working together. But who was the silent third figure? A cloud of wraiths fluttered around the three of them, desperate for whatever yanaa they exuded. Black crowded into Aza's vision as she tried to hold on. *Just make it a little farther.*

"I will say, I was starting to get impatient, but all the pieces have finally aligned," Conrad continued, his voice smug and bloated. "With the Heirs gone, Carceroc will be ours, the throne will fall into my lap, and we'll finally have the power to bring Idriel…"

The blackness swallowed up the last of their words, refusing to be held back any longer. Crashing through the door, she could've sworn Mogens turned his leering face to hers—rotten and bulging. But even as Aza screamed with rage, the pain brought her slamming back into reality.

Aza woke up on her flat bedroll, disoriented and dry-mouthed. She had entered the Shadow Plane before dawn and now the sun's weak light shone through the window. Images of Mogens, Conrad, and the nameless demon shadow of Idriel choked her thoughts. She rubbed her throbbing head with a leaden arm, and sat up with a hiss of pain, a crushing ache running the length of her body.

"Was it worth it?"

Aza flinched at Makeo's voice. How had she not noticed he was there? She turned her stiff neck to see him sitting against the opposite wall with a book in his lap. She shrugged, her head so fuzzy she had to concentrate to collect the right words. Was it a dream or had she really seen Mogens? Perhaps she could use the Plane to find him at last and put an end to this. But she couldn't find the words she needed to explain.

"Maybe."

"Here." Makeo slid over a bowl of noodles swimming in clear broth. "Shad and Witt brought that by before going to the library."

Aza nodded her thanks and picked up the still-warm bowl. She blinked at the window. "How... long was I out?"

"It's nearly dusk."

Aza's mouth fell open. "Oh." Another day gone.

"Are you sure this is safe, Aze?" He waved the book at her, the volume dwarfed in his large paw. "In these accounts, it seems like the Shadow Plane drove Silvix mad."

"But I thought Witt said he imprisoned the Dolobra. Have you spoken to the Wraith-Called about it? They still seem sane."

Makeo sighed. "They only speak to us if they have to."

"All the better. Who wants to waste time on talk anyway?" Aza said, with a smirk that came out more like a wince.

Makeo didn't laugh. "Well, if you're going to cross into the Plane without Seela anyway, maybe we should just leave already."

Chewing a mouthful of noodles, Aza studied him for a moment. Of course, he wanted to go back to Carceroc and help his people, but his ridiculous Maldibor honor wouldn't let him go without her. "You should go, Makeo. It's only over the peaks. You could probably make it in a couple days."

"A couple days there, a couple back. A lot could happen in that time." He shook his shaggy head. "I'm just one sword anyway. It wouldn't make a difference."

Aza's skin prickled, and she rolled her stiff shoulders, trying to ward away the chill. "I went to the Plane last night to look for Silvix and ask about the Dolobra, but while I was there, I heard Mogens and Conrad plotting to resurrect Idriel."

Makeo's paw-like hands tightened on the book, but he said nothing.

"They're trying to get rid of the Heirs to gain the throne, and he mentioned something about Carceroc, but I couldn't stay long enough to reach him." Downing the rest of the broth, Aza placed the bowl next to her, only to realize her fingers were shaking. She squeezed them together. "I know

Silvix will have answers, but I think I'm going to need Seela to show me how to reach him." She frowned apologetically. "I'm going as fast as I can."

Makeo let out a low growl of frustration. "And it seems to be tearing you apart."

"Oh c'mon, Keo." She flexed her aching legs. "I'm made of stronger stuff than that."

Makeo leaned forward, his green eyes intent. "Think twice about everything, Aza. This place feels…" He leaned back. "Dangerous."

Aza shifted on her mat, trying to arrange her cramping limbs in the least painful manner possible. Could Makeo sense that Mogens and Conrad were coming for her? She opened her mouth to tell him, and then closed it again. If he knew, he would almost certainly carry her kicking and screaming from this place, and she was in no shape to put up a fight.

But she *would* need to be more careful, because when Mogens came for her, she'd be waiting for him.

Aza was already in the Shadow Plane, striding toward the dark line of the dead when Seela appeared beside her. "Are you so skilled now that you no longer need the teacher you traveled so far to find?"

"I sought you out this morning, but they said you were otherwise occupied." She didn't look at Seela. "But it looks like you received my message."

"I thought you would take more time to recover from your last experience."

Aza ignored this. She'd gotten distracted, but she wouldn't let it happen again. She could pace herself. "You said we can speak to the dead right? I need to speak to Silvix and figure out what's going on in Carceroc."

Surprise flickered across Seela's face. "Silvix?"

Aza stopped before the black trees looming before her, the now-familiar strain pulling insistently at her thoughts with the pain of a perpetually combusting migraine. "Yes. How do I call him?"

Seela nodded, her face stony. "What do you know of him?"

Aza shrugged. "He was an Heir who discovered and named the Shadow Plane, might've been mad, and sacrificed himself to imprison the Dolobra."

"Yes. He will be an easy one for you to start with."

What did that mean? Aza's gaze bored into the darkness of the Wood. Was she imagining it, or could she see movement amongst those dark trunks?

"Try to hold all that you know in your mind. Picture him as best you can. And reach out with your hand to pull him toward you out of the darkness."

"Like the door."

"Exactly. Except, this will be easier the closer you are to the Mortal Wood, and the closer the dead are to the side of the living."

Aza closed her eyes, her thoughts of Silvix swirling through her mind as she pictured an older, haggard version of her father. "The dead can be closer to the side of the living?"

"Yes. The longer they're dead, the deeper they get. Unless their souls are… disturbed."

Long, gray-streaked, dark hair fell over a weathered face looming before her. Aza's brow furrowed. There he was. She was sure of it. She reached out her hand, cupping the yanaa in her fingers. "Silvix, I need your help." With shadowed eyes pinned to her, he grabbed her hand with an ice-cold grip.

Surprised, Aza's eyes flicked open, and she found the man standing just before her, at the edge of the Wood. Beside her, Seela retreated a step.

"Who?" his voice came out as a strained whisper, but he didn't meet her eyes.

"I'm the Shadow Heir, Aza Thane, your Heir, and I need to—"

"An Heir. An Heir. An Heir," he sang, his body jerking strangely.

"Yes, and I need to know about the Dolobra. How does it connect to the—"

"Do… lo… bra…" He blinked slowly. "The teeth. The dark. The cold."

Aza swallowed. Was this how souls were in death? "Yes. I need to know how it connects Carceroc to the Wraith-Called."

"Ah, my wraiths." He held his arms out and stumbled forward. "Come to me, my sweet wraiths."

Aza pressed a palm to her head and turned to Seela, the pressure of keeping him there building in her skull.

"This is useless. What's wrong with him? Is this what death turns them into? Or was he always mad?"

His cold hands lashed out, seizing her arm. "I'm. Not. Mad." His fingers dug into her skin, the pain pricking her mind. He could hurt her here? "You are nothing compared to me." He threw her to the ground, his hand still locked around her arm.

Aza moved to drive an elbow into his offending hand, but she might as well have been hitting air. She wriggled in his tight grip. "Tell me about the Dolobra."

He released her, jerking back. "The Dolobra? Is it here? We need to bind it."

Aza sat up. "Why?"

"Why?" He stopped, cocking his head. "Who?"

Aza glanced at Seela but found no help in her impassive stare. She would have to be more specific. "Why do we need to bind the Dolobra? Where is it?"

A slow grin spread across Silvix's face. He tapped a finger to his temple. "He is here, of course. Always here."

120

Aza shook her head, the pain in her temples overriding all else. She couldn't stay here anymore and listen to these ravings. "Forget it. I'm going back."

"No, no, no. Don't forget. Never forget," Silvix said, turning his back toward her.

But Aza was already picturing the door.

She opened her eyes to see Seela watching her from her usual mat only a few paces away, a worried, almost warm expression lining her eyes. Dots flickered across Aza's vision and a wave of nausea flowed through her. How did Seela endure it all? A wave of begrudging respect washed through her for the woman.

"I thought you said that would be easy," Aza groaned.

"I said calling him would be easy. I didn't say it would be useful." She sighed, a trace of sorrow curving her shoulders. "He sacrificed his mind to save his students from the Dolobra's unending hunger. But I thought you'd want to see for yourself."

Aza couldn't even argue with that. As annoying as Seela was, she seemed to understand Aza strangely well now. Aza flopped onto her back on the stone floor. "So what do I do now?"

A gentle laugh softened Seela's gaze. "You are so much like me when I was—" But then a shadow crossed her face, sweeping the words away into silence.

Aza tilted her head, trying to understand the sudden change. Was Seela angry? Sad? If only her thoughts weren't so sluggish.

Clearing her throat, Seela stood from her mat. "Perhaps your parents would know this connection you speak of, if you believe it is what killed them. If they passed recently they should be easy to call."

Aza sat up again, her cheeks heating. Was that so obvious? She should've thought of that. "Yes. Of course." Her eyes fell to her arm, expecting to find purpling bruises and the cuts where Silvix's fingernails had dug into her skin. But though she could feel the pain of the wounds, she could see nothing.

"And... if something ever attacks you in the Shadow Plane, you must infuse your blows with yanaa to defend yourself. Just like the door. Just like everything on the Plane." Seela crouched down to inspect her arm, her touch surprisingly gentle as she probed the skin. Aza winced at the invisible wound. "We have some herbs in the kitchen that can take away the sting."

"I'm fine," Aza pulled her arm away. She didn't have time for that.

Seela sighed, and her lips curved in the first real smile Aza had seen from her. "You are strong, Aza. Truly. No one doubts that. And you have an affinity for the shadows that I have never before seen, but that doesn't mean you cannot accept help." She paused, her pale hands fingering her thick, sleek braid. "Alone, you will never be more than Aza Thane, Shadow Heir, but if you reach out, you could grow to be a part of something so much greater."

The long scar that crossed Makeo's chest flashed through her thoughts. She thought of his body carved open and bleeding out, screaming as her brother had held her back, her shirt already red with his blood. She thought of Ioni crying over her father's cold form. Of course, she could accept help. But everything came at a cost.

Aza shook her head. "So, the wraiths can hurt us?" she pressed, as if she hadn't heard Seela.

Seela straightened with another soft chuckle. "My girl, I think you will find very little in this world or the next that cannot hurt you."

17
INTO THE DARKNESS

Aza meandered through the late afternoon, winding her way along the cliff to the kitchens. The strange sensation of being lost washed over her in a wave of vertigo. She paused and sucked in a lungful of cold mountain air, but it did nothing to clear her head. She leaned against the rockface, her gaze finding Makeo sparring on the next landing below with a blindfold securely around his eyes. Attackers whirled on him from all sides, but he moved with fast, sure blows. Aza longed to try it. To stretch out her muscles and feel the nice, uncomplicated burn of exercise.

And yet, even the thought of finding the energy to do so completely drained her. She probably could've used some more of Seela's basic concentration exercises before she had jumped into calling the dead. But she was tough enough to handle the recovery, and she would come back stronger. It was the only way. They didn't have time for anything else.

A sweet fragrance drifted on the breeze, pulling her in the direction of a column of smoke rising from a low building. She opened the sliding door and found Witt stirring a cauldron over the fire while Shad bathed in its orange light.

"What are you two doing here?" Aza crossed her arms with a tired smirk. "I thought you were supposed to be in the library?"

"And just how are we supposed to work with that repulsive drudge they serve here?" Witt took a sip from his wooden spoon. "I mean who can mess up porridge? After this morning's abomination, I had no choice but to step in."

Aza smiled, her eyes drooping in the kitchen's warm embrace "And what about you, Shadmundar?"

He didn't so much as budge. "I'm a 108-year-old cat. I think I'm entitled to a nap by the fire every now and then."

"Speaking of, close the door." Witt waved a spoon at her. "You're letting the heat out."

The fire's crackle and their light chatter was a better balm for her aching head than any herbs she could think of.

"Anything interesting today?" Shad's lazy gaze lingered on the arm she cradled gingerly against her chest.

"Just a waste of time. Silvix truly was… is a raving madman." She pressed a palm to one of her eyes, trying to rub the fatigue out of them. "And Seela… I don't know. I can't seem to read her."

"The other novices are saying she's been acting rather odd lately," Witt said, gathering an assortment of drab vegetables onto a plate. "Disappearing at strange hours and such."

"Sounds like a certain Shadow Heir I know," Shad scoffed.

Aza rested her chin on her palm, the thought of her and Seela's similarity ringing strangely true. She wrinkled her nose. "I thought Makeo said they didn't talk to you."

"Oh Aza." Witt winked at her, flashing his dimples. "Don't you know by now that no one can resist my charms for long?"

"They say he has no yanaa in his veins, but his relentless prattling certainly seems otherworldly to me," Shad muttered.

Aza snatched a slice of raw carrot, and Witt swatted her hand with his spoon. "Be patient."

"Oh, come on, I've been working hard." Aza made a face, letting her hand droop. "I walk the Shadow Plane more than Okarria these days."

Witt pushed a bowl in front of her. "Well, at least you don't seem to be attracting the Hunters anymore."

Aza spooned the thick creamy broth into her mouth, letting it swirl through her with its rich warmth. She let his words settle on her for a moment. In the midst of everything else, she had almost forgotten the Hunters. She should have noticed that earlier. "I wonder why."

"I'm sure it's only a matter of time; the Lost have always been drawn to the Heirs' yanaa," Shad replied, staring into the bustling fire. "Enjoy the reprieve while you can."

Aza stared at her soup. Was that what this was? A reprieve? Then why did she feel more exhausted than ever?

"How's Makeo doing?" she asked absently.

"He seems well-suited to the training of the Wraith-Called," Shad said.

Witt put a shallow saucer of broth on the floor next to Shad. "Yes, they say he is progressing extraordinarily well."

Aza stirred her spoon in lazy circles around her now empty bowl. That sounded right. Makeo's quiet persistence had always been the perfect counterbalance to her breakneck obsessions. A calming hand on her feverish endeavors—but always with her, even if a few paces behind.

"Why is he pushing himself so hard?" she murmured, half to herself.

Witt exchanged a quick glance with Shad. "He does it for you, Aza." He replaced her bowl with a full one. "We all do."

A shiver ran down Aza's spine. But what if that got them hurt?

And why did she keep coming up with these questions but no answers?

For the hundredth time that day, she let the thought dissolve into the shadows of her mind.

"Finding your parents should be even easier than calling Silvix," Seela said, with no trace of her earlier warmth. The wraiths clustered around her today, moths nipping at her clothes and hair. She batted them away with an uncharacteristic scowl. Something was definitely off. "But they might be farther in the Mortal Wood."

Nervous nausea wrapped around Aza's belly. "But Silvix has been dead for years, and I found him."

"Yes, but his mind is still trapped with the Dolobra," Seela replied, her face tight with annoyance. "He never truly crossed over to begin with."

"I thought Silvix was the one who caged the Dolobra."

"Yes, but he didn't get away unscathed, did he? He may have been half-mad before, but after he defeated the Dolobra, his mind was forever stuck in between life and death. Perhaps if you were a loyal Heir you would at least try and put him to rest," she snapped, her words harsh in the silence. "But Odriel knows you only seem to think of yourself."

Aza recoiled. *Skies above.* Why hadn't she said any of this when they called him last time?

Seela smacked at another wraith. "Go on then; call your parents, so you can ask them your questions already."

Shaking her head, Aza closed her eyes. The novices were right, Seela was acting odd. Maybe whatever was bugging her wasn't Aza, after all. She breathed deeply. It didn't matter; she couldn't let that distract her. She had to find her parents and get some answers. Her body trembled as she even thought it. Could they really be dead?

Well, either way, she'd soon find out.

She thought of her mother first. She pictured the copper braid in her long brown hair, her bright smile, her temper, and the ragehound always trailing at her side. She felt her warm, strong arms tight around her in an embrace, and her smooth voice laughing along with her brother. The pressure welled behind her eyes.

She moved to her father. Straight-backed and dark-haired, with that scar through his right eyebrow. She thought of his obsidian blade clanging against her daggers as they sparred with broad smiles. His crinkled hazel eyes flickering with intelligence and pride. She thought of his calloused hand always there to lift her up.

The pressure leaked out in a wetness on her cheeks. She reached out to them but felt nothing. They weren't there—not like Silvix had been.

"Do you see them?" Seela prodded.

"Yes," Aza replied. "But I cannot reach them."

"You must go farther in. You're not trying hard enough," Seela seethed.

Eyes still closed, Aza took a step farther toward the Wood, her body stiffening with the cold of death, the nausea rising in her again, every instinct pushing her back toward the living. But still her parents seemed just as far away. In fact, they seemed to be frowning, worried.

"Mother, Father," she called, "I need your help." No answer. Didn't they love her? Why didn't they come closer?

"Farther." Seela's hard voice pushed at her.

Aza took another step, and a sharp pain lanced through her mind. She cried out and her hands flew to her head. "It hurts."

"Of course, it hurts," Seela barked, a sadistic smile underscoring the words. "Did you think this would be easy? Did you think that since you were the Shadow Heir, you could just walk into the Plane and do whatever you wished?"

Aza took shallow panting breaths, her eyes still clenched shut. "They're not coming. Maybe they're—"

"It's because you're weak." Seela cut her off. "You're just an arrogant girl who's never had to work for anything in your whole little life." The words sizzled with an ire that sounded like a stranger's. "Work. Try harder. Go farther."

Aza swallowed. Maybe she could find someone else. A different Shadow Heir. But who? She only knew one other name. Her grandfather. Orrin Thane. Just snippets of stories passed down from her mother in hushed tones while her father looked away. Killed by the blood plague when her father was young... friend to Tam Dashul and Pryor Brigg... his parents murdered by Mogens when he escaped the corrupt monarchy all those decades ago.

"You're wasting my time," Seela raged behind her. "You were never worthy of the Shadow Plane. Not worthy to be trained."

Aza panted through gritted teeth—she'd have to go deeper for him. She raised her foot and screamed as the pain radiated through her limbs.

"Orrin!" she shouted.

And there he was. A younger version of her father. Dark hair and dark eyes regarded her over his crooked nose. She reached out to him, and he shook his head. "Go back, Aza. There's nothing for you here."

Aza opened her eyes to see him in front of her in the darkness. Her muscles screamed as the yanaa flooded out of them, but she couldn't stop

126

now. Not when she was so close. "Who's causing… Carceroc… to rage," she gasped out. "Where are my… parents? How's it connected to the Shadow Plane?"

He took her hand. "I don't know these answers, daughter, but the Shadow Plane is a double-edged sword, and you are bleeding out. Go back and find a different way."

"No… wait…" she panted, leaning forward. "I have to know."

"Then go look somewhere else. I told your father, and now I'm telling you. You don't belong here."

He shoved her out of the darkness, and with no strength left to catch herself, to conjure the door, Aza fell, crashing through the realm back into the cold world of the living. She hit the floor hard, her head cracking against the stone. Pain ricocheted through her, from her head to her fingernails to the soles of her feet—the bitter aftertaste of the shadows. For a moment, she weakly tried to force her eyes open, but the Plane had bled her strength dry. With no other recourse, she let herself slip into the darkness.

But still there was no relief. Even in her dreams, Aza could not escape the pain or the shadows. The scene repeated itself over and over in her unconscious mind.

Orrin's harsh words. *You don't belong here.*

Seela spitting fire into her face. *Weak.*

And her parents turning their backs on her, like she wasn't even worth their effort. It should've worked. It had been a good plan. But they hadn't come to her. Even in her dreams she continued to reach for them, but they turned away.

The pain throbbed through every muscle in her body, and the shame of it rolled through her. She'd said she wouldn't do that again. She'd left herself weak and vulnerable. The cold leeched the warmth from her skin. Maybe she hadn't come back to the living. Maybe she was like Silvix now, forever doomed to wander the Shadow Plane. Perhaps she was trapped in the Mortal Wood with ancestors who didn't want her.

A tear leaked down her cheek that she wasn't sure was real or dreamed.

And then there was warmth and another wave of pain. She bit down on a scream as the agony threatened to overwhelm her. How long it lasted she couldn't say. A minute? An hour? Finally it subsided, and a low, soft song drifted through the Plane. She couldn't make out the words, but it seemed familiar, pleasant, bringing the scent of fairy-lit forests and shared bonfires. The feeling of tight arms, the sound of laughter, and that blanket of safety that only exists in childhood memories.

It soothed her panicked thoughts like a balm, and at last, she left the Shadow Plane and sank into a dreamless sleep.

◆ ◆ ◆

Aza's eyes fluttered open to find three worried faces crowded over her. She couldn't quite put together who they were, but they pressed warm broth to her lips and made the soothing noises of worried parents before gently tucking the blankets around her as she fell back asleep.

When she awoke again, it was darker, and there was just the one sitting on the edge of the bedroll, crooning a Maldibor tune she had heard many times in her childhood.

For a moment, she didn't move as she assessed her injuries. She felt... damaged. Not just her body, not just her mind, but something else too. She had failed completely and utterly. Had that ever happened before?

"Ah, you're awake." Makeo stopped his humming and moved to stand, taking his warmth with him.

Aza reached out to grab his arm but hissed with the effort. "No... please don't leave." She swallowed. "It's so... cold here."

He nodded. "How are you feeling?"

She opened her mouth. *Fine. I'm fine, of course*, she wanted to say. But the lie just wouldn't come. "I'm sorry."

His tall ear pricked, and he turned to face her. "There's nothing to be sorry for."

"Of course there is... I..." She choked on the words. "This has just been a waste of time."

"So there's no connection between the Shadow Plane and Carceroc?"

"I couldn't find anything. Even my parents..." She pressed her lips together to keep the emotions in check. "Wouldn't help me." Her voice wobbled. "I can't do this alone."

"You're not alone." He squeezed her arm. "And you've been working yourself to death. You need to give yourself time to rest if you want to grow stronger."

"That's no excuse."

He sighed, deep and heavy. "So what would you like to do now?"

She hated that question. That tone. As if they were just waiting for her to emerge from this ridiculous rabbit hole and do the sensible thing again. "I have one last thing I need to do before we go."

"And what's that?"

"I'm going to try to free Silvix from the Dolobra."

"Is that possible?" he whispered.

"I have to try. I can't just let him wander the Shadow Plane, never able to rest." She pictured her own face wandering the Mortal Wood, cold and maddened. "And... with his mind whole again, maybe we'll finally get answers."

"Something bad is coming, Aza," Makeo almost whispered. "I can smell it on the air, like lightning before it strikes."

With his eyes steady on hers, she didn't have to ask to know what he was thinking, what he was remembering. She put a hand to her cheek, running a finger over the long white scar that ran down it like a tear stain. With Mogens, the Dolobra, and Makeo so close, it felt like she was moving back in time instead of forward.

But she was glad for it. It was a night that needed to be redone. When Mogens came for her once again, she would do what she could not last time.

"Yes." Aza lay back down, her heavy eyelids shuttering on the smooth wood of the ceiling. "But I'll be there to meet it."

18

CRUMBLING

Aza woke again in the darkness, her body still sore and her head pounding. The soft snores of Witt and Shad reverberated from their respective corners, but Makeo's deep even breaths were missing. Wincing, she rose as quietly as she could and slid out the door.

Makeo's large shadow glanced over his shoulder at her from farther out on the landing before turning back to the valley. A silver haze dulled the edges of the sharp cliffs of Somisidas, as if the Shadow Plane had curtained the living world in an unnatural fog. The wind whistled between the rooftops, and Aza could've sworn it carried the hushed whispers of unseen voices. Aza ground her fists into her eyes until white sparks flared against her eyelids, and when she opened them, the fog had disappeared. *It's only in my mind. Keep it together.*

With slightly hobbling steps, Aza walked to Makeo's side, and then paused, wondering why she was there. What gave her the right to intrude on his quiet solitude? Perhaps he had come out here to get away from her. The landing was big enough, she really should just find her own piece of it to stretch out her legs and leave him be. But then again… she found she really didn't want to.

"It's the middle of the night." He tipped his nose up to the stars in the sky. "You should be resting."

"I had to get some fresh air to try to clear my head." She pulled her hair back, knotting it with a strip of leather. "What're you doing out here?"

He made a noise somewhere between a chuckle and a scoff but gave her a not-quite smile, his green eyes alight with wistful amusement.

Aza wrinkled her brow and returned her gaze to the sky. In the moonless night, Odriel's guiding star shone brightest of all. Her eyes widened. "Has it been twenty-one days already?"

"See what I mean? You used to be much quicker than that." He laughed, but it rang empty and hollow.

"I just… thought it was after midnight is all." Aza squeezed her temples, her thoughts blurring together with the ache. Was she really losing track of the days?

Makeo flexed his long, clawed fingers. "Nearly there."

Aza sighed at the longing in his voice. She looked to the mountain's jagged peaks, where Carceroc lay only a two-day journey away. It had been five days since she had heard Zephyr on the Shadow Plane. Was he safe? What about Makeo's kin? She sagged under a wave of guilty exhaustion. They should have been there by now.

"You should be back with your people, Makeo. They need you."

He looked at her and opened his mouth, but the change took him before the words could find their way. Paws, ears, fur, tail, gone in a moment, leaving just the smooth fair skin, the green eyes, and the puckered scar crossing his bare chest.

He ran his hands up his arms as if to make sure they had indeed changed. Then, he faced her, his eyes serious. "If you tell me to go, Aza, I'll go." He took a step closer to her. "But I want to stay here as long as you let me."

Aza should've walked away. Should've told him he had put his faith in the wrong person. But, heavy with defeat and regret and pain, she was too tired for those excuses. Instead, she stepped closer and ran her fingers down the long purple scar crossing his chest from shoulder to hip. The one that had allowed her to escape Mogens' grasp. "I thought you were going to die, Keo." Her eyes swam with the memory of his screams. "I was so scared."

"I know." He folded her hand between his smooth palms. "But that night… I'd do it again, you know. I'd follow you." She tried to look away, but his green eyes found her gaze. "It was my choice, and I would make it again."

"That's because you're a Maldibor," she whispered. "Your honor demands—"

"No," he interrupted, his voice harsh. "I rushed the blade because you were my friend." His voice fell again, his eyes boring into her. "But now all you do is push me away."

She took in a breath, his closeness making her head spin. She stood frozen in place as she resisted the urge to forget the danger and curl her arms around him. "I just wanted you to be safe, Keo…"

The Time Heir's last flat words to Aza's parents echoed in her mind, *"You think it's a gift, but we're all cursed. Death follows us like a sickness. If to be an Heir is to die young, tortured at the hands of monsters, then my daughter will* not *be one."*

"…And the Maldibor aren't the only ones who are cursed."

He grinned with a broad radiant gleam.

"Are you laughing?" She slipped her hand from his. "I'm being serious."

His smile only grew. "Then you haven't learned the first thing about being a Maldibor."

"And what's that?"

"The cursed stick together. It's the only defense against our tarnished fate. Otherwise, you're letting the curse win."

She turned away from him but said nothing, his lightness pulling at her. His every word chipped away at her battered walls even as she fought to keep them up… but she was just so tired.

"Am I not worthy of your trust?" He moved to face her again, tension building in his muscled shoulders.

"Of course I trust you."

"Do you doubt my strength? My speed?" He snatched the dagger from her belt and twirled it in a hand.

"It's not you I don't trust, Keo." She swept her hair from her forehead, the pain between her temples throbbing. "It's me."

The words were out before she could catch them, and her eyes widened at the truth of them.

"Ah." Makeo softened instantly, the lines in his face smoothing.

"If you rush the blade for me again…" She shook her head, the night air blowing cold on her cheeks. "What if I can't protect you?"

He took a step closer, her blade still in hand. "What if *I* can't protect *you*?"

"You don't need to worry about that," she scoffed, kicking at the ground. "I can protect myself."

He leaned close and slid the dagger into the sheath at her hip. "*Exactly.*" Holding her gaze, he offered his hand. "A dance to stretch your legs?"

The gesture unknotted something in her, and Aza looked around the deserted cliffside. All lights but the one in the highest building had been extinguished, and only the ruffling of the grizzards punctured the silence. "This doesn't feel like the place for a dance." Even as she said it, she placed her hand in his broad palm.

He pulled her closer, his other hand resting in the curve of her side. "It's not the place that matters, it's the people." With that, he began to hum the soft lilting tune from her dream.

Her shoulders relaxed with the melody, and she pressed into the warmth of Makeo's chest. A rush of relief heated her fingers to her toes, like the feeling of coming home. "I like that one."

"Do you remember the words?" Makeo rumbled in her ear.

"Just snatches."

He nodded, his cheek resting against her hair. "It's the tale of Elika and his love, Janess."

"Love at first sight, I'm sure." Aza wrinkled her nose; all the old tales were like that.

He chuckled. "Not at all. They say Janess spurned him the first time for his impertinence."

Aza met his glance, his face inches from hers. "Did she?"

"And she spurned him the second time for fear of what Ivanora would do to him." Makeo moved them with slow smooth steps, the melody seeming to echo in the still night, but perhaps just in Aza's thoughts. "She only accepted him after he confessed his feelings to Ivanora and turned him into the beast."

Aza's lips twisted. "You don't think it's because she felt sorry for him, do you?"

"After she found out what Ivanora had done, Janess took up a sword in Elika's defense." He shrugged. "Does that sound like pity to you?"

"No. It sounds like my kind of story." A wry smile lifted the corner of Aza's mouth. "It's a wonder Ivanora didn't curse her as well."

"Elika stopped Janess before she could go through with it."

Ah. That made sense. Ivanora would probably curse a child for toddling on her shadow.

"So, Janess went to Everard instead, and at her prodding, he made the bargain."

Aza nodded, her scarred cheek pressed against Makeo's scarred chest. "A human night every dark moon in exchange for passing on the curse."

"It was a mistake."

Aza stopped. "What do you mean?"

"The curse could have died with Elika, but instead it spread through generations. It was a selfish choice." He pulled away from her, and Aza immediately missed his touch. "We should go in. It's too cold to stay out here."

Aza snatched at his wrist, her words still forming in the muddle of her slowed mind. "Okarria is a better place for Everard's bargain."

When he didn't speak, she rubbed her hands up the goosebumps of his bare arms. "You wouldn't be here if you weren't cursed, Makeo."

He tried a sagging smile. "Perhaps. But maybe we'd be happier somewhere else." He put a large hand over hers, something unreadable flashing in his eyes. "You know, I transformed only a few months after… that night. I was so worried of what you would think when you came back." He tapped his fingers nervously against hers. "But then you never did."

Aza swallowed, the guilt thickening with the pain in her head. She couldn't imagine how hard that must've been. He had been brought to the brink of death, turned into a beast, and she had turned away from him. Just like his scummy father. In his darkest moment, she hadn't been there.

"I told myself I should be relieved that you didn't have to see me that way. With the curse, we could never be…"

He shook his head, his cheeks burning red with the confession, and something in Aza shuddered with the unsaid words. Defiant almost. Of course, they couldn't be, but not because of some jealous magus' curse.

"But I still missed you," he breathed.

And then Aza couldn't stop herself anymore. She laced her arms around his neck and pulled him close. He stiffened at first, as if surprised by her embrace, and then hesitantly wove his arms around her. Together, they swayed, still locked in the dance of the moonless night.

"I didn't know," she said into his chest. "I'm so sorry I..." The words were on the tip of her tongue. The ones she knew she should say. The truth. *I missed you too. More than you could ever know.* But for some reason, they wouldn't budge. Her cheek brushed against his, his lips so close to hers, and all she had to do was turn her head... and they would meet.

She trembled with the want of it.

But she couldn't. She *would* not.

So she gave him a different truth instead. "I was never a good friend."

He snorted, and then threw his head back, chuckling deep in his chest.

Aza looked up at him, her cheeks burning. "What? I'm serious. Why do you keep laughing when I'm being serious?"

His grin broadened. "For a Shadow Heir, you're a terrible liar."

He gazed down at her, his face now only a hands-breadth from hers, and any retort she had dried up on her tongue.

"Do you remember the first time you saw me as a beast?"

Aza shuffled her feet. Of course, she did. He had come to the festival with his uncle, Tekoa. More than a head taller and nearly unrecognizable, except for the slant of his shoulders and the way he cocked his head when he laughed, his left ear flopping in the breeze just as his mop of hair had once done. It had been almost a year since she had last seen him, but in Catalede there was nowhere to hide. So she'd stood at the gate and greeted them. Cold. Business-like. As she would a stranger. Trying to prove to herself she could do it. That she could keep him away—keep him safe.

"When I changed, my own sister didn't recognize me." He ran a finger along her cheek. "So, how did you know me right away?"

Because she had been looking for him. She rested her head on his chest, strangely breathless. "I don't miss much."

"You saw through the beast to the real me," he whispered. "You always have. And that's why I'll be here for you before all others."

Even as she tried to brace the walls that she'd built, she could feel them crumbling away in her hands. She turned her face to his, and then clear as anything, a ghostly voice rang through the air.

"Here, Shadow, Shadow, Shadow..."

Aza broke away, her heart leaping into her throat. "Did you hear that?

Makeo tensed beside her, his head swiveling. "Hear what? What is it?"

"A voice. You didn't hear it?" Aza's pulse pounded in her ears, the world turning silvery once more, as if the Shadow Plane were sucking her in. Had that been real? Or had she imagined it?

Green eyes shining with worry, Makeo took one of her shaking hands in his. "You really should rest, Aza. You're not yourself."

Even as he said it, a spike of pain lanced through her head, ricocheting through her body. She winced with a grimace, her shoulders shuddering. "I... okay... yeah. You're probably right." He led her back to the room, and her gaze swept the silver fog one more time, the whispers once again rustling on the wind.

What was happening to her?

Aza woke with a gasp and rivulets of sweat coursing down her temple, adrenaline churning her fried thoughts into drivels of panic. Zephyr bleeding in the dark. The children's cries. Mogens' rasping voice. "What's happening, what's happening, what's happening?" Her hands scrambled at her mat in a frantic madness. "The Shadow Plane. I need the Shadow Plane. I need to see. I'll hear them. I have to know."

Smooth, warm hands gripped her arms. "Aza, wake up, Aza!" Still in his human form, Makeo's emerald eyes peered into hers. "It's okay. You're safe here."

"No, no, no, no, no, no," she muttered, her whole body shaking and her eyes rolling. "You don't understand. They're in trouble, Makeo. My brother, your tribe. They were in the forest, and his fire went out. Something got to them. I know it did. I have to see."

"It was just a nightmare, Aze," Makeo said.

"No!" she shook her head back and forth, furious and desperate. "It couldn't have been. It was real. It was real. It was real." She looked up at him, the Shadow Plane already sucking her back into the fold of its arms, dragging her away. Like she was the prisoner instead of a master. "I have to know. Now. I have to."

With that, she gathered the shadows and opened the door, leaving Makeo and plunging into the Plane where her brother's voice waited for her. She raced toward it feverishly, consumed with guilt and fear and desperation. "Zephyr!"

"They have to run, or we'll never make it." Strain cracked his voice. "They're coming from all directions. Get behind me."

"Zephyr!" she screamed again in the void of black.

"I'll burn this whole cursed forest down if I have to."

"Can you hear me?" Aza called, still running.

"Hoku! They took her," Zephyr yelled. "You two, go after her, I can't leave these children. Hoku!"

She stopped, falling to her knees with the agonized realization that there was nothing she could do to help him here.

"No one else leaves! We've lost too many already. If we don't get out of here soon, we won't make—" A strangling gurgle cut off his words, and his voice disintegrated into the wind.

"No!" Aza leaned into it, straining for more. Was he there? What had happened? Were they in the forest like she had heard? Was it already too late? She curled her trembling fingers into fists.

Distantly, an unhinged laughter shook the air—raspy and cruel and familiar. *Mogens.*

And a certainty hardened in her core. He was coming for her. Whatever they were planning had already begun.

Aza didn't know how long she sat there with that one dismal thought echoing in her empty mind, her yanaa slowly trickling out of her as the worm wraiths snaked up her boots.

When a hand squeezed her shoulder she jumped to her feet with a whirl, daggers out and ready to fight whatever had found her in this strange land.

Her eyes widened. "Keo? Is this a dream? How are you here?"

Chest heaving, Makeo staggered before her in his gray robes, his body tense among the swaying grass. "I can only cross for very short times, but I needed to make sure you were okay." He took her hand, his blond hair falling across his intense gaze. "You've been here for over an hour, Aze. Let's go back."

"Did you hear them?" she whispered, her voice trembling. "Did you hear the screams?"

His lips tightened, and he squeezed her hand. "C'mon, Aze. Please."

She nodded dumbly, the shock freezing her arms and legs and thoughts. Summoning the door, she stumbled through it almost without thinking. The shadows faded, and she was back on her bedroll with a weary Makeo in front of her. Shad and Witt crowded in behind him with worried expressions.

Witt opened his mouth. "Are you okay?"

"No," Aza said, still in the fog she couldn't quite shake.

"What happened?" Shad asked, leaning forward.

"My brother is in danger. The Maldibor are screaming. The children are…" She trailed off, her urgency returning as their cries echoed in her mind. "You have to go to them."

"Then you must come too." Makeo squeezed his forehead, unused to the toll of the Shadow Plane.

"Not yet," she whispered. "I have to find Seela. I have to free Silvix. I can't leave without the answers I came for. Otherwise their sacrifice would all be for nothing."

"We won't leave without you, Aza," Witt said, running an anxious hand through his curls.

"We can wait—" Makeo started.

"No!" She snapped to her feet. "Your people are *dying*, Makeo. You heard them screaming. Some are probably already gone. I will *not* be the reason you were too late to save them." Not with Mogens coming after her. Not again. Makeo needed to be anywhere but here, and she would say *anything* to make that happen. Because this time, there would be no healing Heir to save him.

"Aze..." he tried, his voice still soft. "I'm just one person."

The tenderness almost broke her, but then she remembered how he'd lain on the forest floor, the dark crimson blood pooling around him. *No.*

"*Leave*, Keo. I don't want you here. I never wanted you here," she said through gritted teeth, backing toward the door. "How *many* times do I have to say it? A reeking beast, an old one-eyed stray, and a kitchen maid? Useless. What have you done for me?" She pointed to each of them, her sharp double-edged words cutting into her even as she lashed out. But she had to get them away from her. "I don't want *any* of you."

She tried not to look at their betrayed faces. She didn't want to see the hurt flashing from one to the other like a lightning storm—the sorrow that shone in Witt's eyes or the way that Shad leaned away from her, like a cowed kitten. But she couldn't look away as Makeo's warm and welcoming face turned hard as stone.

He nodded, his smooth voice almost too quiet for her ears. "If that's what you want."

"More than *anything*," she said, her voice too loud in the quiet.

And with that, she turned her back on them and walked away.

19

FREE

Aza stood in the Shadow Plane once again, trying to erase the raw memory of Makeo climbing the cliffside without her, with Shad in the crook of his arm and Witt probably pulling up the rear somewhere out of sight. After they'd come all this way, stayed by her side, believed in her… And she had turned on them like a rabid dog. How they must despise her now. The thought rolled through her with an aching nausea.

But with Mogens so close, this was the only way she knew to protect them. And there was one more thing she needed to do before he arrived.

Seela appeared in front of her. "You called for me."

Aza met her strangely steely gaze. "I want to free Silvix from the Dolobra." She looked away at the lonely Plane, trying to collect the thoughts that seemed to spool away in the space between life and death. "If I free him, perhaps he may yet hold answers for me."

A cold smile curved Seela's lips—almost smug. "That's noble of you, Shadow Heir."

"How do I call the Dolobra?"

"Defeated as it is, the Dolobra cannot be called." She beckoned with a curt hand. "But I can take you to where Silvix has caged it."

As they walked through the Plane, an uncomfortable feeling nagged at the edge of Aza's mind, like a child pulling on its mother's skirt. Freeing Silvix was exactly what she should be doing. Seela had even suggested it. So why did she feel so ill at ease? Over the past couple weeks, she had grown accustomed to the tolls and oddities of the Shadow Plane. So surely it wasn't that. Unless there was something different on the wind today.

She wished Makeo were here. Perhaps he'd be able to tell her what was true and what was just a figment of her tired mind. Because she *was* tired.

Makeo had been right. This place had mashed and drained her thoughts into a weak, cold soup. She practically longed for the burn of her muscles, to see the problem—the enemy—clearly in front of her.

Spending so much time here among the shades of gray seemed to have leeched the very color from herself, and she wholly understood how Silvix could've lost his mind to it. How much time did she have left before she suffered the same fate?

But she couldn't stop. Not now. Not when she was still so close. She would get her answers, she would find Mogens, and then she could rejoin the others. She *had* to.

"There." Seela pointed to a sizable thicket that grew out of the edge of the Plane, waving away the first gnats of wraiths that had begun to cling to her. "Silvix imprisoned the Dolobra there, inadvertently trapping himself as well."

"How do I set Silvix free?"

"You must find his shadow and lead it to the Plane. There, it will be free to reunite with its other half." She crossed her arms. "Only a Shadow Heir can enter the trap he has snared, but beware, though the Dolobra sleeps, you must not awaken it."

Anticipation crawled Aza's skin on spider legs. "The Maldibor tell stories of the Dolobra," she said, cracking her knuckles. "They say it slumbers deep in Carceroc, rising on the coldest nights to snatch children from their beds."

"Like Silvix, the other half of the Dolobra—its physical body—is trapped in the depths of Carceroc. Lured by the magi when they imprisoned Okarria's mankillers there centuries ago." Her hard eyes pierced Aza. "As for the rest of it, I'm surprised you would listen to such childish tales."

Aza let Seela's foul mood wash over and off her. While Seela had always been cold, she'd never seemed ill-tempered like she had in the last few days. Perhaps she was angry that Aza hadn't been able to reach her parents.

She shook it away. After she got her answers, Aza would be gone and the Shadow Plane would no longer rule her—no longer consume her every moment.

"I'll be quick."

As she moved into the thicket, her fingers rested on the hilts of her daggers, calming the nervous twisting of her stomach. The black, broad-trunked trees grew up out of the slate grass. Exposed roots, as thick as Aza's middle, twisted through the broken ground in the shadows pooling on the forest floor.

She paused before she entered. It wasn't quite as dark as the Mortal Wood had been, and she didn't feel the same stabbing pain. It reminded her more of the dusky foreboding of Carceroc.

But, she wasn't after the Dolobra this time. She was just there for Silvix. Inhaling deeply, she stepped into the wood. A pair of wide white eyes glowed in front of her, and Aza whipped out her dagger. But it was only a strange squid-like wraith drifting by.

She exhaled, her heart still jumping. Just because the Dolobra had been trapped didn't mean there weren't other things here that could hurt her. She experimentally allowed a thin stream of yanaa to flow into her dagger as Seela had instructed her. Not that she had ever tried it—she could only hope it would work.

Aza rolled her feet from heel to toe as she crept half-crouched through the trees. If the worst happened, she could always crash back into the world of the living... although with Mogens nearing every day... it would have to be a last resort.

The wraiths rustled around her in the gloom, their soft feather-like touch brushing her arms and legs, drawing on her yanaa. How could she find a shadow in this darkness?

She stopped. Of course. She'd been in and out of the Shadow Plane for days now, and still she relied on her eyes. She closed them and thought of Silvix—the long hair, the lined face, the obsession with the darkness, the sacrifice he had made to protect his students. Unlike her. She thought of turning away as Witt nearly drowned in the sea.

She wouldn't. She inherited the darkness, the Shadow Plane obsession, and even the long dark hair, but she couldn't imagine a situation in which self-sacrifice would be the smartest option. There was no victory there, only a hollow compromise—and she could never settle for that.

A sound rippled through the darkness, somewhere between a sigh and a beast-like grunt. Aza opened her eyes and walked in that direction. The wraiths fluttered about her thickly now, their long tentacles prickling her skin.

She swatted at a few beetle-like creatures crawling up her arms, and in her distraction almost missed the great heaving mountain in front of her. She stopped mid-step, her muscles tense and her heart thrumming. The sigh hadn't come from Silvix, it had come from this... thing. The Dolobra—deep in its imprisoned slumber.

The Maldibor had told many hair-raising stories of the Dolobra around the fire to frighten the children. Some had described it as a great hairy beast, while some said it was blacker than the darkest souls. They'd all been wrong.

Its pale white skin seemed almost luminescent in the darkness. It was tall like a giant but with thin, sinewy arms wrapped around bony knees drawn to its chest. Spikes lined its spine and forearms, while spiraling horns grew out the sides of its head. Long needle-like fingers and toes twitched in its slumber while its sharp ribs rose and fell in the slowest of comatose breathing.

Though she would never have admitted it, she had feared this creature as a child just like the others. That's why she had gone into the forest that night, to prove to herself she wasn't scared. But she had been a fool. And she had been a liar.

Her throat tightened as her instincts screamed for her to step away. To forget Silvix and go back to the warmth of the light. She reigned in those emotions with a sharp tug. *Don't be a coward. It's bound. It cannot harm me.* She breathed deep and slow, forcing herself to look closer.

A black spiderweb of shadow crisscrossed the creature's body, like a net holding it to the ground. It flinched in its sleep with another grunt, baring long fangs from a lipless mouth. Aza swallowed. So, if she had found the Dolobra, then Silvix could not be far. But where?

On creeping feet, she tiptoed around the beast, wishing she could render herself invisible and safe. The netting around it seemed delicate against its bulging muscle, and if it woke up to find her there, she wasn't confident the shadows would hold it.

The monster twitched again, but this time Aza caught sight of something else moving at its feet. She squinted. It looked like the shadow of a person leaning against it, their head bowed, and an elbow resting on a bent knee, as if resigned to waiting.

Aza crouched down next to the person to see that it wasn't quite a shadow. She could make out Silvix's features in the dark. A straight nose and a square chin, bags sagging beneath the eyes, and the blank expression of the condemned. Everything bent toward the ground in the unmistakable language of the world-weary.

Aza frowned. She wondered if he had spent the last century regretting his sacrifice. Or if his students had truly appreciated what he'd done for them. A gladness raced through her. This was the right thing to do. This was where she was supposed to be. She could help him.

She let yanaa trickle through her fingers and took his hand in hers. His brow furrowed like he was trying to see something he couldn't quite make out, but he didn't resist as she pulled him away from the Dolobra. She glanced at the creature over her shoulder, but its body continued its unconscious rise and fall.

The wraiths practically spun around her, their excited whispers like an indecipherable hiss in her ear. The fear and uncertainty lifted from her with each step toward the edge of the copse. She had come so far in her short time here to make this seem easy. Now she could leave with at least this small victory to warm her.

Aza stepped out into the Plane, and Silvix tugged back on her hand, his feet stopped at the brink of the thicket. Aza turned to see confusion and doubt lining his face. Was he frightened? Of death? Of change?

"It's okay, Silvix. I'm your Heir. I'm here to help you." She squeezed his cold fingers. "You can finally rest."

His expression didn't change, and Aza wasn't sure if he was able to hear or see her. She pulled again on his hand, but still he resisted. The wraiths flew around him as if trying to push him out themselves.

"I know you've been in here for a long time," Aza whispered. "But this isn't where you belong."

Silvix opened his mouth to say something, but Aza couldn't hear the words.

"What?" She leaned closer, the slightest whisper tickling her ears, when a pair of strong hands seized her from behind and yanked her into the Plane.

Her hands tightened around Silvix's, and a yanaa that wasn't her own, something dark and slippery, funneled through her into him, wrenching him forward.

In the twilight of the Plane, Silvix's shadowed face squinted as though he'd just stepped into the noon sun. He blinked rapidly until at last, his gaze flitted down to the grass at his feet and then the forest behind them.

"Well done," Seela said.

Aza smiled at Silvix's shadow. "How does it feel to be free?"

Silvix's head whipped to her, his eyes wide. The darkness of him faded into the gusting Plane wind, but even though his words were soundless, Aza didn't need to hear them to know what he said.

"What have you done?"

20
BURNING

A tremendous crack rent the placid air, like an avalanche crashing into the Shadow Plane. The very ground beneath Aza's boots trembled, and a hair-raising roar thundered out from between the trees.

With Silvix nowhere to be seen, Aza turned to where Seela stood calmly beside her, a wide smile spreading across her face for the first time. The creature bellowed, and Aza cringed, her heart pounding.

"Seela, what's going on?"

Seela laughed in throaty triumph. "And to think you're supposed to be the cunning one." The chuckle rumbled through her words. "Seela was so sure you would figure it out, and yet…" She spread her arms. "Here we are."

Panicked confusion whooshed in and out of Aza with quick breaths. "Who are you?"

The ground shuddered with huge footsteps, and the splintering of trees crackled closer. Seela frowned with mock sympathy. "Tsk. Tsk. Now, that would be cheating."

Aza tightened her grip on her daggers. "I'm not playing your games."

Seela continued as if she hadn't spoken. "The way I see it, you have three options. You can follow in the footsteps of dear Silvix and sacrifice yourself to bind the Dolobra, you could challenge it here in the Plane and let it feed on your soul, or you can come back to Somisidas, and we'll kill you there. All excellent choices." She sighed, her eyes all soft and dreamy. "The wakened Dolobra will kill your brother in Carceroc, and our Heir problems will be solved. All thanks to you."

Bile swelled in Aza's throat, the bitter nausea coating her mouth. "Mogens," she choked.

"Close," Seela winked. "But not quite."

Aza lunged for Seela, just as the Dolobra crashed out of the wood.

Seela disappeared in a blink, and Aza cut through the thin air. She cursed under her breath and whirled to face the monster of her childhood nightmares. With its freedom, the Dolobra had swollen in size. Though still lean, it stood easily four times taller than her, with gnarled arms like thorny tree limbs and a great gaping maw dripping into its spiky beard. It stared at her from the black holes of its eyes, and the bone shards along its back twisted as if they had a mind of their own.

Aza adjusted her stance as it crept toward her on all fours. It lowered its head between its wiry forearms, its gaze holding hers. "Poor, lost girl, do not fear," it crooned. "You've saved me from my prison. Please allow me to return the favor."

Though fear and adrenaline coursed through her limbs, Aza found herself frozen, her mind locked on the white flames in those dark eyes. What had she done? The Dolobra reached out its long, spined fingers, saliva dripping from its widening jaws. This is not how Aza thought she would end, as some passive recipient of death's fangs.

A screech on the wind tore through her paralysis. "Run, girl!"

Aza blinked, the Dolobra's strange hold on her broken, and leapt away as its fingers closed around air.

"Don't look at its eyes!" Silvix's voice seemed like a shout from far away.

The Dolobra's claws snapped at her in fast succession. Aza slashed at its fingers, her daggers leaving shallow, bloodless slits in its pale skin. She dodged between the trees, her mind still reeling. Silvix hadn't inadvertently gotten trapped with the Dolobra, he had purposefully sacrificed himself to imprison it.

And she had freed it.

A searing shame turned her cold. A claw raked across her arm, and a lick of pain flared up her skin. Should she try to capture it again? But how would she even do that?

"What do I do?" she yelled into the wind.

"Leave, girl, while you still can," Silvix replied. "You've already lost this battle."

Fury rushed through Aza, and she weaved in to stab through the Dolobra again. She hadn't lost yet. She could still fix this. The Dolobra swiped at her, its claw grazing her leg with another spike of pain.

"I can't just run away!" She dodged behind trees as the Dolobra tore through the forest for her. "Tell me how to kill it!"

"This is its kingdom," Silvix snapped. "You must kill both its spirit here and its body in Carceroc to truly destroy it, and you are far too weak to trap it." His voice rose to a frustrated yell. "Go before you make things worse."

Aza opened her mouth to say something else when the Dolobra's claw closed around her foot. With a scream, she stabbed and slashed at its fingers, but it held fast, dragging her toward its gaping jaws and the eyes she couldn't meet.

"Come to me, my luscious Shadow. You would not believe how I've hungered all these years. How I've dreamed of you."

"The door, girl, think of the door!" Silvix shouted.

Aza screamed again, the claws tightening on her leg. Through the pain, she panted shallow breaths and tried to visualize the door back to the living. The Dolobra's hot breath misted on her face, but if she crashed back out this time, someone would be waiting on the other side to kill her—she had to find her way out.

She let the yanaa trickle into her fingers, and the Dolobra reared its head back, ready to crunch into her. With one last breath, the jaws snapped down, and she flung open the door.

Her eyes flashed open, and she moved before she even saw the blade. She rolled forward in a dive, the swipe of the steel ruffling her hair. Pain shot through her body from the wounds she had sustained in the Plane, but it looked undamaged, and most importantly, she still had yanaa. With a thought, she pulled the shadows to her and melted into the air.

"You missed her?" said a familiar posh voice.

Valente Conrad.

Aza took in the trio standing in the empty training room. Conrad leaned against the wall, unruffled in his ornate navy doublet, with his thick blond hair coiffed upon his head. Behind him, Seela stood with eyes glowing green. Aza's heart clenched. Had Conrad been... controlling her?

The next voice was unsurprising, even as Aza turned to face him. "You said she was going to be half-dead. She looks in fine form to me."

Mogens—the Heir killer.

The hood fell back as he rose from his crouch, the long lank hair on his mottled skull draping over the wrinkled, gray skin of his face, the bones of his teeth and cheeks protruding through the rot under his nose cavity in an eternal smile. The green haze of yanaa curled around him, pooling in the dark pits of his eyes. Rags draped over the rest of his skeletal remains—the skin fallen away where the yanaa had failed to preserve it, and his white-boned fingers gripped the jagged dagger that had once cut her grandfather's throat. The same one that had scarred Aza's face.

They faced each other, two assassins balancing on the scale. Odriel's and Idriel's. One living, one rotting—both deadly.

Conrad arched an eyebrow with a nonchalant smile, but anger sparked in his eyes as he stared at Mogens standing in the middle of the room. "She may be conscious, but she's still weak. The wraiths have been gnawing at her for days now. She'll be sluggish and stupid."

Mogens stalked toward Conrad with his dagger out, and for a moment Aza thought he might punish his impertinence. Instead, he flashed a skeletal smile. "Then, we don't need this anymore."

Aza's eyes widened. "No, don't—"

With one slash of his blade, Mogens sliced through Seela's neck. She crumpled to the floor, the green light gone from her eyes and a pool of dark blood burgeoning from her body.

Conrad stepped away from the fresh corpse with a grimace. "You always make such a mess."

Aza's grip tightened on her daggers as she shifted to conceal her position. *The monsters.*

"This is more fun anyway." Mogens tapped his blade against his teeth with a chuckle, Seela's blood dripping from the steel, and glanced in Aza's direction. "And she's been looking forward to this for years."

Aza's brow creased. How would he know that? Had he been watching her? *No.* A cold understanding washed over her. He'd been listening to her on the Shadow Plane. Every time she had spoken to the wraiths, her voice would have echoed over those gray grasses. Just like she had heard him.

"You led me here," she breathed.

Mogens' chuckle turned to a rattling laugh. "A little bit of the stick." He gestured to Conrad. "A little bit of the carrot…"

"Here, Shadow, Shadow, Shadow," Conrad taunted, as if calling a hound.

The blood drained from Aza's face with an icy chill.

"…And you practically flew to us," Mogens finished.

"But now that you've done your bit, I'm afraid it's time for us to part ways. I'd hate to miss the Dolobra snuffing out the final Heir." Conrad stood and straightened his doublet. "Mogens, clean this up, would you?" He strode to the doorway with smooth long strides. "And don't miss—"

Aza rushed him. Her muddled mind was still putting together the pieces, but she wouldn't let him escape until she knew everything. True to his word, her muscles were sore and stiff, but she could still Shadow Step, and even at half-strength, she was more than a match for this dandy.

Aza brought her dagger down to stab into Conrad's back, and another blade rose to meet it with a clang. Mogens' face loomed inches from hers as their steel locked together. But… how did he see her?

A sly smile spread across Conrad's face. "Always a pleasure, my lady."

Mogens' other hand thrust forward with a second dagger, and Aza twisted out of the way. She made another lunge for the door, only to find Mogens' cloaked form blocking her way. She slashed to cut his head from his body, but he beat her away with ease. He slashed, thrust, and feinted with smooth advances, his every move astoundingly accurate until she pressed up against the back wall. His blade crashed into the wood as she rolled away.

"You scurry faster now." Mogens turned toward her, his teeth open in a wide smile. "But I do quite like how my beauty mark turned out."

Her breaths came in huffs, and her limbs ached where the Dolobra had cut into her. But Mogens shouldn't have been able to see her. This should've been easy. "How can you see me?"

"And here I thought Seela had told you not to trust your eyes."

Aza stepped back and nearly stumbled on Seela's body, the sound of paper crinkling as a blood-stained letter fluttered from her robe.

Sensing her distraction, Mogens advanced again. Her muscles burning and sweat beading on her forehead, Aza matched him blow for blow. She struck for his neck and heart again and again, but his inhuman speed was too much for her lethargic mind. He easily took the upper hand, keeping her on the defensive. Even battered as she felt, she could keep up with him, but he was wearing her down—and she wouldn't win that game. Not today.

She got some distance to catch her heaving breath and tasted the oily scent of smoke.

Mogens sniffed at the air. "Conrad is of such little faith." He cocked his head to Aza. "I'm afraid our play time is running out."

He closed the gap between them, and Aza retreated, trying to conserve her strength while she looked for a weakness, for an opening, for anything that could give her the upper hand. Steel on steel rang out as their battle ranged onto the stone landing.

Flames billowed black smoke from each end of the long snaking train of buildings. The ropes that led up and down the cliffside had been cut, and students clambered up the bare cliff wall to escape the fire's fingers. A tiny gush of relief shot through Aza. At least Keo, Shad, and Witt were safe.

The blaze crackled around them as their battle raged on, a new urgency in Mogens' attacks. Aza's bid for victory had turned into a scramble for survival. If she was to survive the flames, this had to end. And soon.

A band of two-dozen figures clad in the gray robes of the Wraith-Called emerged from the smoke on either side of the landing. Hope sang through Aza. The numbers were in her favor. They could take care of Mogens and get out of here. Then she noticed the blood on their robes. *The Lost.*

Mogens' gravelly laugh rang through the air. "Well, at least he sent reinforcements."

But she had fire. Grabbing a burning spar, she heaved it toward Mogens. He dodged, just barely, and it crashed to the ground in an explosion of embers. With an inhuman shriek, Mogens raised his brittle, corpse arms, smothering the eager sparks. Aza grabbed another fiery plank, brandishing it before her, and a hint of fear tightened Mogens' skeletal jaw.

Mogens straightened, his green eyes narrowing. "As much as I'd love to make you scream, I'm afraid I'll have to leave you to the flames… but don't worry." He smirked. "The Dolobra will be waiting either way."

With that, he turned and shambled to the cliffside.

"Coward!" Aza screamed, running after him.

She cut through the Lost one after the other, dodging their clumsy strikes and shoving the abominable creations away. But even as she put them down, they'd already accomplished their task. The fire had cut her off from the exit, and Mogens now clambered to freedom. She coughed as the smoke clogged her lungs.

You don't have time for this, girl, Silvix's voice shouted in her head. *Get the letter from Seela's robe and flee if you want your answers.*

"Letter?" Stumbling with exhaustion, Aza didn't have a chance to second guess the strange words smashing through her mind. Cutting through one more attacker, she turned and raced back to where Seela's body lay in the practice room. She snatched the letter from the floor and stuffed it in her pocket before a cry from the landing turned her attention outside.

"Help!" someone called.

Coughing, Aza barreled out of the burning building to find a knot of adolescent Wraith-Called on the landing beside her, struggling against their Lost brethren. In one leap, Aza crossed the landings, dispatching the creatures with quick, efficient flashes of her daggers. Precious time burned away in the fire until Aza gasped for breath over a scattering of bodies, their blood slicking the stone. She turned to the five trembling novices cringing against the cliff face. They looked younger than her by a couple years, and soot smudged their pale faces, their eyes wide with fear.

"The flames are too hot to climb," one whimpered.

"Down," Aza barked, her voice hoarse and her wounds aching. "There has to be another way down."

With a gasp, one of the younger boys nodded. "Y-yes, this way."

On quick, shuffling feet, he led them to the lowest landing. Showers of sparks rained down on their shoulders with agonizing stings as he took them to a square hole cut into the stone where a rope hung down to pull up supplies. Covering her mouth with her arm, Aza eyed the flaming building beside them. They had to get away before it collapsed, or they would be caught in the spray of fire.

"Hurry, down the rope!" Aza ushered the cringing students one after the other, their faces already blackened by smoke.

Four went down without a word, but the fifth hesitated, sobs racking his body. The building crackled ominously beside them.

"Go!" Aza shouted.

The boy shook his head, shock freezing him to the spot. "I can't."

The building groaned as it leaned to one side. She should just leave him. It wasn't worth the risk.

You can't leave him, Silvix cut into her thoughts.

"I'm not," Aza growled. She grabbed his arms and looped them around her shoulders. "Hold on!" As the building gave way beside them, Aza leapt through the hole, the rope loose in her gloves.

Fire and debris rained down, and she squeezed the rope to slow their sliding, the heat of the friction burning her hands while the boy squealed into her ear. Time slowed, Aza's hands on fire as she tried to control their descent, the sand sliding reluctantly through the hourglass while the fates weighed their lives in the balance.

But at last, her luck gave out, and the rope snapped somewhere high above them. Together she and the boy plummeted the last fifteen feet to land in a heap of dense brush already sizzling from the embers.

Ignoring the scream of pain in her ankle, she grabbed the boy and dragged him away from the cliff's edge, away from the flaming debris tumbling in earnest now.

Aza sucked in the fresh air of the valley and deposited their last member at the feet of the other novices. Then, together, they watched Somisidas burn.

21
ANSWERS

Vision swimming, body aching, and smoke still choking her lungs, Aza collapsed against a tree with a groan. The novices clustered somewhere off in the distance, but she pointedly ignored them. She could only think of Seela's bloodied body somewhere high above her in the ashes of the monastery.

For a moment, Aza hesitated, seeing two people at once. Seela had taken her in hand, taught her the secrets of the Shadow Plane, and connected her to a past long forgotten. But she had also betrayed her to Idriel's Children, hadn't she? She'd led her into the waiting trap set to snap not just on her, but her entire family. Now her friends were gone, and the creature that she had set loose was roaming free, lusting after her brother's life. Aza had thought she'd earned Seela's respect at least once. Had it all been an act? Had she been working with Mogens and Conrad all along?

The letter, girl, open the letter, Silvix's voice prodded.

And now she was hearing voices from the Shadow Plane in broad daylight. Perhaps she really was going mad.

She withdrew the square of blood-streaked parchment from her pocket and considered the three looping letters of her name on the front. Bracing herself for the worst, she unfolded the thick paper.

Aza,

I can only hope you have survived to find this letter. But if you are reading this, then that means I'm not alive to explain myself, and the Dolobra now roams free. I expect you have many unanswered questions, so with this, your final lesson, hopefully I can grant you some understanding.

Valente Conrad first arrived at Somisidas several months ago. His orders were simple. I would call the younger Shadow Heir to Somisidas. As I had already wished to train you, it didn't take much convincing for me to agree. I had heard you in the Shadow Plane and written to your father, but he had been unmoving in his wishes to keep you away.

Conrad arrived again four days before you with new orders. I would let the Plane drain your strength and then instruct you to release the Dolobra. I resisted. Conrad tried to entice me with his dream of Idriel's resurrection and gift of eternal life.

This did not wholly surprise me, as I have had students in the past who have fallen into Idriel's empty promises of immortality as a Lost soul. But this was the first true child of Idriel I'd beheld. I turned him away, but he seized control of my students, filling their minds with dark yanaa. Many of my students were too weak to resist him. They were as the living Lost, their lives twisted in his horrid hands.

My students are everything to me. So, in an attempt to buy time, I acquiesced. He didn't have the strength to control me, so I thought I could stall. I thought I could drive you away. You arrived, and I tried to send your friends away to keep them safe. I tried to wear you down. But you were so much stronger than I could have ever imagined. The tenacity and speed with which you learned nearly overwhelmed me, and I could truly see you were a descendant of Silvix. I wanted to tell you more but with Conrad and that abomination, Mogens, listening, I could say nothing.

I've made a plan to evacuate the school and get you away from here. I can't risk the countless souls the Dolobra would take, even at the risk of my students. But I expect I have stalled too long, for I sense something else... more powerful approaches.

The Dolobra is a terrible creature. A devourer of souls in the living world and in the Shadow Plane. Like the Lost, it hungers for yanaa and will seek out you and your kin. To bind it is to sacrifice your mind and lock the two of you together in an endless struggle. To defeat it, you would have to kill both halves at the same time—a nigh impossible task.

Though you are young and still have much to learn, you are strong, Aza. Perhaps even stronger than Silvix. But even you cannot do this on your own. I wish I could be there to guide you, but I have every faith that one way or another, you will right this wrong.

Please forgive me for my weakness and my mistakes that have led us to this dark path. And I hope that one day, you, a victorious Shadow Heir will find me in the Mortal Wood and put my aching, shamed spirit to rest.

Until then, be safe Aza.

Seela

Aza thought of the soul-eating Dolobra loose on the Shadow Plane and swallowed.

"Will the Dolobra be waiting for Seela when she tries to cross?" she asked aloud, her breath crystallizing in the crisp mountain air. "Will she make it?"

"She did not."

Aza looked up and there was Silvix standing before her, as if he had crossed straight from the Shadow Plane. His presence didn't even shock her. Her mind was too far gone. "I... see." She knocked her head against the tree. "Odriel take it," she swore bitterly. "Just run me through."

Memories of her mother reciting to them from *The Heir's Way* drifted to her—how they honored their own. Seela wasn't an Heir, but she deserved such a send-off. She swam through those warm memories now gone cold and scraped up the only words she could remember, whispering them to herself in the quiet of the valley:

A fallen ally, a friend, a teacher,
The battle claims those we hold most dear,

But we carry them with us,
Their strengths become ours,

And through their memory, we will be more,
Then we ever were before,

For you, the fallen, we will walk on,
With you not here, but never far beyond.

Silvix stood, silvery in the overcast light, and put his fingers solemnly to his lips. "May Odriel guide us all."

Perhaps it was the shock, or her wounds, or her sheer exhaustion, but all of Aza's thoughts and emotions froze into a solid block of nothing.

"Just leave me alone," she muttered to the ghost. With that, she let the blood-stained letter fall to the ground, rested her forehead on her knees, and let the darkness take her.

Aza woke up to something heavy around her shoulders and a low fire crackling in the dusk. For a moment, she blinked her heavy eyelids, hoping to remain in unconscious oblivion for just a few moments longer. But her thoughts refused to obey, and the day's events came rushing back to her all at once.

Keo, Shad, and Witt were gone, Somisidas had burned, and Seela was dead. All because of her. Because she wouldn't listen to anyone but her damned self. If she had just followed her father's advice from the beginning, she would have followed her brother to Carceroc, helped the Maldibor, and gone back home. Instead, she had fallen straight into Mogens' trap, again. And now, who even knew if her brother was still alive?

What if she was the only Heir left?

The sorrow built in her forehead, threatening to trace the permanent tear-stain scar Mogens had marred her with all those years ago. How could she have been so stupid? She, a Shadow Heir, with their *legendary* cleverness.

Instead, she'd been the fool who had destroyed an ancient monastery and unleashed a soul-devouring monster onto her friends and family. Silvix's look of astounded horror would forever be branded in her memory. Her father in the Mortal Wood must be so ashamed of her.

A flash of movement caught her eye, and Aza looked up to see Witt walking toward her out of the dusk-drenched foliage. Her eyebrows raised in surprise. Of course, someone had to have built the fire, but what was he doing here? Hadn't he left with the others? If he had any sense at all, he should have abandoned her and her fool's quest. Just like Keo. Just like Shad. They'd been the smart ones.

"You're awake." He smiled at her, his unguarded, happy expression completely bereft of guile or blame. What was wrong with him? "You know, when you sleep, you really sleep hard. I had to check to make sure you were breathing like five times."

"What are you doing here?" she croaked. "Where did the novices go?"

He nodded next to a satchel by the fire. "The novices left some supplies and then started toward the village where they get their provisions." He shrugged. "And me... I couldn't leave. I didn't make it far before I decided to turn around."

Aza's throat clogged. *Not in front of Witt. Don't let him see you cry. Don't cry. Crying is weak. Shadow Heirs don't cry.*

"Anyways, we should get you something to fill your belly, Aza. There's not much in the bag, but it should be enough for something decent."

His talk was so easy, so familiar, she half-expected her brother to emerge from the brush behind him with his own fish and bantering insults. Her brother who might be dead already. Aza pulled herself in tighter, trying to keep the emotions from spilling out. She didn't deserve this. Why was he here? Why couldn't he just go away? Then it occurred to her. He didn't know.

He didn't realize it was her fault.

Witt looked up at her again, and his smile fell away. "Aza?" He crouched beside her. "Are you okay?"

"No." And for some odd reason, that simple word let loose the floodgates. The sobs and tears gurgled out of her throat in a deluge she could no longer hold back. "It's all my fault."

He put his arm around her shoulders. "It's okay, Aza," he crooned as if trying to soothe an infant. "It's okay to not be okay."

Aza shook her head, her words only half coherent through the hitched gasps. "No. You don't understand." She pointed to the letter, the blood on the parchment now a rusty shade of brown. "I did this. It was me."

He squeezed her lightly as her grief dripped from her cheeks. "I do understand, Aza. I know what it says."

Aza leaned away, and he withdrew his arm as she tried to calm her uneven breaths. She scrubbed her cheeks with her sleeves in a vain effort to reclaim some of the dignity that now stained Witt's shirt. "If I had just listened to my father, none of this would have happened."

Witt nodded, his placid expression unruffled by this revelation. "Maybe. You can't really ever know what would have happened if you'd gone with your brother. Maybe those Hunters would've gotten to you, like they did your parents."

"Yes, if those Hunters killed my parents, then there's no reason to believe my brother and I would've survived either. There has to be a different reason they wanted to unleash the Dolobra."

Witt's mouth twisted. "Well, we always said we couldn't trust Ivanora's word for it anyway."

Aza's brow wrinkled, and she sat up straighter. "That's right. Which is why I never saw them in the Mortal Wood. Because they're not dead." Her mind spun slowly like a fire trying to catch on damp wood. "And that's why Mogens and Conrad need the Dolobra. Because you have to go into the Shadow Plane to kill it. And my father doesn't walk the Shadow Plane."

Witt's eyes widened, and he looked up to where Somisidas lay in ashes somewhere above them. "And they've killed Seela and... and if they think you're dead too then there'd be no one there to stop it."

A sudden bark of laughter erupted from Witt, and Aza looked at him incredulously. He'd finally cracked under the weight of their desperate situation. "Why are you laughing?"

His laughter continued, loud and unabated, until tears ran down his face.

Even as Aza resisted the urge to slap him, her traitorous mouth lifted up at the corner. "There's nothing funny about this."

"No, there's not." He wiped his tears away with his palms. "I'm just so relieved, Aza. Your parents are *alive!*"

Her smirk grew into a tiny smile, but she waved him away. "Oh, I always knew they weren't dead," she mumbled to the damp soil beneath her hands.

Witt leaned against the rocks, the air whooshing out of him in a massive gust of a sigh. "Thank Odriel."

"But we still have a massive problem."

Witt hummed happily to himself as he popped to his feet. "Yes, but you"—he pointed at her—"are alive."

"I'm the one who caused all this to begin with."

"But you are also the only person who can fix it."

Aza pressed her palms to her forehead. "I'm not sure I can. I tried to fight that thing in the Shadow Plane, Witt." She chewed her lip. "I hardly made a scratch."

"That's because you needed someone to weaken its physical body as well." He wrinkled his nose at her. "Did you even *read* the letter?"

Aza threw a dirt clod at him. "Of course I read the letter."

"And Zephyr and the Maldibor are in Carceroc right now ready to fight this thing."

She struggled to her feet. "You're right. We need to get moving."

"No. Before we go anywhere, you need to eat, recover, and get your strength back."

Aza rolled her eyes but said nothing. Just standing had made her head spin.

"Besides," Witt continued, squinting at the cliff walls. "I'm pretty sure the only way to get out of here is up. So, until you're strong enough to climb, we need to regroup." He smiled again, a wistful shine in his eyes. "And *eat*."

Aza let her shoulders relax and wrapped the cloak around herself tighter. She'd always written Witt off as her brother's friend, but here he was, beside her at the bottom of all things. The one person she hadn't scared off.

Her thoughts turned to the holes around their fire that should've been filled by Keo's warm bulk and Shad's dry sarcasm. She didn't blame them for abandoning her on her fool's errand. Especially after the things she'd said. Honestly, she respected them for it. She'd been stupid and stubborn, so they'd made the smart move without her. It's what she would've done.

But it still didn't keep her from missing them.

22
MOVING FORWARD

The sun bloomed on the valley with fire-lined clouds of navy cotton. Aza stoked their dying fire while experimentally leaning on her bad foot. A dull pain still radiated up her leg, but it would bear her weight. She debated going back into the Shadow Plane to listen for her brother or her parents, but she couldn't risk alerting Mogens that she was still alive.

They were already a day behind Mogens and Conrad, and if she remembered the map correctly, it would take them at least two days to reach Carceroc on foot. That was two days the Dolobra had to murder her brother, Makeo, and the Maldibor.

She tested her ankle again. It would hold. It would have to.

She turned to where Witt snored, his legs kicking like a ragehound in its sleep. "Wake up, Witt."

With a groan, he opened one eye. "What?" He passed a hand over his face. "Oh yes, that's right. We're in the middle of the wilderness, preparing to scale a cliff, so we can go chase after a monster."

"We're leaving now."

He sat up. "Not before breakfast!"

"We're running out of time."

Witt winked with a gleaming smile. "There's always time for breakfast."

Aza glared and crossed her arms.

"You know you need it," he coaxed.

Aza sighed and glanced up at the rockface before them. She really couldn't argue with breakfast. They would need their strength.

After a hasty meal of berries and a snared rabbit, there was nothing left to do but begin the climb. Hand-over-hand, Aza and Witt pulled themselves up the sheer face to the blackened stone landing that had once held the

156

Wraith-Called of Somisidas.

Catching her breath, Aza let her eyes trail down the smoking wreckage of the monastery. The buildings lay in ashy rubble, the dorms and training rooms all but leveled. Charred and still bodies littered the wreckage in blackened lumps, but Aza couldn't bring herself to investigate. All that remained were the trail of stairs cut into the cliff between the stone landings.

Maybe the students would be able to rebuild it, but the thought of heaving the timber and supplies up here made Aza's already raw hands burn.

Witt pulled himself up beside her and collapsed onto the rock slab like a fish gasping for air.

"Don't tell me we're really only halfway?"

Aza gazed up to the peak above them. "If that."

He shook his head at her, his mop of curls bouncing. "Couldn't you just lie to me for once?"

She fixed him with a flat look.

"Well fine then." He sniffed. "See if I find wool berries for *you* again." He sat up and brushed his hands on his pants, but he paused, catching sight of the destruction around them. "Wow. I thought we'd be able to scavenge for more supplies but..."

"There's nothing left," Aza said.

"I hope most of the students were able to get out."

Aza's mouth pressed into a tight line. The fire had been too fast, too sudden, and the only exits had been purposely cut. She didn't even want to know how many of the students mixed with the ashes on the wind, but she wouldn't lie to herself—there were many.

Even so, there was no point in burdening Witt with the truth. She only hoped the fallen Wraith-Called would be able to cross the Shadow Plane safely. With a sigh, she rose to her feet. She didn't have time to dwell on these ghosts.

"Come on, the easiest place to climb out of here will be where we arrived."

This time, Aza made Witt go on ahead of her up the rocky face. If she fell, she didn't want to take him down with her. She followed a few body lengths behind, her hands and toes seeking the same holds he'd found, her foot trembling under the strain.

She flinched as a grizzard cut through the air behind her, its rattling caw echoing off the cliff walls. "Follow."

How long would they continue to parrot the words of a Somisidas that no longer stood? Were they feeding on the remains of the Wraith-Called, or was it her fresh body they were waiting for? She was high enough now that a fall would be deadly.

She thought back to the dark night they'd descended this very wall, confident and fearless of the height they could not see. Now, she climbed out, battered, afraid, and ashamed. She cried out as her ankle crumpled beneath her, wrenching her hand away from the wall.

The agitated grizzards fluttered behind her, parroting their cryptic messages. "Feel your way."

Aza whipped her body back to the rockface, her free hand scrambling for a hold and her bad foot sliding down.

"Step forward."

Sweat pouring and heart racing, she reached higher, her fingers wedging in a tiny unseen crack.

"Come now, or do not come at all."

She pulled herself up, her toes finally finding a solid foothold. She leaned her forehead against the cold, hard mountain. Her eyes widened with a realization. If she died here, she wouldn't get a chance to right her wrongs. She'd wander the Mortal Wood, waiting for her family to join her or wondering if the Dolobra had silenced them. She'd carry the shame for eternity.

The grizzards continued their lines. "The wraiths—"

"SHUT UP!" Tenacious adrenaline surged through Aza's muscles, the pain fading away. "Somisidas is gone, and I've got to get up this sky-cracked mountain, so I can do something about it."

With another squawk, the grizzards flapped away, and Aza moved up the cliff with strong, smooth movements.

"Uh... are you okay?" Witt called down.

"I'm fine," Aza said through gritted teeth.

She lost track of time as she focused on moving one hand after the other, thinking of nothing but her next hold and listening to her breath going in and out. The same concentration that got her into the Shadow Plane could get her up this mountain. Small clouds of her warmth billowed from her lips into the crisp air as dust and pebbles spilled from her boot soles to the ruins below.

"Here's the top, Aza," Witt shouted, relief dripping from each word.

With one last surge of strength, Aza pulled herself over the precipice. She rolled onto her back as Witt peeked over the edge. She followed his gaze down the steep wall of rock, skipping over the dark splotch of ash that used to be Somisidas, until her eyes landed where they'd started the day in the wooded valley.

"Near the end, I wasn't sure I was going to make it." He laughed. "But I knew if I fell, I'd be taking you with me, and I didn't want you to kill me again on the Shadow Plane."

Aza smiled, the adrenaline fading from her limbs, and the pain rushing back all at once. It didn't matter that her wounds from the Dolobra weren't open and bleeding, her mind seemed to think they were. She squeezed the bridge of her nose. They'd gotten out of the valley. The first step was always the hardest, even when it wasn't vertical. She looked up at the snow-dusted peak still so high above them, and then let her head droop between her knees.

Witt nudged her. "Eat. You'll feel better."

"Does food solve all your problems, Witt?" Aza asked with a dry laugh.

He craned his neck at the peak before them. "No, but it couldn't hurt after we just climbed half the mountain."

"Better save it for the half of the mountain we have left."

"It's okay to celebrate halfway."

Drawing the tough, herb-rubbed meat from her bag, Aza chewed thoughtfully. "Does anything ever get you down, Witt?"

"Sure, but I've always had you and Zephyr to pick me back up again."

"You mean Zephyr." Aza took a swig from the waterskin. "I'm not sure I've ever picked *anyone* up."

"No, I mean you too." He wrapped his arms around his lanky legs. "Sure, you didn't talk much, and sometimes I'm sure you probably weren't even listening." His smile widened. "But sometimes, it's enough just to be there."

Aza crunched into a handful of tart wool berries and thought of what she'd be doing if she had come out here on her own. She'd probably still be wallowing on the valley floor. For all his fool-headed chatter and relentless optimism, it was his hope that was propping her up—keeping them moving.

"Thanks, Witt," she said, her voice soft. "Thank you for being here. I wouldn't have made it this far without you."

He waved her off. "Of course, you would have. But I like to think my charm does make the journey more pleasurable."

Aza rolled her eyes, but she didn't deny it.

As dusk fell, what little scrap of victory Aza had achieved in climbing the cliff face had fallen away. The trail was nonexistent, their supplies were gone, and on the bare rocky mountainside, they didn't even have enough firewood to make a flame.

Instead, they took shelter from the wind in the lee of a boulder, their bodies drooping from more than just exhaustion.

"How's your foot?" Witt asked, his earlier cheer vanished. "Better or worse?"

Aza hid her numbed fingers in her armpits. "The same."

"Do you think we'll make the pass tomorrow?"

"Probably."

"And from the top, we'll be able to find a trail, right?"

A wry smile twisted Aza's lips. Witt just couldn't shake that unflappable optimism. "Perhaps. But it's more important that we find water first."

"And food," Witt added sternly.

Aza sighed. "And that."

For a moment the silence stretched between them, tired and empty.

"Do you think we'll make it in time?" he whispered.

Not at this rate. Aza bit back the words. They were of no use. There were no towns between here and Carceroc. No way to go any faster. They would have to make do with the best pace they could muster. "I don't know."

But in her dreams, the wraiths screamed.

They started again at first light, their spirits rising with the sun as the mountain's crest loomed just above them. Witt practically bounded the last few steps to the saddle between the peaks, his arms lifted in a mock victory dance.

"It's all downhill from—" He stopped short, his face falling.

Alarm rushing through her, Aza pushed past the pain of her throbbing ankle to join him at the top. On the blue-sky day, they could see for miles across the forests and fields of Okarria, but there was no mistaking the streak of smoke on the horizon.

Carceroc was burning.

By her brother's hand? Or Conrad's?

Aza started down the other side, sliding on the shale. "C'mon, we have to hurry."

"Hey, wait up," Witt called from behind her.

But Aza barely heard him as she hurtled down the slope. Her ankle hurt, but she could stand it. She had to use every bit of speed the slope had to offer, just as she did on the mountains back home. Her eyes glued to the ground, she hopped from one sturdy rock to the other and let herself slide on the shale. Faster and faster, she leapt down the mountain.

"Aza, you're going too fast! You're going to—"

Witt didn't get to finish his sentence before Aza's bad ankle gave out beneath her. In a whirl of stone and sky, she tumbled head over heels down the slope, the rocks tumbling after her. She raised her arms to protect her head as her body clattered against the mountain again and again. Finally, she crashed into the crevice of an outcropping, her hands and knees scraping against the gravel to bring her to a stop. But she only had a second to breathe, before a shower of rocks battered down onto her.

"Aza!" Witt yelled, scrambling to her side. "Are you okay?"

For a moment, Aza just lay there, hiding her scratched face in her bloodied arms. *Get up*, she told herself. *You have to keep moving. You have to fix this.* Head pounding and fuzzy with hunger, fatigue, and thirst, Aza assessed her injuries. The crimson red of blood bloomed around her hands and knees, but nothing seemed broken. She shook off the rubble and tried to pull herself out of the crevice. She moved her right hand, then her left, her right foot, and then her left... stuck.

"Odriel's teeth." She looked down to where a chest-sized boulder had trapped her foot in the crevice. "I'm stuck." She reached down to try to pull against the rock, but it stuck fast. Breaths quickening, she heaved and strained against the rock, her panic rattling her bones. "Witt, can you help me?" Her voice pitched in a near scream even as she struggled to control it.

Witt jumped down next to her boot, his face creased with worry. He strained against the rock with her, but it didn't so much as budge.

Witt met her gaze with wide eyes, his face white and bloodless. "I'm... I'm sorry, Aza."

Her heart thumping frantically, Aza's gaze raced to the black smudge in the distance where Keo and the others waited for her. Needed her. With a concentrated effort, she dragged her attention back to her wedged foot. How was she going to get out of this?

"Witt, do you see anything that might be close by. Villages? Campfires? Trails?"

He shook his head. "I... don't see anything."

Aza scraped her gaze across the landscape again. Witt was right. There was nothing.

Just the unforgiving mountain wilderness.

Her gaze trailed back to the smoke in the distance. It would take Witt days to travel to Carceroc and back, and their supplies had run dry.

Witt chewed on a shaking knuckle. "What should we do?"

Behind him, Silvix had reappeared, his face tight and drawn, but he said nothing.

"We need help," Aza whispered. "I need Keo."

"But—" Witt started.

"I can reach him through the Shadow Plane." The chill of shock soaked into her bones in a thousand icy needles. "But there's a chance Mogens or Conrad will hear me instead." She swallowed, locking eyes with him. "You can't be here when they do."

Witt shook his curls furiously. "I'm not going anywhere."

"Witt—"

"You're wasting time you don't have," Silvix snapped from behind them.

Witt glanced toward Silvix and then turned back to Aza, his expression abnormally hard. "I'm not leaving."

Confusion ricocheted around Aza's already jagged thoughts. Could Witt see Silvix? She shook her head. It didn't matter. "Fine."

"With your leg trapped, you will not be able to physically cross over. You can open the door, but you will not be able to step over the threshold," Silvix said. "Reach out with your mind, but do not linger. The Dolobra hunts the Plane now."

Aza nodded and reached out for the door in her mind, pulling the shadows to her. She opened the door, the darkness of the Plane stretching before her, but when she tried to step through, a jolt of pain tore through her trapped leg. Still in the open doorway, she sucked in a hiss of pain. *Please, Keo.* With her desperation icing into resolve, her hands curled into fists, and she screamed into the Plane.

She screamed words; she screamed her fury and desperation. She screamed for Keo; she screamed for her parents. She screamed for anyone and anything. She screamed until her voice was hoarse and cracking. But no one answered her. Not even the Dolobra. Finally, exhausted, she let her mind slip back into the world of the living.

Witt sat patiently beside her, his body sagging with resignation, but a hopeful smile still edging his mouth. "Anything?"

She turned to the smokey horizon where the lingering haze seemed to grow darker by the hour and shook her head. Then she lifted her chin and released a sorrowful howl, like a Maldibor mourning their dead.

Beside her, Silvix crossed his arms, his face unreadable.

And all Aza could think was, *I truly have gone mad.*

She was wiping the blood from her face when the wind started to sing. So now, even the elements were taking pity on her. Her lips curled in a scowl. She didn't need their sympathy. But still, the notes grew louder on the breeze. And for a moment, Aza froze in the fear that the Shadow Plane had finally claimed her. That it was the wraiths calling to her one last time.

"Sing all you want, you bloody wraiths!" she yelled, her voice still hoarse. "I'm not listening anymore."

"I didn't think you really listened to me to begin with," rumbled a familiar voice.

Aza whirled and squinted up in the fading sunlight to see Makeo mounted on his tall Dalteek at the top of the slope. The antlers of a second Dalteek edged closer to them. Not even on a lead, it stayed as close as a trained ragehound.

She watched, speechless, as the graceful mounts picked their way down the incline as gracefully as two mountain goats until they stopped before her. "How…? How are you here?" Aza asked, her voice scratchy and rough.

Makeo softened with something that looked like relief mixed with worry. "I rode through the night. I was already here searching for you when I heard your call." His green eyes combed over the scratches and scrapes littering her body before snagging on her foot. He dismounted and knelt at her side. "Skies, Aza, are you all right? What happened?"

"I'm okay. My leg's just trapped," Aza rasped. "What about the others? Is my brother all right? Your people? Where's Shadmundar?"

"They were doing fine when I left." Makeo fitted his huge hands around the rock, and with one huge heave, lifted it free.

With a wince Aza withdrew her leg, bloodied but not broken... and most importantly—free. She blinked stupidly up at Makeo, still trying to absorb his presence. "I thought I'd be stuck forever out here." His gaze swiveled to her, and she had to look away. The last time she'd seen him, she'd thrown words like knives. And now here he was, saving her life. "I released the Dolobra by mistake," she said softly. "I have to get back to Carceroc before Conrad turns it on Zephyr and then your clan." She licked her lips and finally met his eyes. "I'm sorry... for everything."

He squeezed her shoulder with a huge paw, his green eyes as gentle as his voice. "Aza, when I saw Somisidas, I wasn't sure you had survived. I searched the rubble for you for ages."

"If it weren't for Witt..." She nodded to him crouched beside her, a strange sorrow glinting in his eyes. "I don't think I would have."

Makeo paused, blinking once, twice, three times. Then he slowly edged closer to her, as if she were a frightened animal. "Aza..." He cleared his throat. "I found Witt... down in Somisidas."

"What?" Aza looked to Witt on her other side next to Silvix, his image strangely silvery. "What are you talking about? He's right here." But even as she said it, her heart stuttered in her chest, something unraveling inside of her.

Witt shook his head, tears glistening in his brown eyes. "I'm sorry, Aza, I... lied to you. I never actually left Somisidas. After the fire... Silvix told me where you were, and I just... couldn't leave you like that." His face was translucent now, like a fog lifting in the afternoon sun.

Aza's breaths came fast in panicked flurries of air. *No, no, no, no, no, no, no.* She had touched him, hadn't she? She couldn't have imagined that. He was right there in front of her.

"With your strength, you have blurred the line between the Plane and the living." Silvix rested a hand on Witt's shoulder. "As I once did."

"But you can't have." Aza shook her head, tears spilling from her eyes now. She reached out for Witt, but her fingers could no longer feel him, and the grief threatened to strangle her. Not Witt. Not her funny, cheerful kitchen boy. She would've gone back for him if she had known. She would've saved him. "Why didn't you leave with the others? I was supposed to be alone."

"Come on, Aza. You've been ordering me around since we were kids; you know that doesn't work. You can't make other's choices for them." He exchanged a glance with Silvix. "I stayed in case you needed me." He ran a translucent finger over the back of her hand, and she choked on a sob. "My only regret is that it's a little tough to cook for you like this." He chuckled, just a faint outline now. "But I was glad I could be there for you, for just a little longer."

This was it. Witt was slipping through her fingers. And as he faded away, Aza could think of just one more gift she could give to him—the boy who had longed for legendary adventure. Gaze still wide with shocked sorrow, for the second time in as many days, *The Heir's Way* flowed from Aza's trembling lips:

> *How can I let you go from here,*
> *When through the years, you've always been dear,*
>
> *Though through my fingers, you slip free,*
> *Into our stories, you'll always be,*
>
> *With the other legends of old,*
> *The ones that will be told and retold,*
>
> *There you'll be close forevermore,*
> *Till we join you among Odriel's lore.*

As her words faded into the mountain air, so, too, did Witt Corser. The one who'd always been there for her, even when she hadn't been there for him. The boy who'd taken her hand when she'd most desperately needed it. The boy who'd stayed by her side, even when she'd shouted for him to go.

And in that moment, as her heart broke open and tears cascaded down her cheeks, there was nothing Aza wouldn't have given to save him.

"Aza…" Makeo whispered, his huge paw squeezing her shoulder.

"You have to go now, Aza. Your time runs short," Silvix said. "But know that we're always with you. As a Shadow Heir, you're never truly alone."

Makeo turned her toward him with gentle hands; the concern practically radiating from him in a hot wave. "Aza, what are you seeing? Are you still with me?"

Numbly, Aza started to nod and then shook her head instead, her breath cracking in painful wracking sobs. "The Shadow Plane has…" *Consumed me,* she choked on the words. "Witt's gone." She leaned into him until her head rested on his chest and buried her fingers in his thick fur. "You're not a ghost too, are you?"

Slowly, tentatively, Makeo wrapped his bulky arms around her. Enveloping her in his soothing warmth, in his ring of safety. "I'm here, Aza. I promise."

Her words rushed out between her hitched breaths "Everything is falling apart, and I have to put it back together before everyone else…"

Makeo gave her a squeeze, his breath warm on her cheek. "It's okay, Aza, you can lean on me. We'll fix it together." Underneath his thick fur, his heart beat steady against Aza's ear.

"How can you say that after I said all those hateful things?" she whispered.

"I left because I needed to get the Dalteek." His voice lowered. "You couldn't frighten me off that easily. You're not that scary. And…" He smiled, his green eyes tinged with sorrow. "You're a terrible liar."

"Right." Aza wiped away the tears from her sopping cheeks. "But we're running out of time. Conrad is already days ahead of us." She looked once more at the space where Witt had been, and she clenched her fists, hating that they had to move on. With a shuddering breath, she gently tucked her grief into the back of her mind. There, it would have to keep for now. She pressed a kiss to her fingers, and let the breeze whisk it away.

Goodbye, my friend.

Rising to her feet, Aza held out a hand to the dark bay Dalteek beside Windtorn, and it pushed its soft nose into her palm as though it had always fit there. She glanced at Keo. "Do you think he'll let me ride him?"

"Rainracer belongs to my aunt. He's stubborn, but he knows the way," Keo said.

Aza stroked the thick ring of black mane surrounding Rainracer's neck. "Am I doing the right thing this time?" she whispered. "What if it's just another trap?"

"When in doubt, you're already thinking twice as much as when you were certain." Makeo mounted, and Windtorn eagerly pawed the ground with a cloven hoof. "My uncle says doubt is like fear. We can't be courageous unless we're afraid. We can't be shrewd unless we've weighed all the options." His gaze trailed to the smoking horizon. "So as long as we can move forward without the doubt and fear weighing us down, then we'll be brave, and we'll be wise."

Aza nodded and mounted the tall Dalteek, the antlers climbing to the sky in front of her. "You know, I think it's time I started laying a trap of my own."

23
A PLAN

The sting of Witt's death and Aza's scratched and bruised body summarily sucked away the thrill of riding the Dalteek across the twilit Naerami valley. But at least she was moving in the right direction. And if she stumbled, she would have Makeo beside her to make sure she didn't fall. They rode through the night until Aza threatened to fall out of the saddle, and Makeo finally made her stop to rest.

Catching her reflection in the stream, Aza grimaced. Her hazel eyes stared flatly back at her, her dark hair falling across her pale face. The blood from her tumbles onto the rocks had crusted over on nearly every inch of her skin. She let the cold water run over her, washing the cuts clean. Her fingers scrubbed at her arms, neck, and face. Nothing serious, nothing too deep, except the heavy ache in her chest.

Makeo knelt beside her, letting the water run between his long, clawed fingers. "If we're going to battle the Dolobra tomorrow, I need you to promise me something."

Aza dipped her flask into the water, the air bubbling up as it filled. "What is it?"

"If things don't go as we planned, I need you to promise you won't sacrifice yourself to cage the Dolobra."

"Why would I promise that?"

"Because you'd be damning yourself to an eternity of imprisonment with that monster."

"Silvix did it."

"Yes, but there wouldn't be another Shadow Heir to save you."

"My father's still alive. I know he is. He could do it," Aza whispered, letting her fingertips numb in the water. "If I just bought him some time."

"Even if he is alive, you don't know if he could walk the Plane." Makeo's voice tightened. "With Seela gone, who could teach him?"

"There were survivors who could teach him." She rose and stretched out her cramped legs. "I don't think there's much my father couldn't do."

"Every child thinks that about their father," Makeo murmured. "That doesn't make them right."

"So what if it doesn't? Isn't my life worth the hundreds of others I would save?"

Makeo met her gaze. "Not to me, it isn't."

Aza softened at that. She let the breath go out of her, the dark falling thickly between them now. The chattering of the brook and the rustling of leaves above them filling their silence. Not comfortable. Not painful. Just silence.

"It won't come to that," she said at last. "Zephyr and I will bait the Dolobra. Two traps at the same time. Together, it won't be able to resist the lure of our yanaa."

Without her constant visits to the Shadow Plane, her mind was finally sharpening once again, her energy returning. Everything seemed so much clearer to her now. With fresh muscles and mind, she would be stronger than when she had last faced Mogens. And with her brother fighting beside her, together they would strike fast and hard—killing the Dolobra in both realms once and for all.

"And if Conrad and the others come, then the Maldibor will be there to buy time," she continued.

And once she defeated the Dolobra, she'd have to move quickly to claim Mogens. If he disappeared again, who knew how long it would be before she got another chance to even the score. He would never stop coming for them, and she wouldn't spend her years wondering where he was and what he was plotting—looking over her shoulder, checking her drinks, sleeping with knife in hand, never truly resting… like her mother did. She would end this here.

"So you won't promise then?" he pressed.

She raised an eyebrow at him. "Do you lack faith in my plan?"

"Do you?" He straightened, towering over her. "You seem to have thought a lot about trapping the Dolobra in case we fail."

"I've learned lately that my confidence isn't always well placed, but I'll do what has to be done." She crossed her arms. "Isn't that what you said about Ivanora?"

Makeo growled and raked a paw through the fur between his ears. "That's not the same."

"Of course, it's not. Just two different kinds of life-changing sacrifice." She shared a half-smile. "I guess we're just not very good at making promises."

He grunted, his ears flattened against his head.

"But how about a small wager?"

"A wager with a Shadow Heir? That doesn't sound wise."

She eyed Windtorn as he bent his antlers down to the stream. "If the plan goes without a hitch, then—"

"That confident are we?"

She went on as if he hadn't spoken. "You put in a good word to Tekoa about maybe getting me a Dalteek."

He broke into a great booming laugh she hadn't heard in weeks. The very sound of it made her ache just a little less.

"You're still going on about that? And here I thought you'd finally given up."

"I'm just saying, put in a good word." She smirked. "You know, after I kill the monster I brought to life in the first place."

He nodded, eyes glinting with a smile. "Okay, I can do that. But what do I get if there is... a hitch?"

"What would you like?" she said lightly, the devil-may-care pre-battle high coursing through her now.

"Maybe we could be... like we used to be." He fiddled with the bags on Windtorn's saddle. "Close"

"We've always been close," she answered automatically, but even as she said it, she knew it wasn't true.

"No, Aza." He took a step toward her, the green of his gaze deepening with an urgent sincerity. "I want to be there for you, I want you to talk to me, I want us to laugh and have fun, I want us to be... together."

She cocked her head, her heart skipping with the idea of it. "Together?"

"N-no. Not like that." He looked away quickly, and if it had been a dark moon, Aza was sure his cheeks would've turned red. "You know... like before."

Before. When they'd been unscarred. When they'd shared worries, fears, and joy. When their eyes had sought each other's across a campfire. Could she even be that person anymore? She wasn't sure. But she was willing to try.

"The deal is struck." She stuck out a hand, and his paw swallowed hers. "Now, let's go kill a Dolobra."

The scent of smoke and death hung thick in the air when they arrived at Carceroc in the early morning, mounts heaving. The trees grew taller here, with branches that wove a thick canopy overhead, sheltering the lush forest floor sprinkled with stormblooms and starclover. Blue-backed singing bees fluttered among the dewy, scarlet flowers, humming softly. But between the massive trunks, Aza could just make out the movement of people and flicker of campfires.

A young, dark-furred Maldibor sentry emerged from the shadows to intercept them. Atop his brown Dalteek, he reached out to grasp arms with Makeo.

"Cousin, it's good to see you back. We worried something had befallen you." His green eyes shifted to Aza, and he bowed his head. "Shadow Heir."

Makeo slowed Windtorn to match the walking pace. "And you, Alakai. How's the camp since I left?"

"We were able to relocate the clan. But the strange Lost continue to ambush us from Carceroc. The Dragon Heir thinks something in the forest is creating them, but we haven't been able to get deep enough to find out what without the other creatures attacking."

"Casualties?" Aza asked.

"Three of our own," Alakai replied. "And a few of the humans the Dragon Heir brought with him, but everyone is tiring of the never-ending battle. They attack every night now."

Aza winced. Those would have been the Greens who had followed Zephyr down here. That probably hit him hard, and she still had to tell him about Witt… But the Dolobra hadn't attacked yet. So what were Mogens and Conrad waiting for?

The trees thinned into a small open lea, and the camp spread out before them. A handful of hastily erected tents ran in rows down the verdant field still wet with morning dew. And though men, women, and Maldibor strode between small fires, a strange, tense quiet stretched between the warriors. They nodded at Aza and Makeo with weary, preoccupied faces and whispered to each other over steaming tin mugs.

Energy and cheer seemed to have drained from the camp like water through sand. How many days had they been fighting? Aza turned to Alakai. "Where's my brother?"

The small Maldibor tipped his head and led them to a slightly larger tent. Even before they entered, Zephyr's raised voice cut through the air.

"We can't stay here forever. Can't we just leave Carceroc for the creatures and move the village to Catalede? They'll wear us down at this rate."

Tekoa's deep rumble answered, "But you've heard the yanaa prison of Carceroc cracking. The creatures of the forest are trying to escape their bonds. If we retreat now, we may just be leading them back to Catalede, where more innocents will be hurt."

"But surely no man has the power to break the magi's yanai barrier," Hoku cut in.

Makeo pushed aside the heavy canvas flap and gestured for Aza to enter. Zephyr, Hoku, Shadmundar, and the barrel-chested, rust-furred Maldibor chief, Tekoa, turned to her as she stepped inside. But Zephyr's black ragehound was the first to respond. She rushed at Aza with a happy yip, planting her paws on her chest and snuffling at her hair.

Aza ruffled the hound's fur with a wry grin. "Luna-girl, I missed you."

Zephyr's arms were around her next, his words equal parts ecstatic and angry. "Where have you been? I can't believe you *literally* disappeared." He stabbed an accusing finger at Makeo. "And you're late getting back, we thought something had happened."

She pushed him away. "Yes, yes. I'm sorry, all right? It wasn't my finest moment."

Zephyr looked over her shoulder. "But where's that lout Witt? I've missed his obnoxious face."

"Yes, he'd be appalled at the state of the food here," Shad added from behind Zephyr's leg.

Aza stilled, and Zephyr's gaze shifted from her crumpled expression to Makeo's solemn one. His back straightened even as his face fell. "Ah." He swallowed. "I see. Something *did* happen."

"Yes." Aza sighed. "It did." She smoothed her mussed hair from her face. "But I think I have some answers to your questions."

Tekoa and his daughter, Hoku, with bandages wrapped around one arm, listened to her story with patient, expressionless faces, while Zephyr paced back and forth, interjecting far more than necessary with questions, comments, and whatever other thoughts popped into his head. She fought the urge to throttle him as she finally came to her hastily concocted plan.

"So, I think the cracking you're hearing must be the Dolobra fighting to get free somehow. But if Zephyr and I act as bait and draw it to us, I think we'll be strong enough to destroy it."

"You *think*?" Zephyr cut in.

"What makes you think you can defeat it?" Hoku asked with a milder tone.

"When I faced it the first time, I was exhausted, surprised, and my mind was gone, and even so, I could hit it." Her hands tightened into fists. "Now that I'm full strength and ready, it'll be a fair fight. And with Zephyr attacking its physical body, my blows on the Shadow Plane should actually affect it."

"What makes you think that my fire can harm it?" Zephyr asked, the purple shadows dark beneath his eyes. "While my flames seem to keep most of the Carceroc creatures at bay, it harms very few of them. My fire is meant for the Lost... not these other beasts."

Tekoa held out a hand to calm him. "It sounds like there are a lot of things we don't know, but if Aza is right, we won't have much time before the Dolobra escapes, and we're forced to do something."

"The fighter who lands the first blow always has the advantage," Makeo said.

Tekoa reached out and squeezed his daughter's good arm. "We're familiar with the creatures of Carceroc and will be able to do our part while you handle the Dolobra."

A cold smile curved Aza's lips. Maybe it wasn't the best plan, but the Maldibor were behind it, and their strength was a force to be reckoned with. "Be on the lookout too. Conrad and Mogens are also here somewhere, and they're the ones controlling people."

"Do we need to worry about them taking control of us?" Hoku asked, concern creasing her forehead.

Makeo stepped forward. "From Seela's letter, it seems like the more yanaa you have, the more you can resist their control. And through the curse, the Maldibor have yanaa running through their veins."

"But Seela said the novices were overcome, so the other humans…" Aza licked her lips. "Could be a liability."

"We'll send them away." Zephyr ran an agitated hand through his wild nest of brown hair. "We can't have our own turning on us and… this is beyond them anyway."

Tekoa nodded. "Do it now and take your rest while you can. The longer we wait, the more time our enemies have to strike first. But this eve, before the sun is set, we will call the Dolobra." He sighed, a big heavy breath. "And let's just hope he's not waiting for us."

24

INTO BATTLE

Zephyr and Luna's footsteps shuffled behind Aza as she watched the red sun burrow into the dark tangle of Carceroc, the billowing clouds turning navy with the promise of night. The forest crackled in front of her, like a far-off storm, the sound rising and falling like something was chipping away at the magical barrier from within. For a moment, the silence weighed heavily between them.

"I'm sorry about Witt," Aza whispered.

Luna whined, and Zephyr absent-mindedly scratched behind her ears. "Don't say that, Azy." An urgent undercurrent steeled his soft words. "I'm the one who sent him after you in the first place, and then he was the one who decided to stay, even when you tried to warn them off." He sighed and Luna seemed to sigh with him. "We do the best we can to protect the people we love, but we aren't the masters of their fate." He nodded, as if speaking more for his own benefit than hers. "Still, I'll miss the clown."

"Me too."

A call pulled their attention back toward the camp. "Tekoa's rallying the others." Zephyr took a deep breath beside her, and she could practically feel the nervous energy rolling off him.

"Good." Aza ran a hand along the belt of knives crossing her chest and the daggers resting against her thighs. "Have you heard from Mother and Father since you left Catalede?"

He lit and extinguished a flame in his hand over and over. "There was a harehawk some weeks back. They wrote to the Maldibor of finding a Lost army amid the Rastgol. They were having luck rallying the soldiers of Faveno, so they didn't expect it to bleed this far west. But they might call for reinforcements if things turn bleak."

Aza sagged with relief. Proof of life. Even if she failed here, Mogens and Conrad would have to fight through two more Heirs. She tapped her lip. Could they also be responsible for the Lost in the West? They had to be. A shiver ran down her spine. How much power did Idriel's Children have?

"Did you tell them of the troubles of the Maldibor?"

He shook his head. "Tekoa didn't want to disturb them further while they were already embattled." He tossed his fireball from hand to hand. "But I still worry about them."

Tekoa and Makeo's howls rang through the camp as they mustered the Maldibor to arms. The warriors clustered in their heavy leather armor, broadswords hanging from their backs, while Tekoa barked out a plan. All forty stood steady with practiced hands resting on gleaming weapons, more green-eyed women than beasts. Strong as they were, they wouldn't be able to hold out for long with so few.

Zephyr separated the fire into two and then three spheres swirling between his fingers. "So this, Dolobra, the soul-eating creature. Is it as terrifying as the Maldibor grandmothers say it is?" He tried to laugh, but she could hear the edge to his words. The fear of the unknown. Luna nosed his leg with a low growl.

"Not as scary as your morning breath," Aza replied.

His smile turned genuine as Makeo and Tekoa joined them. They loomed even larger than usual with their armor and weapons, their green eyes hard.

Makeo's arm brushed Aza's, his voice loud enough for only her ears. "As much as I'd like to win our wager, I'd much prefer this went without a hitch, and I help you pick out a Dalteek fawn."

She reached out and squeezed his paw. "No hitches."

His eyes held hers for a long, agonizing moment, the unspoken feelings twisting together between them, but they didn't have time to voice the words.

Tekoa unsheathed the broadsword from his back. "Call the monster."

Aza nodded, looking from Makeo to Zephyr. "Remember to wait for the signal. The timing has to be perfect." Taking a deep breath to calm her racing heart, she stepped forward into the cusp of the forest. Zephyr held out a hand to order Luna back before he joined her. With a shared glance, he let the fire grow in his hands, his yanaa building in an impressive inferno that billowed up toward the dying sun. The shadows of Carceroc melted away before it, and Aza held up a hand to shield herself from the heat.

His flames crackling and snapping, Zephyr shouted out into the still forest. "Enough of these games, Conrad." Farther in the depths of the forest, Aza could make out something shifting in the darkness. "Show your face and bring your pet."

With slow, measured steps, a line of Rastgol emerged from the forest. Gaping wounds and crusted blood adorned some, while others seemed whole and healthy as they marched—the line between Lost and human blurred with this new dark yanaa.

They outnumbered the Maldibor, but not by many. This was something they could handle. Behind them, monsters of darkness slid through the shadows, but they wouldn't be able to step beyond their bounds unless the barrier failed. From among their shifting, a towering figure resolved in Zephyr's flickering light.

Its jaw swung as if on a loose hinge, and Zephyr's flames illuminated the black greed in its eyes. The same pale creature that had haunted the Shadow Plane now stalked the Carceroc trees. "Oh, my dear child, my mouth drools for your sweet ignorance."

The creature stepped forward and shrilled a piercing note. With it, the translucent barrier of Carceroc crackled and shuddered around them, its fissures shimmering like green lightning bolts in the wavering air.

Alarm flooded through Aza. If it broke the barrier the mankillers would be loose… But she didn't have time to think as Conrad's army lurched forward. Howling, the Maldibor charged to meet them, Makeo rushing forward with his kin. A pang of fear ripped through Aza as she lost sight of his flashing blade. *Odriel spare him.*

Zephyr stepped toward the trees with their small army, their warriors giving him a wide berth. His light illuminated the Rastgol, the Maldibor, and the looming Dolobra. But then there was someone else. A dim green glow in the far off somewhere.

Mogens was out there.

Her brother's fire lashed out toward the Dolobra and with the clash of steel-on-steel ringing through the air, Aza knew she couldn't delay. She had to follow the plan. She would have to come back for Mogens.

Her back braced against a tree, she let the battle fade away. Rested and strong, it took her only moments to imagine the door and let her yanaa unlock it, sweeping her from the battle.

The adrenaline surged through her even in the quiet Plane. She'd been prepared to take off in search of the Dolobra, but there was no need.

"Duck," shouted Silvix from somewhere on the wind.

Aza leapt forward with a roll, and the Dolobra's long, clawed arm raked through the air where her head had been. She drew her daggers and swirled to face it. Though it looked the same as she had last seen it, a strain tightened its face, and its muscles twitched and jumped.

"So you're fool enough to come—"

Aza didn't give the creature time to prattle on. Darting forward, she slashed her daggers through its ankles, and the beast cried out in rage. It kicked at her, and she sprang away before closing in again to stab at its underbelly.

With a shrill scream, the monster brought its spiked fists down to crush her, and she rolled to the right, breathing fast. She was definitely hurting it, but the longer the battle stretched out, the smaller her chances. She needed a mortal blow—and fast.

She rushed it straight on, and its reaching fingers grabbed at her. She leapt onto its wrist, and with quick feet ran up its spindly arm. Its other hand moved to swat her like a biting fly, but she jumped again onto its shoulder, plunging her dagger, one, two, three times into its chest. The impact of bone on metal rattled through her fingers and up to her shoulder, its stringy muscles cutting loose beneath her blades as she stabbed again and again.

Roaring, it dropped to its knees, and Aza could practically feel the victory close at hand. The Dolobra snapped its jaws at her, and she pushed away. She fell to the ground and rolled between its feet before its claws found her once more. Her muscles tensed to scale its back, when Silvix's disembodied voice cut through the air once more.

"Behind you!"

This time when Aza whirled, she wasn't quite fast enough to avoid the blade trying to plunge into her back. The edge cut through her arm instead, and its partner slashed at her throat. She ducked the second and danced away, her arm burning with pain.

It turned out, she wouldn't have to go back for Mogens. He stood before her now, his skeletal bones gleaming white from his sloughing gray skin.

"It's rude not to die when expected, but I'm glad to add a fourth Heir to my trophies. Maybe an ear to go with your grandfather's? A lock of hair perhaps?" He rushed forward again, and Aza parried his onslaught, her arm burning.

This was definitely a hitch.

"Maybe you should set the example." She darted away, trying to find her bearings, while one eye tracked the Dolobra stumbling to its feet. Its head shook as though warding off invisible blows, its attention no longer on her. Her brother was making good on his end of the attack. She could not waste this moment.

"But you'll have to wait your turn." She knocked Mogens' blade out of the way, and raced toward the creature, letting her yanaa spill from her body in wide ripples. "Come on, you big ugly beast, aren't you hungry?"

"The wait only makes the marrow sweeter," the Dolobra replied with a jagged smile.

Her heavy limbs weighed her down while the Dolobra surged forward, his eyes pinned on her like a light in the darkness. Mogens gave chase, but even he had to spin away from the Dolobra's swinging limbs. Mogens' dagger just brushed her shoulder as she slashed at the Dolobra's hands.

"Too slow," she taunted, beating away Mogens' stabbing thrusts.

She whirled back again, but the Dolobra's fist caught her this time, whipping her across the field in a crunch of bone. She wheezed and clutched her cracked ribs. The Dolobra stalked closer to its wounded prey, and she pulled the knives from her belt, throwing them with shaking hands.

"Hush now, my lovely, we can go slow," crooned the Dolobra.

She staggered to her feet, blade at the ready, but knowing she wouldn't be able to evade again.

Silvix's voice whispered in her ear, the only aid he had to offer. "Now's your chance girl, release all your yanaa onto the Dolobra. You can trap it here."

Aza smiled at his words, and Mogens snarled from across the field. "You overestimate her. She has neither the skill nor the heart." He laughed. "The Shadow Heir works alone, after all."

She coughed, the iron tang of blood in her mouth. "Who wants to repeat old tricks anyway?" And with that, she lifted her head back and howled long and loud. The Dolobra's fingers closed around her, and black edged her vision as it squeezed her already broken bones.

"One down," Mogens said. "Now for the boy."

Before Aza, the Dolobra's snapping jaws opened wide, drool dripping from the long mess of teeth. Struggling, she screamed with rage and pain and fear. She had been too late after all. Her timing had been off. She only hoped Zephyr and Makeo would have the sense to retreat.

Then the Dolobra paused. Aza squirmed as its foul breath misted hot against her face, just before its head slumped forward to reveal Makeo on its back, his broadsword gleaming black and a gaping wound all but decapitating the Dolobra from the rear.

His chest heaving and the Dolobra's head hanging from a sinewy strand, Makeo met her eyes for only a pained moment before disappearing back into the living world.

But Aza didn't have time for relief. Still encased in the Dolobra's tight death grip, she fell to the ground. Mogens turned toward her once more, strangely unaffected by the death of the Dolobra they'd gone through so much effort to free.

"Such a clever rabbit, and yet here you are still wriggling in the trap. Too stupid to know you've already lost." He raised his dagger. "It's really a shame you won't get to see what happens next."

Aza struggled to get free, her arms hidden by the Dolobra's claws. Gasping with pain and vision dotted with black splotches, she shifted her dagger in her off hand. It was suitably loose, but the other was still hopelessly pinned in the Dolobra's grasp.

Still, she only needed one.

Mogens' dagger arced down onto Aza's head, and she threw herself back, burying the blade into the meat of the Dolobra's fist. Not missing a beat, her free hand snaked from its hiding place to slash across Mogens' throat.

"Come now, Mogens," she tutted. "Eyes deceive."

Still the green light burned in his eyes, and panic coursed through Aza. If she didn't kill him here, she might not get another chance. Flooding yanaa into her blade, she slashed again and again, hacking until his head rolled from his body. And still she was unsatisfied. She struggled to free herself from the Dolobra's fingers, but not before a mass of dark worm-like creatures wriggled from the silver grass, swarming over Mogens' body with circular, leeching jaws.

"Fear not, girl. Even *he* cannot escape this fate," Silvix said, his silvery form looking on beside her. "In the Shadow Plane, nothing goes to waste."

She watched in transfixed horror, as thousands of the wraiths dismantled Mogens before her eyes, until even the rotten smell of him had been whisked away on the wind.

"Thank Odriel. He's finally gone." With that, Aza let herself slump over with relief, her strength still bleeding away with every second.

But she didn't have but a moment before the black worms swarmed toward the Dolobra. Her mind scrambled for the door as the wraiths frantically wriggled between the creature's fingers. At last, she tugged open the door and slipped back into the world of the living.

The noise of the battlefield ripped through the quiet of the Shadow Plane, and Aza opened her eyes to dark chaos. Farther back in the trees, the ghostly white mass of the Dolobra had collapsed into a dead heap. But the battle raged on nearly oblivious to this victory. Shouts and screams ripped through the chaos of the night, the Maldibor and the Rastgol clashing together between the trees and the field beyond.

So Mogens hadn't been the one controlling them. That left just one other option.

Her brother was easy to find with his fiery blade cutting through the night. She stumbled toward him, ribs and arm screaming with unseen wounds. *It's all in my head. It's all in my head,* she repeated to herself, her teeth grinding together. *There's nothing wrong with my bones and muscles.* But that didn't stop the pain.

"Zephyr," she yelled, her voice lost amid the din of battle.

She opened her mouth to shout again, when a Rastgol turned toward her. She pulled a knife from her belt and threw it with a cry of pain. The blade sank into his green eye, but still he surged forward. As his blade lashed out, she stepped to the side and slashed at him. Another approached her from the left, blocking her from her brother's flame. She parried their blows, pain lancing through her with every jarring clash.

Finally, seeing an opening, she stepped into the Rastgol, separating his neck from his shoulders, but she couldn't turn fast enough for the second. She raised her daggers just a moment too late and braced for the slice of the edge.

Instead, a broadsword smashed down on the man, and Makeo was there beside her, his breath coming fast and blood matting his blond fur. "Are you all right?"

"Mogens is dead." She stumbled forward. "I have to reach Zephyr. Conrad has got to be controlling these things. If we can kill him, the battle will be over."

Makeo took her elbow, steadying her as she lurched forward. "Is he here?"

"Aza!" Zephyr had spotted them now and battled through the throng of Rastgol surrounding him, lashing out with his flaming sword. "The Dolobra has fallen."

She nodded and parried the blade thrusting for her. "We still have to kill the necromancer. Have you seen a green aura?"

Zephyr whirled, taking out the two approaching from behind. "There are two." He pointed. "But they're deeper in the forest, and the Carceroc creatures are protecting them." His expression darkened. "I think they're being controlled as well."

"It could be another trap," Makeo said with a grunt as he swung his sword again.

"But if the Dolobra is dead, why haven't they retreated?" She surveyed the battlefield. Though it raged on, the Maldibor clearly had the upper hand. "Mogens acted as if they were planning something else."

"And if we don't strike now, we may be unfortunate enough to find out what," Makeo finished for her.

Aza squinted into the darkness at the two glowing, green figures. One closer and one farther off. Cloaked in shadow, she could make it without drawing any attention to herself. But which one?

She straightened and crossed the gloom to Zephyr's side. "Zephyr, if you distract the creatures, I will deal with Conrad… and whoever stands beside him."

"Take the farther." Makeo raised his broadsword. "With the flames as a distraction, I'll be able to make it to the closer."

She flashed a smile at him, ignoring the pain. "No hitches."

"I think I've already won that bet." His eyes shone with a weary glint of humor.

She snorted. "And I thought it was going rather well." She slapped her brother on the shoulder. "Put on a good show, Zeph."

Then with that, she let the shadows fall over her.

25
IDRIEL'S CHILDREN

Sliding through the trees, Aza focused on her breathing. Small, silent puffs of air. She rolled her steps heel to toe as silent as a cat in the night. With the shadows around her, the eyes of the warriors all slid away, the noises of battle dimming behind as she cut into the darkness of the forest. Her childhood monsters vanquished, she felt no fear. No whispers called to her.

Pain and exhaustion stabbed through her focus, but they were familiar friends by now. Even as they needled her, Seela's voice echoed in her thoughts, strong and true. *"Control your mind first, and your body will follow."* Aza could practically see her straight back and arched eyebrows challenging her. *"The mind always fails before the body. Focus. Believe it possible and feel your own limitations disappear."*

A glowing pair of green eyes loomed in front of her, and at first, she thought Seela had awoken from the grave to stand in front of her. In another breath, she realized it was a beautifully translucent woman—a syrish— standing oddly still in the darkness. Her very voice could draw a soul from its body. She padded past the monster and found herself in a veritable thicket of life. Cyclogres, griegals, giants, and terraverms, surrounded her, green eyes unnaturally fluorescent in the dark. Like the Hunters. Marked with yanaa. Waiting for something.

Zephyr had been right. These creatures were being controlled. But why? Without the Dolobra to break the yanai barrier that imprisoned them, they had no chance of escaping Carceroc. Was Conrad just planning on staying here with this as his personal guard? She smiled to herself. If so, he had severely underestimated her. There were many things in Carceroc that couldn't be killed with fire and steel... but she didn't need to kill them. And

179

she had a feeling Conrad bled just like her.

She found him wedged between the feet of a cyclogre, his eyes rolled in the back of his head as his hands twitched, like a strange puppeteer above his marionettes. *Let's see how quickly I can cut those strings.* On silent, weary feet, she crept up behind Conrad, the perfumed smell of his oiled hair tickling her nose. She gripped one of his shoulders and—

"Don't do it, Shadow Heir," a cold, familiar voice cut through the darkness. "Or your pet dog dies."

Aza paused, her dagger edge at Conrad's throat and his hands scrabbling fruitlessly at her arm. Did she mean Luna? Locking Conrad's neck in the crook of her elbow, she turned toward the voice and froze.

Makeo's huge, prone body floated in front of Ivanora, her green aura connecting him to her.

"What are you doing here, Ivanora?"

"Yo—" Conrad started.

Aza pressed the blade edge harder against his throat, silencing him. "Put Makeo down and just walk away from all of this," she called. "You're not a necromancer. You're not one of *them.*"

"Oh, girl." A smile curved her crimson lips. "I'm much more than just another magus, now." She curled her fingers tighter into a fist, and the audible snap of a bone cracked through the air. Makeo howled with pain.

"Stop it!" Aza shouted. "Why are you doing this?"

"You know…" Ivanora brought a mocking finger to her cheek, disgust twisting her beautiful features into something vile. "I used to think it was just Elika I hated, these brutish beasts that he spawned, and the repulsive humans who killed my sister for no reason at all." She curled her hand and another bone in Makeo's body snapped. His yell grated on Aza's heart. "But then, Valente here revealed what I had missed. I hate *all* humans."

"Conrad *is* human!" Aza held him up as if to brandish the proof of his flesh and blood—of his mortality. "He's fooling you."

Ivanora wagged a finger at her, like a scolding teacher. "No, no dear. Valente, myself, and our dear Mogens who sacrificed himself for the cause…" She raised a hand with a flourish. "We are the children of Idriel."

"Idriel is a demon of death." Confusion swirled through Aza's mind as she tried to piece together the rest of Ivanora's plan. "And he's dead. My parents killed him."

Ivanora rolled her eyes, though a smile curled her lips. A glutted predator toying with its prey. "All that time with the Wraith-Called and still so slow-minded. Weak. Arrogant."

Aza's stomach turned at the familiarity of the words.

"Idriel will wipe Okarria clean," Ivanora continued. "We will start anew, free of the tragedy of death."

"And I thought you were smart enough not to be wooed with lies and false promises," Aza snapped, her mind desperately racing for a way out of this.

"It's really no matter if you believe me or not." She shrugged. "You will see the proof before we're done."

"The Dolobra is dead. Mogens is dead. Your Rastgol corpses are overwhelmed." Aza scoffed. "Are you just going to hide here in Carceroc with your other puppets?"

"And so short-sighted at that." Ivanora sighed theatrically. "Best just to show you, but I am afraid I do need that one first, please."

Conrad struggled, and Aza tightened her grip on him again, the warm blood trickling from his throat down her arm. She should just kill him. Whatever Ivanora was planning would surely take many more lives. That possible future for Makeo's one life. It wasn't worth the trade. And yet... her hand stilled.

Ivanora flexed her fingers, and two more bones snapped.

Makeo roared in pain, but even as he did, he managed to get three words out against whatever spell was holding him. "Do it, Aza."

Cold sweat slid down Aza's temples. "Even if I let Conrad go, you'll kill Makeo anyway."

"I will not," Ivanora said, her face firm. "You can have your creature. I swear it on Idriel himself. A magus keeps her word, unlike you humans."

"And reverse his curse as well," Aza added, trying to buy herself time to think. Her gaze swiveled in the night, looking for anything she could use to her advantage, anyone who could help her. But the forest was emptied, and her brother's flame was still too far away, embroiled with Conrad's creatures.

Ivanora laughed, long and hard. "Do you know? He had the nerve to ask the very same thing. Practically offered himself to me. I do regret that curse." Her face hardened. "I should have worn Elika's pelt like a coat instead." She stalked toward Aza, her long caramel hair flowing behind her. "You get his wretched life. And that's only because I'm feeling generous this evening." Another bone snapped, and Makeo bit down. "But you best do it quickly, or I fear he will never be the same."

Ivanora curled her fingers as if to squeeze the life from Makeo. His strangled screams shredded the darkness, and Aza wilted under them. To lose Makeo would be to die herself. She could *not* lose him too. No matter the cost.

"Fine. I let Conrad go, and you leave us be." She spread out a hand to encompass the battle behind her. "All of us."

Ivanora shrugged as if this were her plan all along. "Of course."

With that, Aza pushed Conrad toward her, and Makeo dropped to the ground with a sharp cry. She rushed toward him, nearly brushing by Ivanora as she practically floated to where Conrad knelt, cursing and holding a hand to his bleeding throat.

Then he started to laugh, a maddened, frenzied sound. "You'll regret this, you stupid girl." His smile was blinding white in the dark. Behind him, two hulking cyclogres dragged something away into the blackness. "Just remember, all of this was made possible by you."

Aza said nothing as she stood over Makeo's groaning form. No matter what choice she'd made, she would've regretted it. But one of them would've taken a piece of her soul. She was a killer, yes. But she was a protector first. And if she didn't protect her friends, well then, she might as well follow Ivanora into the darkness. Makeo... and the rest of them... made everything else bearable. Without them, she'd be lost.

Ivanora took Conrad by the arm and pulled him to his feet. "Come, my dear. That's enough for one night. I think it's time we depart." She looked over her shoulder, her eyes catching on Zephyr's flames edging closer. "Oh, but there is that one thing I almost forgot. The real reason we're here. Thank you so much for giving me time to finish the spell." She lifted her hands, and her green aura rose into the forest. High in the canopy, it shot away like an explosion of shooting stars. The crackling of the forest rose in a great thunderous crashing that ended in a deafening shatter like a thousand mirrors breaking at once.

The still creatures of Carceroc suddenly came to life, surging forward in a great churn, and Aza's heart went cold. With Carceroc broken, the man-killers were free. At best, a whole host of predators had been released into the world. At worst, a formidable army at the hands of... Aza snapped to Conrad disappearing into the night with Ivanora gliding alongside him. Far, but not too far.

She drew a knife from her belt and let it sing into the air. Just missing, it buried itself into the back of Conrad's shoulder. He cried out in pain, and the green faded from the creatures' eyes. She threw the second, and Ivanora lashed out in a flash of light, the knife grazing his cheek instead of burying into his neck.

"Wretched child." A weak rush of Ivanora's depleted yanaa swept Aza off her feet. When she looked up again, the magus and the necromancer were gone.

Freed from both their puppeteer and their cage, the Carceroc creatures bellowed with rage and fury, claws and teeth primed to rip through anyone in their path. With her last bit of strength, Aza dragged the now unconscious Makeo into the shelter of a tree trunk as the mankillers, large and small, stampeded toward her brother's fire.

"To me!" Zephyr yelled as the murderous creatures surrounded the battle's survivors. Zephyr's fire billowed in a protective ring around them. But he was too weak. His shoulders shook as he struggled to hold the creatures at bay.

And Aza had even less to give. She pulled a knife from her sheath as something crept toward them in the darkness, tall like a man but with only a gaping mouth for a face. Like something out of the Shadow Plane, but there was no escape here. Staggering to her feet, Aza put herself between Makeo and the mankiller, wheezing with every movement. If they were going to the Mortal Wood, she would be going first.

Sweat stinging her eyes, she lifted her hand to throw the knife, when something hurtled out of the dark. Aza wheeled around to take on the new threat, and steel flashed in front of her face. Her heart seemed to stop as she flinched away, but the blade was not meant for her.

The dagger flew into the creature's middle, glancing off its strange armored skin. Screeching with fury, the creature backpedaled as the invisible onslaught continued blow after blow after merciless blow.

Her brother's scream drew her gaze back to his dying fire, where a mob of cyclogres and terraverms closed in. She opened her mouth to scream his name, when an explosion of flames billowed through the darkness, like a sudden dawn hurtling from the earth into the sky.

Aza threw her body over Makeo as a gust of burning air rippled over them. With her skin prickling in the intense heat, and the trees scorching around her, Aza looked up to see Carceroc's mankillers scattering in a mad stampede to escape the column of molten fire pouring down from the sky that was Kaia Dashul Thane.

The Dragon Heir had arrived.

Aza looked to where a now visible figure in black rested the flat of his obsidian blade on his shoulder, and she broke into a hiccup of hysterical laughter. "Papa," she whispered. "How did you…?"

In three strides he had her wrapped in a gentle embrace. "I heard you calling me, Aza. I don't know how you did it, but I *heard* you."

"I'm so sorry." She shook her head, her eyes swimming with tears of relief and pain and sorrow. "I couldn't do it on my own."

"Oh, Aza," he said, his own words choking. "No one ever asked you to."

And behind him, Silvix's silvery form nodded with approval.

The dawn glowed navy blue on the dew-laced meadow, a quiet breeze cleansing the air. Aza shifted Makeo's bulky form onto a blanket in the long grass. She tended to his smaller injuries while the more seasoned healers addressed the critical cases in the open field of the injured. His breaths were still shallow and weak, and his body was covered with bleeding cuts she couldn't assess under his thick fur. Groaning, his eyelids fluttered on the brink of consciousness and a jolt of hope raced through her.

"C'mon, Makeo," she whispered. "I just traded the world for you, so you have to hang in there."

"Shouldn't... have done that," he managed through his wheezes of pain.

She lightly placed her hand on his and wrinkled her nose with a smile. "Well, it was a bit of a hitch, so I had to make sure I could still make good on my bet."

She swallowed, still trying to wrap her head around what had happened. Hoku had been right, a human would never have had enough yanaa to break the magi's barrier, but a magus... It hadn't been the Dolobra cracking the barrier after all. It had been Ivanora. *That's* what she'd been researching in Dorinar's libraries. That's the great power Seela had sensed, and that had been the third figure standing with Mogens and Conrad in the Shadow Plane. The power that had forced Seela to trick Aza into releasing the Dolobra. Aza knocked her head against the tree trunk. How had she not made the connections?

"Don't blame yourself," Makeo said weakly, eyes still closed. "The Dolobra is dead. Mogens is dead. And you are alive." Makeo's paw lightly squeezed hers. "The rest we can fix."

Aza nodded. It was a hollow victory. But with the Heir killer gone, maybe she would sleep a little better at night. "*We* are alive." From across the field, she heard her mother calling her name.

Makeo drew in a rattling breath. "Did you really ask Ivanora to revert the curse?"

"Did you?" Aza returned. "I was just trying to buy time." She ran her fingers through the fur on his arm. "But when she's gone, and the curse is broken, I'll miss this side of you."

"When she's gone?"

Aza nodded. "I don't know how to kill a magus, Keo, but if she's trying to revive Idriel, you can bet your hide I'll figure it out."

26
NOT ALONE

Aza sat beside Makeo's bed in the now mostly empty Carceroc. The flickering lantern light glowed over Makeo's curled form, his breath huffing evenly from his bandaged body. Outside the cabin in the early night, the Maldibor gathered for the dark moon, wisps of music and laughter drifting on the breeze. Her eyes wandered to where her parents laughed with Tekoa by the fire. Her father's arm wound tightly around her mother's shoulders, and Shadmundar perched on a nearby stump, his black fur finally glossy and thick again.

For a moment, she flashed back to telling her parents the whole ghastly story on the edge of the still-bloody battleground. From abandoning Zephyr, to freeing the Dolobra, to killing Mogens on the Shadow Plane. Aza had expected heated words and a harsh rebuke, but instead her mother had just wrapped her arms tightly around Aza.

"Thank you, Aza, for doing what I couldn't," she whispered. "I knew the moment he was gone, like a knife had been finally pulled from my chest." Her brown eyes had gleamed as they'd met Aza's. "At least one nightmare has ended."

Luna's happy bark returned Aza to the present. Not far off, her brother held a bottle of wine out of Hoku's reach while she chased him around the grassy square, with Luna playfully nipping at his heels. The Maldibor children pointed and giggled from a nearby fire, just as she and Makeo might have done years ago.

After two weeks of tending the wounded and mourning their losses in the battle of Carceroc, the Heirs and the Maldibor tribe were finally ready to celebrate the lives that still went on—celebrate survival and hope and perhaps even the death of a monster... or two. Still, the cheerful anticipation of the dark moon was quieter than in days past. On the village edge, hulking Maldibor sentries diligently searched the night where they'd once celebrated freely, even in a forest of monsters.

Aza returned her gaze to the crinkled letter in her hands. A note from the Faveno shields still guarding the west, where the Rastgol had suddenly retreated for now... probably with Conrad and Ivanora safely in their midst. Aza rested her chin on her fist with a sigh. There was still so much to do. As soon as Makeo was well, they would have to go after Ivanora and Conrad. They had to be stopped before they raised Idriel from the dead—however they were managing that. The Heirs would probably have to visit Dorinar's library again to figure it out. Not to mention the bloodthirsty creatures of Carceroc now roaming freely across Okarria...

Makeo stirred in front of her, and she smiled. But those problems would have to wait. Now was the time to rest and regroup. Hard-won time. But time nonetheless.

Groaning, Makeo sat up, bandages wrapping both of his arms and his chest. "How long was I out this time?" he grumbled, his voice thick with sleep.

"A little more than a day."

"You have to tell your mother to stop giving me that pain tonic; it makes me sleep too much."

"That's what it's supposed to do, so you give yourself time to heal." She nudged a plate of food toward him. "And your uncle brought this for you too."

Makeo cocked his head to the commotion outside, his words lined with longing. "It's a dark moon night, isn't it?"

Aza's mouth curved up, and she offered him her arm. "Would you like to go out?"

He raised an eyebrow at her. "How are you going to help me when you're still injured yourself?"

"It's better than it was." She stretched her arms experimentally, and her invisible wounds protested with a stiffening ache. "And besides, my injuries are just in my head."

"The things in your head are still real, Aza."

Her smile widened. "You don't even want to know what's going on in my head, Keo."

"Maybe not." He accepted her hand with a chuckle and put his bandaged arm around her shoulder, leaning against her as little as he could. "But sometimes, I like guessing all the same."

She opened the cabin door into the mild summer night. Families clustered around fires in the grassy square, their necks craned to the stars as they waited for midnight. Though more subdued than usual, smiles, food, and wine flowed aplenty.

Aza led Makeo in a wide circle around the fires, smiling and nodding to friends and family. Her mother's gaze landed on them, her brown eyes flicking from Aza to Makeo, and she nodded at Aza with a knowing smile. Even though there were still monsters in the night and Idriel's Children at work, together they savored this sweet moment of peace—the lull in the storm.

They looked on from the edge of the square as her parents, Zephyr, Tekoa, Shadmundar, and Hoku all sat together, sharing plates of smoked meat and honey cakes. And if Aza looked hard enough, she thought she could even make out the silvery shape of Witt's smile glimmering beside Zephyr, his own plate heaped high with food. She stilled at the sight, her heart skipping a beat and a wistful smile crossing her face. Then, with a wink, he dissolved into the smoke of the fire, and his place was empty once more.

"About that bet..." Makeo started, gesturing away from the square.

Aza raised a brow at him, her heart beating again, now with a bittersweet ache. "What about it?"

"I believe your plan went very much without a hitch, don't you think?" His eyes twinkled with mischief.

She pursed her lips to hide the grin. "Sure, Keo, I totally meant for Carceroc to break open and to let the necromancer get away."

He nodded in mock seriousness. "I thought so. And as you know, I'm a Maldibor of my word."

Aza didn't dare herself to speak as he led her to a low building smelling of hay and beast.

"Not to mention, when Windtorn's mate foaled last spring, I may have asked my uncle to let me place the fawn."

"No, you didn't," Aza whispered.

Makeo led her to a stall with a bright-eyed Dalteek, its coat a blue-black of the midnight sky and a fluffy mane of creamy wheat encircling its neck.

"What do you think of her?" Makeo murmured, reaching out to pet the Dalteek's soft nose.

"I... I... don't know if I can accept this." Aza ran her fingers through the thick lion-like mane, resisting the urge to wrap her arms around the creature.

"Of course, you can," Makeo snorted. "Because we all know there were all kinds of hitches in your plan, so that makes us friends again, which means it would be downright rude not to accept my gift of your heart's desire."

Aza smothered a laugh. "Okay, I suppose." She shrugged, feigning reluctance. "If I must... but what's her name?"

"Starsong."

Outside, the Maldibor counted the seconds to midnight with raucous abandon.

"Starsong." As Aza whispered her name, a bell tolled in the square, and

Makeo began to change beside her. Fur, tail, and ears all receded, leaving the shaggy-haired boy she'd known all her life. This time though, his loose bandages sagged to reveal the many additions to the old scar down his chest.

He smiled down at her with soft eyes, his happiness melding with hers as a fiddle began to play with an enthusiastic cheer outside.

Aza looked away. "There is one problem though."

"Oh?" he said, raising his eyebrows.

"I don't think we can be friends."

His shoulders sagged just a touch. "…Oh well I…"

Aza crossed the charged air between them, pressing her mouth to his quickly and without hesitation, his lips soft and warm against hers. An echo of the kiss she'd been thinking about for the last three years.

She pulled back, her fingers lacing with his. His eyes widened, his long golden eyelashes blinking with surprise.

"I don't care about your curse or mine. I just want us. I want to be there for you… to make up for all the times I wasn't." She edged closer, her chest nearly touching his as she looked up into his emerald eyes. She pressed his hand to her cheek with a smirk. "Besides, I don't have friends."

Still, he said nothing, and she let her gaze drop to the floor, doubt fluttering in her stomach. "Is… that all right?"

His confusion melted into the widest smile she'd ever seen, his eyes gleaming. He bent his head and kissed her long and hard, his bandaged arm pulling her at the waist. Her lips caught fire under his searching kiss, her body molding to his and her mind emptying of everything but him. Only Keo.

With a sigh, he finally pulled away, still smiling, his forehead leaning against hers. "You have no idea how long I've wanted to hear you say that." He paused, a flicker of worry wrinkling his bliss. "I thought after I changed…"

She silenced him with another kiss, this one slow and tender. Flushed and breathless, she squeezed his hand. "I never once cared about that. I want to be with you, Keo. For one day in twenty, or one in a hundred. You're worth any curse."

His smile widened again, setting Aza's heart aflame, the cold shadows in her melting away into a warmth that filled her from her fingers to her hair. She had never really been heartless. Makeo had just been keeping it for her all along. He pressed his lips to her forehead and then to her cheek, the jubilant fiddle slowing to a soft croon.

"Dance with me then?" he breathed into her ear.

"With you?" She nodded. "Always."

EPILOGUE

"Years of work and patience." Conrad paced his marble floors, hands flying about in a rage. "And now Mogens is dead, and the Heirs are still alive." He picked up a vase and hurled it against a portrait on the wall in an explosion of ceramic and glass shards. "How did she even kill him? I thought his body was supposed to be eternal."

"Calm down," Ivanora purred, reclining on the nearby lounge. "He made a mistake, facing her on the Shadow Plane, and lost more than just his body. It was disappointing that Mogens couldn't kill the girl, but if he couldn't fulfill his purpose, then what do we need him for? The cyclogres collected the Dolobra's corpse, and I have everything I need for the next piece of the puzzle."

"But the bloody Heirs will ruin everything."

"Patience, dearest. Do you not understand the gifts Idriel has bestowed upon us? Once, it took persuasion and charm to turn the people against the Heirs. Now with your growing control, and my unparalleled wealth of yanaa, we can do it by force." She smiled her sweet, saccharine grin. "And do you think the Heirs will really have the heart to turn on their own people? Between that and the man-killers, we have more than the army we need to keep the Heirs busy."

Conrad took a deep breath, the rage fading from his countenance. "And you're sure you have all you need to call Idriel from the grave?" His lips twisted under his wispy mustache. "I don't know if I can resurrect something in another's body."

Ivanora chuckled dryly. "Of course, you can. It's all clearly explained in Dorinar's texts, Idriel bless him."

Conrad frowned. "But that's all theoretical."

"Come now, darling." She rose from her repose and leaned toward Conrad. "Did you learn nothing from the Wraith-Called? All it takes is time, practice, and the right materials. You've only just begun to tap into the talents Idriel has gifted you." She ran a finger along the side of his angular face and pointed to the stack of Dorinar's books. "But with my guidance, together we will rise to heights you never knew we could reach."

"Will it still be strong enough after they took its head off?"

"Fixable." Ivanora sniffed with a dismissive wave. "Even stitched together, it is the most powerful beast in this world. The Dolobra *will* host Idriel." Her smile turned feral. "And we will wipe Okarria clean."

AUTHOR'S NOTE

Thanks so much for reading! I hope you enjoyed Idriel's Children. If you have time to leave a review on Amazon or your favorite book site, I would be so grateful to any words you'd be willing to leave. Even just a line or two can make a huge difference. Reviews are vital for any author, but as an indie author especially, encouragement from readers like you keeps me going and gives these stories wings.

If you're interested in reading more, you can find updates on the sequel, Time's Orphan, as well as my other works on my website at hayleyreesechow.com. You can also connect with me on Twitter or Instagram @HayleyReeseChow.

Thanks for
Supporting local
authors with your
reviews!

ACKNOWLEDGMENTS

When I first published Odriel's Heirs, I told my husband if even one person liked it, I would write the sequel… and even then I wasn't sure it would actually happen. Honestly without encouragement from my family, my writing village, and readers, this book would have forever stayed only a daydream. So, as always, I'm so grateful to any and everyone who's taken the time to read or just passed on a kind word.

More specifically, thanks to my husband, Adam, for always being there to encourage and support me… even after I killed his favorite character. For what it's worth, Witt will always live on in our hearts.

To my wild boys, Decker & Dashiell, for always offering a smile and a hug… and for going to bed on time tonight so I could write this.

To my parents, two of the biggest supporters of my books who have imparted the tenacity and resilience that have made my writing journey possible.

To my editor, Martha, for her incredible attention to detail and grammar knowledge that keeps me learning.

To my cover designer, Dominique, for bringing my characters to life.

To my beta readers for taking the time to read my words—your support lifts me up. Special shout-out to Caleb, who knows way more about story-telling than I ever will. I can't wait to see your book on the shelf one day! And another big shout-out to Kayleigh for her endless well of positivity.

And to all the others who have given their kind encouragement—thank you so much. Trust me when I say, your words have given me the confidence to make this book a reality.

ABOUT THE AUTHOR

Hayley Reese Chow has done of lot of things that have nothing at all to do with writing. Her hat collection includes mother, wife, engineer, USAF veteran, reservist, four-time All American fencer, 100 mile ultramarathoner, world traveler, book inhaler, and super nerd.

Hayley is also the author of Odriel's Heirs, The Gatekeeper of Pericael, and Burning Shadows. She currently lives in Florida with two small wild boys, her long-suffering husband, and her miniature ragehound.

But in the night, when the house is still, she writes.

Made in the USA
Columbia, SC
21 July 2021